Conan put his back against the wall and lifted his ax. He stood like an image of the unconquerable primordial—legs braced far apart, head thrust forward, one hand clutching the wall for support, the other gripping the ax on high, with the great corded muscles standing out in iron ridges, and his features frozen in a death snarl of fury—his eyes blazing terribly through the mist of blood which veiled them. The men faltered —wild, criminal and dissolute though they were, yet they came of a breed men called civilized, with a civilized background; here was the barbarian—the natural killer. They shrank back—the dying tiger could still deal death.

King Conan sensed their uncertainty and grinned mirthlessly and ferociously.

"Who dies first?" he mumbled through smashed and bloody lips. . . .

—from *The Phoenix on the Sword*

CONAN THE USURPER

Chronological order of the CONAN series:

CONAN
CONAN OF CIMMERIA
CONAN THE FREEBOOTER
CONAN THE WANDERER
CONAN THE ADVENTURER
CONAN THE BUCCANEER
CONAN THE WARRIOR
CONAN THE USURPER
CONAN THE CONQUEROR
CONAN THE AVENGER
CONAN OF AQUILONIA
CONAN OF THE ISLES

Illustrated CONAN novels:

CONAN AND THE SORCERER
CONAN: THE FLAME KNIFE
CONAN THE MERCENARY
THE TREASURE OF TRANICOS

Other CONAN novels:

THE BLADE OF CONAN
THE SPELL OF CONAN

CONAN

8

THE USURPER

BY ROBERT E. HOWARD AND L. SPRAGUE DE CAMP

ACE FANTASY BOOKS
NEW YORK

The Treasure of Tranicos was originally published, as revised by L. Sprague de Camp, under the title *The Black Stranger*, in *Fantasy Magazine* for March, 1953; copyright 1953 by Future Publications, Inc. It was reprinted under its present title in *King Conan*, by Robert E. Howard, N.Y.: Gnome Press, Inc., 1953.

Wolves Beyond the Border is published here for the first time. In 1965, Glenn Lord, literary agent for the Howard estate, discovered, in a batch of Howard's papers, the first half of this story and a brief summary of the rest. L. Sprague de Camp edited the existing text and completed the story according to Howard's summary.

The Phoenix on the Sword was originally published in *Weird Tales* for December, 1932; copyright 1932 by Popular Fiction Publishing Co. It was reprinted in *Skull-Face and Others*, by Robert E. Howard, Sauk City, Wis.: Arkham House, 1946; and in *King Conan*.

The Scarlet Citadel was originally published in *Weird Tales* for January, 1933; copyright 1933 by Popular Fiction Publishing Co. It was reprinted in *Skull-Face and Others* and in *King Conan*.

CONAN THE USURPER

An Ace Fantasy Book/published by arrangement with
the Estate of Robert E. Howard

PRINTING HISTORY
This printing / May 1983

ISBN: 0-441-11602-7

Ace Fantasy Books are published by Charter Communications, Inc.
200 Madison Avenue, New York, New York 10016.
PRINTED IN THE UNITED STATES OF AMERICA

Contents

Cover painting by Frank Frazetta . . . with grateful acknowledgment to Roy Krenkel, advisor

The biographical paragraphs between the stories are based upon *A Probable Outline of Conan's Career*, by P. Schuyler Miller and Dr. John D. Clark, published in *The Hyborian Age* (Los Angeles: LANY Coöperative Publications, 1938) and on the expanded version of this essay, *An Informal Biography of Conan the Cimmerian*, by P. Schuyler Miller, John D. Clark, and L. Sprague de Camp, published in *Amra*, Vol. 2, No. 4, copyright © 1959 by G. H. Scithers, used by permission of G. H. Scithers, *Amra* (Box 9120, Chicago, 60690) is the magazine of the Hyborian Legion, a group of enthusiasts for heroic fantasy and for the Conan stories in particular.

Pages 6 and 7: A map of the world of Conan in the Hyborian Age, based upon notes and sketches by Robert E. Howard and upon previous maps by P. Schuyler Miller, John D. Clark, David Kyle, and L. Sprague de Camp, with a map of Europe and adjacent regions superimposed for reference.

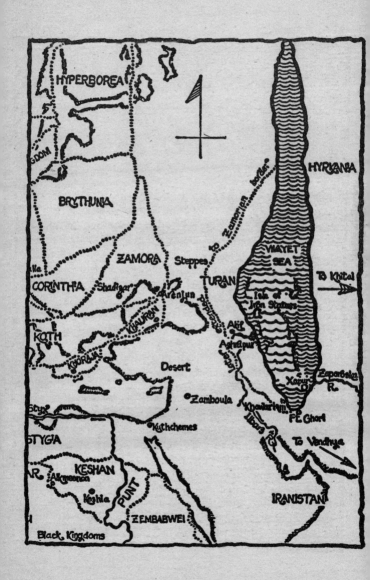

Introduction

ONE OF THE WORLD'S GREAT natural storytellers was Robert Ervin
Howard (1906–36) of Cross Plains, Texas. Although Howard
was a versatile and prolific writer—he wrote, for instance, a
series of hilarious humorous western stories—his narrative sorcery reached its climax in his swashbuckling adventure-
fantasies. Through these tales of swordsmen and sorcerers,
demons and dooms stalk his unforgettable, larger-than-life
heroes: King Kull of Valusia, Bran Mak Morn, Solomon
Kane—and, mightiest and most colorful of all, Conan the Cimmerian, hero of over two dozen rousing tales.

Conan is supposed to have lived about twelve thousand years
ago, in Howard's imaginary Hyborian Age, between the sinking
of Atlantis and the beginning of recorded history. A gigantic
barbarian adventurer from the bleak northern land of Cimmeria
(see the map), Conan waded through rivers of gore and over-
came fell adversaries, both natural and supernatural, to become
at last the king of the Hyborian kingdom of Aquilonia.

Eighteen Conan stories were published in Howard's lifetime,
and several more have been discovered in manuscript—some
complete and some fragmentary—during the last two decades.
It has been my privilege to edit these stories for posthumous
publication and to complete most of the incomplete ones.

Of the four stories in this volume, the first two have compli-
cated histories. In 1951 I discovered, in a stack of unpublished
Howard manuscripts in the house of the late Oscar J. Friend,

then the literary agent for the Howard estate, a story entitled "The Black Stranger." In preparing this manuscript for publication, I edited and rewrote it somewhat drastically, condensing it by more than fifteen per cent and adding a number of interpolations to tie the story in with King Numedides, Thoth-Amon, and the subsequent revolution in Aquilonia, to fit the story snugly into the saga.

The editor of *Fantasy Magazine*, who first published the story, made further additions and deletions. This version was reprinted in 1953 in the volume *King Conan*. The magazine editor retained the original title; but, when the story was published in *King Conan*, I changed the title to "The Treasure of Tranicos" because "The Black Stranger" was confusingly similar to the titles of a number of other Howard stories, at least a dozen of which had "black" in their titles.

For the present publication, I have gone back to the original Howard manuscript and have edited it much more lightly, not trying to condense it and making only such changes as seemed urgently necessary. I have omitted the magazine editor's changes; I have, however, kept the interpolations I introduced the first time to tie the story in with the rest of the saga—e.g. Conan's account of his escape from Aquilonia. What you read is, therefore, a good deal closer to Howard's original than the previously published version.

In addition, Glenn Lord, the present literary agent for the Howard estate, found "Wolves Beyond the Border" in a cache of Howard papers in 1965. The story seemed to be in final draft; but it stopped halfway through (at the fight in the cabin) and gave only a brief summary, of about a page, of the rest. Whether Howard had grown tired of the story and had put it aside, meaning to round it out later, or whether he had something else in mind, will probably never be known. I have undertaken to complete the story in Howardian style, following the summary.

The two remaining stories, "The Phoenix on the Sword" and "The Scarlet Citadel," are—save for a few minor editorial corrections—in the form in which Howard wrote them and *Weird Tales* published them in the 1930s.

The Conan saga runs as follows: Conan, the son of a Cimmerian blacksmith, was born on a battlefield in that hilly, cloudy land. As a youth he took part in the sack of the Aquilonian frontier post of Venarium. Subsequently, joining in a raid with a band of Æsir into Hyperborea, he was captured by the Hyperboreans. Escaping from the Hyperborean slave pen, he wandered south into Zamora and adjacent counties, making a precarious living as a thief. Green to civilization and quite lawless by nature, he made up for his lack of subtlety and sophistication by natural shrewdness and the herculean physique he had inherited from his father.

Eventually, he enlisted as a mercenary in the army of King Yildiz of Turan. He traveled widely through the Hyrkanian lands and acquired a knowledge of archery and horsemanship. Later he served as a *condottiere* in the Hyborian lands, led a piratical band of black corsairs on the coast of Kush, and served as a mercenary in Shem and the adjacent counties. He returned to outlawry among the *kozaki* of the eastern steppes and the pirates of the Sea of Vilayet. After mercenary service for the kingdom of Khauran, he spent two years as a chief of the Zuagirs, the nomadic eastern Shemites. Then followed wild adventures in the eastern lands of Iranistan and Vendhya, in the course of which Conan confronted the Black Seers of Yimsha in the Himelian Mountains.

Returning to the west, Conan again became a freebooter with the Barachan pirates and the Zingaran buccaneers. Then he served again as a mercenary in Stygia and among the black kingdoms. He wandered north to Aquilonia and—now about forty years old—became a scout on the Pictish frontier. When the Picts, with the help of the wizard Zogar Sag, attacked the Aquilonian settlements, Conan tried but failed to save Fort Tuscelan from destruction, but he did save the lives of a number of settlers between the Thunder and Black rivers. At this point, the present book begins.

L. Sprague de Camp

The Treasure of Tranicos

After the events of the story "Beyond the Black River," in Conan the Warrior, Conan rises rapidly in the Aquilonian service. Becoming a general, he defeats the Picts in a great battle at Velitrium and breaks the back of their confederacy. Then he is called back to the capital, Tarantia, for a triumph. But, having aroused the suspicion and jealousy of the depraved and foolish King Numedides, he is plied with drugged wine and chained in the Iron Tower under sentence of death. The barbarian, however, has friends as well as enemies in Aquilonia, and soon he is spirited out of his prison and turned loose with a horse and a sword. Riding back to the frontier, he finds his Bossonian troops scattered and a price on his head. Swimming Thunder River, he strikes out across the dank forests of Pictland toward the distant sea.

1. *The Painted Men*

ONE MOMENT the glade lay empty; the next, a man stood poised warily at the edge of the bushes. There had been no sound to warn the gray squirrels of his coming; but the gay-hued birds that flitted about in the sunshine of the open space took fright at his sudden appearance and rose in a clamoring cloud. The man scowled and glanced quickly back the way he had come, as if fearing that their flight had betrayed his position to someone unseen. Then he stalked across the glade, placing his feet with care.

For all his massive, muscular build, the man moved with the supple certitude of a leopard. He was naked except for a rag twisted about his loins, and his limbs were crisscrossed with scratches from briars and caked with dried mud. A brown-crusted bandage was knotted about his thickly-muscled left arm. Under his matted, black mane, his face was drawn and gaunt, and his eyes burned like those of a wounded wolf. He limped slightly as he followed the faint path that led across the open space.

Halfway across the glade, he stopped short and whirled catlike, facing back the way he had come, as a long-drawn call quavered out across the forest. To another man it would have seemed merely the howl of a wolf. But this man knew it was no wolf. A Cimmerian, he understood the voices of the wilderness as a city-bred man recognizes the voices of his friends.

Rage burned redly in his bloodshot eyes as he turned once more and hurried along the path. This path, as it left the glade, ran along the edge of a dense thicket that rose in a solid clump of greenery among the trees and bushes. A massive log, deeply embedded in the grassy earth, paralleled the fringe of the thicket, lying between it and the path. When the Cimmerian saw this log, he halted and looked back across the glade. To the average eye there were no signs to show that he had passed; but the evidence was visible to his wilderness-sharpened eyes and therefore to the equally keen eyes of those who pursued him. He snarled silently, like a hunted beast ready to turn at bay.

He walked with deliberate carelessness down the trail, here and there crushing a grass-blade beneath his foot. Then, when he had reached the further end of the great log, he sprang upon it, turned, and ran lightly back along it. As the bark had long been worn away by the elements, he left no sign to show the keenest eyes that he had doubled on his trail. When he reached the densest part of the thicket, he faded into it like a shadow, with hardly the quiver of a leaf to mark his passing.

The minutes dragged. The gray squirrels chattered again—then flattened their bodies against the branches and were suddenly mute. Again the glade was invaded. As silently as the first man had appeared, three other men materialized out of the eastern edge of the clearing: dark-skinned men of short stature, with thickly-muscled chests and arms. They wore beaded buckskin loincloths, and an eagle's feather was thrust into each black topknot. Their bodies were painted in intricate designs, and they were heavily armed with crude weapons of hammered copper.

They had scanned the glade carefully before showing themselves in the open, for they moved out of the bushes without hesitation, in close single file, treading as softly as leopards and bending down to stare at the path. They were following the trail of the Cimmerian—no easy task even for these human bloodhounds. They moved slowly across the glade; then one of them stiffened, grunted, and pointed with his broad-bladed stabbing-spear at a crushed grass-blade where the path entered the forest again. All halted instantly, their beady black eyes questing the forest walls. But their quarry was well hidden. Seeing nothing to awaken suspicion, they presently moved on, more rapidly now. They followed the faint marks that implied their prey was growing careless through weakness or desperation.

They had just passed the spot where the thicket crowded closest to the ancient trail, when the Cimmerian bounded into the path behind them, gripping the weapons he had drawn from his loincloth: a long copper-bladed knife in his left hand and a hatchet of the same material in his right. The attack was so quick and un-expected that the last Pict had no chance to save himself as the Cimmerian plunged his knife between the man's shoulders. The blade was in the Pict's heart before he knew he was in peril.

The other two whirled with the steel-trap quickness of savages; but, even as the Cimmerian wrenched the knife out of his first victim's back, he struck a tremendous blow with the war-ax in his right hand. The second Pict was in the act of turning as the ax fell, splitting his skull to the teeth.

The remaining Pict, a chief by the scarlet tip of his eagle feather, came savagely in to the attack. He was stab-bing at the Cimmerian's breast even as the killer wrenched his ax from the dead man's head. The Cimmerian had the advantage of a greater intelligence, and a weapon in each hand. The hatchet, checked in its down-ward sweep, struck the spear aside, and the knife in the

14

Cimmerian's left hand ripped upward into the painted belly.

An awful howl burst from the Pict's lips as he crumpled, disemboweled. The cry of baffled, bestial fury was answered by a wild chorus of yells from some distance east of the glade. The Cimmerian started convulsively and wheeled, crouching like a wild thing at bay, lips asnarl and shaking the sweat from his face. Blood trickled down his forearm from under the bandage.

With a gasping, incoherent imprecation, he turned and fled westward. He did not pick his way now but ran with all the speed of his long legs, calling on the deep and all but inexhaustible reservoirs of endurance that are Nature's compensation for a barbaric existence. Behind him for a space the woods were silent. Then a demoniac howling burst out, and he knew his pursuers had found the bodies of his victims. He had no breath for cursing the drops of blood that kept falling to the ground from his freshly-opened wound, leaving a trail a child could follow. He had thought that perhaps these three Picts were all that still pursued him of the war-party that had followed him for over a hundred miles. But he might have known that these human wolves would never quit a blood trail.

The woods were silent again; that meant they were racing after him, marking his path by the betraying blood-drops he could not check. A wind out of the west, laden with a salty dampness that he recognized, blew against his face. Dully, he was amazed. If he was that close to the sea, the chase must have been even longer than he had realized.

But now it was nearly over; even his wolfish vitality was ebbing under the terrible strain. He gasped for breath, and there was a sharp pain in his side. His legs trembled with weariness, and the lame one ached like the cut of a knife in the tendons every time he set the foot to earth. He had followed the instincts of the wilderness that had bred him, straining every nerve and sinew, exhausting every subtlety and artifice to survive. Now, in his extremity, he was obeying another instinct—to find a place to turn at bay and sell his life at a bloody price.

He did not leave the trail for the tangled depths on either hand. It was futile, he knew, to hope to evade his pursuers now. He ran on down the trail while the blood pounded louder and louder in his ears and each breath he drew was a racking, dry-lipped gulp. Behind him a mad baying broke out, token that they were close on his heels and expected swiftly to overhaul their prey. Now they would come as fleet as starving wolves, howling at every leap.

Abruptly he burst from the denseness of the trees and saw, ahead of him, the face of a cliff that rose almost straight from the ground without any intermediate slope. Glances to right and left showed that he faced a solitary dome or crag of rock that rose like a tower from the depths of the forest. As a boy, the Cimmerian had scaled the steep hills of his native land; but, while he might have attempted the near side of this crag had he been in prime condition, he knew that he would have little chance with it in his present wounded and weakened state. By the time he had struggled up twenty or thirty feet, the Picts would burst from the woods and fill him with arrows.

Perhaps, however, the crag's other faces would prove less inhospitable. The trail curved around the crag to the right. Following it, he found that at the west side of the crag it wound up rocky ledges between jagged boulders to a broad ledge near the summit.

That ledge would be as good a place to die as any. As the world swam before him in a dizzy red mist, he limped up the trail, going on hands and knees in the steeper places, holding his knife between his teeth.

He had not yet reached the jutting ledge when some forty painted savages raced around from the far side of the crag, howling like wolves. At the sight of their prey, their screams rose to a devilish crescendo, and they ran to the foot of the crag, loosing arrows as they came. The shafts showered about the man who climbed doggedly upward, and one stuck in the calf of his leg. Without pausing in his climb, he tore it out and threw it aside, heedless of the less accurate missiles that cracked against the rocks about him. Grimly he hauled himself over the rim of the ledge and turned about, drawing his hatchet and shifting his knife to his hand. He lay glaring down at his pursuers over the rim, only his shock of hair and blazing eyes visible. His chest heaved as he drank in the air in great, shuddering gasps, and he clenched his teeth against a tendency toward nausea.

Only a few more arrows whistled up at him; the horde knew its prey was cornered. The warriors came on howling, war-axes in hand and leaping agilely over the rocks at the foot of the hill. The first to reach the steep part of the crag was a brawny brave, whose eagle feather was stained scarlet as a token of chieftainship. He halted briefly, one foot on the sloping trail, arrow notched and drawn halfway back, head thrown back and lips parted for an exultant yell. But the shaft was never loosed. He froze into motionlessness as the blood lust in his black eyes gave way to a look of startled recognition. With a whoop he gave back, throwing his arms wide to check the rush of his howling braves. Although the man on the ledge above them understood the Pictish tongue, he was too far away to catch the significance of the staccato phrases snapped at the warriors by the crimson-feathered chief.

They all ceased their yelping and stood mutely staring

up—not, it seemed to the man on the ledge, at him, but at the hill itself. Then, without further hesitation, they unstrung their bows and thrust them into buckskin cases at their girdles, turned their backs, and trotted back along the trail by which they had come, to disappear around the curve of the cliff without a backward look.

The Cimmerian glared in amazement. He knew the Pictish nature too well not to recognize the finality expressed in this departure. He knew they would not come back; they were heading for their villages, a hundred miles to the east.

But he could not understand it. What was there about his refuge that would cause a Pictish war-party to abandon a chase it had followed so long with all the passion of hungry wolves? He knew there were sacred places, spots set aside as sanctuaries by /the various clans, and that a fugitive, taking refuge in one of these sanctuaries, was safe from the clan that raised it. But the different tribes seldom respected the sanctuaries of other tribes, and the men who pursued him certainly had no sacred spots of their own in this region. They were men of the Eagle, whose villages lay far to the east, adjoining the country of the Wolf Picts.

It was the Wolves who had captured the Cimmerian when he had plunged into the wilderness in his flight from Aquilonia, and it was they who had given him to the Eagles in return for a captured Wolf chief. The Eagle men had a red score against the giant Cimmerian, and now it was redder still, for his escape had cost the life of a noted war chief. That was why they had followed him so relentlessly, over broad rivers and rugged hills and through long leagues of gloomy forest, the hunting grounds of hostile tribes. And now the survivors of that long chase had turned back when their enemy was run to earth and trapped. He shook his head, unable to understand it.

He rose gingerly, dizzy from the long grind and scarcely able to realize that it was over. His limbs were stiff; his wounds ached. He spat dryly and cursed, rubbing his burning, bloodshot eyes with the back of his thick wrist. He blinked and took stock of his surroundings. Below him the green wilderness billowed away and away in a solid mass, and above its western rim rose a steel-blue haze that, he knew, hung over the ocean. The wind stirred his black mane, and the salt tang of the atmosphere revived him. He expanded his enormous chest and drank it in.

Then he turned stiffly and painfully about, growling at the twinge in his bleeding calf, and investigated the ledge on which he stood. Behind it rose a sheer, rocky cliff to the crest of the crag, some thirty feet above him. A narrow, ladderlike stair of handholds had been niched into the rock, and a few feet from the foot of this ascent a cleft, wide and tall enough for a man to enter, opened in the wall.

He limped to the cleft, peered in, and grunted. The sun, hanging high above the western forest, threw a shaft of light down the cleft, revealing a tunnel-like cavern beyond with an arch at its end. In that arch, illuminated by the beam, was set a heavy, iron-bound, oaken door!

This was amazing. This country was a howling wilderness. The Cimmerian knew that for a thousand miles, this western coast ran bare and uninhabited except by the villages of the ferocious sea-land tribes, who were even less civilized than their forest-dwelling brothers.

The nearest outposts of civilization were the frontier settlements along Thunder River, hundreds of miles to the east. The Cimmerian knew that he was the only white man ever to cross the wilderness that lay between that river and the coast. Yet that door was no work of Picts.

Being unexplainable, it was an object of suspicion,

19

and suspiciously he approached it, ax and knife ready. Then, as his bloodshot eyes became more accustomed to the soft gloom that lurked on either side of the narrow shaft of sunlight, he noticed something else. The tunnel widened out before it came to the door, and along the walls were ranged massive, iron-bound chests. A blaze of comprehension came into his eyes. He bent over one, but the lid resisted his efforts. He lifted his hatchet to shatter the ancient lock; then changed his mind and limped toward the arched door. Now his bearing was more confident, and his weapons hung at his sides. He pushed against the ornately-carven door, and it swung inward without resistance.

Then, with a lightninglike abruptness, his manner changed again. He recoiled with a startled curse, knife and hatchet flashing as they leaped to positions of defense. An instant he poised there, like a statue of fierce menace, craning his massive neck to glare through the door.

He was looking into a cave, darker than the tunnel, but meagerly illuminated by the dim glow that came from the great jewel that stood on a tiny ivory pedestal in the center of the great ebony table, about which sat those silent shapes whose appearance had so startled the Cimmerian.

These did not move, nor did they turn their heads toward him; but the bluish mist that overhung the chamber seemed to move like a living thing.

"Well," he said harshly, "are you all drunk?"

There was no reply. He was not a man easily abashed, yet now he felt disconcerted.

"You might offer me a glass of that wine you're swigging," he growled, his natural belligerence aroused by the awkwardness of the situation. "By Crom, you show damned poor courtesy to a man who's been one of your own brotherhood. Are you going to—"

His voice trailed off into silence, and in silence he

stood and stared a while at those bizarre figures sitting so silently about the great ebon table.

"They're not drunk," he muttered presently. "They're not even drinking. What devil's game is this?

He stepped across the threshold. Instantly the movement of the blue mist quickened. The stuff flowed together and solidified, and the Cimmerian found himself fighting for his life against huge black hands that darted for his throat.

2. Men from the Sea

Belesa idly stirred a sea shell with a daintily slippered toe, mentally comparing its delicate pink edges to the first pink haze of dawn that rose over the misty beaches. Dawn was now past, but the early sun had not yet dispelled the light, pearly clouds that drifted over the waters to westward.

She lifted her splendidly-shaped head and stared out over a scene alien and repellent to her, yet drearily familiar in every detail. From her small feet, the tawny sands ran to meet the softly-lapping waves, which stretched westward to be lost in the blue haze of the horizon. She was standing on the southern curve of a wide bay; south of her the land sloped up to the low ridge that formed one horn on that bay. From that ridge, she knew, one could look southward across the bare waters into infinities of distance as absolute as the view to the westward and to the northward.

Glancing listlessly landward, she absently scanned the fortress, which had been her home for the past year and a half. Against a vague, pearl-and-cerulean morning sky floated the golden and scarlet flag of her house. But the red falcon on its golden field awakened no enthusiasm in her youthful bosom, although it had flown over many a bloody field in the far south.

She made out the figures of men toiling in the gardens and fields that huddled near the fort, seeming to shrink from the gloomy rampart of the forest that fringed the open belt to the east, stretching north and south as far as she could see. She feared that forest, and that fear was shared by everyone in that tiny settlement. Nor was it an idle fear. Death lurked in those whispering depths—death swift and terrible, death slow and hideous—hidden, painted, tireless, unrelenting.

She sighed and moved toward the water's edge, with no set purpose in mind. The dragging days were all of one color, and the world of cities and courts and gaiety seemed thousands of miles and ages of time away. Again she sought in vain for the reason that had caused a count of Zingara to flee with his retainers to this wild coast, hundreds of miles from the land that bore him, exchanging the castle of his ancestors for a hut of logs.

Belesa's eyes softened at the light patter of small bare feet across the sands. A young girl came running over the low, sandy ridge, naked and dripping, with her flaxen hair plastered wetly to her small head. Her wistful eyes were wide with excitement.

"Lady Belesa!" she cried, rendering the Zingaran words with a soft, Ophirean accent. "Oh, Lady Belesa!"

Breathless from her scamper, the child stammered and gestured with her hands. Belesa smiled and put an arm about her, not minding that her silken dress came in contact with the damp, warm body. In her lonely, isolated life, Belesa had bestowed the tenderness of a naturally affectionate nature on the pitiful waif she had taken away from a brutal master on that long voyage up from the southern coasts.

"What are you trying to tell me, Tina? Get your breath, child."

"A ship!" cried the girl, pointing southward. "I was swimming in a pool that the tide left in the sand, on the other side of the ridge, and I saw it! A ship sailing up out of the south!"

She tugged timidly at Belesa's hand, her slender body aquiver. And Belesa felt her own heart beat faster at the mere thought of an unknown visitor. They had seen no sail since coming to that barren shore.

Tina flitted ahead of her over the yellow sands, skirting the little pools that the outgoing tide had left in shallow depressions. They mounted the low, undulating ridge. Tina poised there, a slender white figure against the clearing sky, with her wet, flaxen hair blowing about her thin face and a frail arm outstretched.

"Look, my lady!"

Belesa had already seen it: a billowing white sail, filled with the freshening south wind, beating up along the coast a few miles from the point. Her heart skipped a beat; a small thing can loom large in colorless, isolated lives, but Belesa felt a premonition of strange and violent events. She felt that it was not by chance that this sail was wafting up this lonely coast. There was no harbor town to the north, though one sailed to the ultimate shores of ice; and the nearest port to the south must be nearly a thousand miles away. What had brought this stranger to lonely Korvela Bay, as her uncle had named the place when he landed?

Tina pressed close to her mistress, apprehension pinching her thin features. "Who can it be, my lady?" she stammered, the wind whipping color to her pale cheeks. "Is it the man the count fears?"

23

Belesa looked down at her, her brow shadowed. "Why do you say that, child? How do you know my uncle fears anyone?"

"He must," returned Tina naïvely, "or he would never have come to hide in this lonely spot. Look, my lady, how fast it comes!"

"We must go and inform my uncle," murmured Belesa. "The fishing boats have not yet gone out, so that none of the men has seen that sail. Get your clothes, Tina. Hurry!"

The child scampered down the low slope to the pool where she had been bathing when she sighted the craft and snatched up the slippers, tunic, and girdle that she had left lying on the sand. She skipped back up the ridge, hopping as she dressed in mid-flight.

Belesa, anxiously watching the approaching sail, caught her hand, and they hurried toward the fort. A few moments after they had entered the gate of the log palisade that inclosed the building, the strident blare of a trumpet startled the workers in the gardens and the men who were opening the boathouse doors to push the fishing boats on their rollers down to the water's edge.

Every man outside the fort dropped his tool or left his task and ran for the stockade without pausing to look about for the cause of the alarm. As the straggling lines of fleeing men converged on the open gate, every head was twisted over its shoulder to gaze fearfully at the dark line of woodland to the east; not one looked seaward.

They thronged through the gate, shouting questions at the sentries who patrolled the footwalk below the up-jutting points of the logs that formed the palisade: "What is it?" "Why are we called in?" "Are the Picts coming?"

For answer, one taciturn man-at-arms in worn leather and rusty steel pointed southward. From his vantage point, the sail was now visible to the men who climbed up on the footwalk, staring toward the sea.

On a small lookout tower on the roof of the manor house, which was built of logs like the other buildings in the inclosure, Count Valenso of Korzetta watched the on-sweeping sail as it rounded the point of the southern horn. The count was a lean, wiry man of medium height and late middle age; dark, somber of expression. His trunk-hose and doublet were of black silk, the only color about his costume being that of the jewels that twinkled on his sword hilt and the wine-red cloak thrown carelessly over his shoulders. He nervously twisted his thin black mustache and turned his gloomy eyes on his senescal, a leather-featured man in steel and satin.

"What do you make of it, Galbro?"

"A carack, sir," answered the senescal. "It is a carack trimmed and rigged like a craft of the Barachan pirates —look there!"

A chorus of cries below them echoed his ejaculation; the ship had cleared the point and was slanting inward across the bay. And all saw the flag that suddenly broke forth from the masthead: a black flag with the outline of a scarlet hand. The people within the stockade stared wildly at that dread emblem. Then all eyes turned up toward the tower, where the master of the fort stood somberly, his cloak whipping about him in the wind.

"It is a Barachan, all right," grunted Galbro. "And unless I am mad, 'tis Strombanni's *Red Hand*. What is he doing on this naked coast?"

"He can mean us no good," growled the count. A glance below showed him that the massive gates had been closed and that the captain of his men-at-arms, gleaming in steel, was directing his men to their stations, some to the ledges, some to the lower loopholes. He was massing his main strength along the western wall, which contained the gate.

A hundred men—soldiers, vassals, and serfs—and their dependents had followed Valenso into exile. Of these, some forty were men-at-arms, wearing helmets and suits of mail, armed with swords, axes, and crossbows. The rest were toilers, without armor save for shirts of toughened leather; but they were brawny stalwarts, skilled in the use of their hunting bows, woodsmen's axes, and boar spears. They took their places, scowling at their hereditary enemies. For more than a century the pirates of the Barachan Isles, a tiny archipelago off the southwestern coast of Zingara, had preyed on the people of the mainland.

The men on the stockade gripped their bows or boar spears and stared somberly at the carack as it swung inshore, its brasswork flashing in the sun. They could see the figures swarming on the deck and hear the lusty yells of the seamen. Steel twinkled along the rail.

The count had retired from the tower, shooing his niece and her eager protegée before him. Having donned helmet and cuirass, he betook himself to the palisade to direct the defense. His subjects watched him with moody fatalism. They intended to sell their lives as dearly as they could, but they had scant hope of victory, in spite of their strong position. They were oppressed by a conviction of doom. More than a year on that naked coast, with the brooding threat of that devil-haunted forest looming forever at their backs, had shadowed their souls with gloomy forebodings. Their women stood silently in the doorways of their huts, inside the stockade, and quieted the clamor of their children.

Belesa and Tina watched eagerly from an upper window in the manor house, and Belesa felt the child's tense little body quiver within the crook of her protecting arm.

"They will cast anchor near the boathouse," murmured Belesa. "Yes! There goes their anchor, a hundred

26

yards offshore. Do not tremble so, child! They cannot take the fort. Perhaps they wish only fresh water and supplies; perhaps a storm blew them into these seas."

"They are coming ashore in the longboat!" said the child. "Oh, my lady, I am afraid! They are big men in armor! Look how the sun strikes fire from their pikes and helmets! Will they eat us?"

Belesa burst into laughter in spite of her apprehension. "Of course not! Who put that idea into your head?"

"Zingelito told me the Barachans eat women."

"He was teasing you. The Barachans are cruel, but they are no worse than the Zingaran renegades who call themselves buccaneers. Zingelito was a buccaneer once."

"He was cruel," muttered the child. "I'm glad the Picts cut his head off."

"Hush, Tina!" Belesa shuddered slightly. "You must not speak that way. Look, the pirates have reached the shore. They line the beach, and one of them is coming toward the fort. That must be Strombanni."

"Ahoy, the fort there!" came a hail in a voice as gusty as the wind. "I come under a flag of truce!"

The count's helmeted head appeared over the points of the palisade. His stern face, framed in steel, surveyed the pirate somberly. Strombanni had halted just within earshot: a big man, bare-headed, with hair of the tawny hue sometimes found in Argos. Of all the sea-rovers who haunted the Barachans, none was more famed for deviltry than he.

"Speak!" commanded Valenso. "I have scant desire to converse with one of your breed."

Strombanni laughed with his lips, not with his eyes. "When your galleon escaped me in that squall off the Trallibes last year, I never thought to meet you again on the Pictish coast, Valenso!" said he. "But I wondered at the time what your destination might be. By Mitra, had I known, I should have followed you then! I got the start of my life a little while ago, when I saw your scarlet falcon floating over a fortress where I had thought to see naught but bare beach. You have found it, of course?"

"Found what?" snapped the count impatiently.

"Do not try to dissemble with me!" The pirate's stormy nature showed itself in a flash of impatience. "I know why you came here, and I have come for the same reason. I will not be balked. Where is your ship?"

"That is none of your affair."

"You have none," confidently asserted the pirate. "I see pieces of ship's mast in that stockade. It must have been wrecked somehow, after you landed here. If you'd had a ship, you would have sailed away with your plunder long ago."

"What are you talking about, damn you?" yelled the count. "My plunder? Am I a Barachan, to burn and loot? Even so, what should I loot on this bare coast?"

"That which you came to find," answered the pirate coolly. "The same thing I'm after and mean to have. But I shall be easy to deal with. Just give me the loot and I'll go my way and leave you in peace."

"You must be mad!" snarled Valenso. "I came here to find solitude and seclusion, which I enjoyed until you crawled out of the sea, you yellow-headed dog. Begone! I did not ask for a parley, and I weary of this empty talk. Take your rogues and go your ways."

"When I go, I'll leave that hovel in ashes!" roared the pirate in a transport of rage. "For the last time: will you give me the loot in return for your lives? I have you hemmed in here, and a hundred and fifty men ready to cut your throats at my word."

For answer, the count made a quick gesture with his hand below the points of the palisade. Almost instantly, a shaft hummed venomously through a loophole and splintered on Strombanni's breastplate. The pirate yelled ferociously, bounded back, and ran toward the beach,

28

with arrows whistling all about him. His men roared and came on like a wave, blades gleaming in the sun.

"Curse you, dog!" raved the count, felling the offending archer with his iron-clad fist. "Why did you not strike his throat above the gorget? Ready with your bows, men; here they come!"

But Strombanni checked the headlong rush of his men. The pirates spread out in a long line that overlapped the extremities of the western wall; they advanced warily, loosing their shafts as they came. Although their archery was considered superior to that of the Zingarans, they had to rise to loose their longbows. Meanwhile the Zingarans, protected by their stockade, sent crossbow bolts and hunting arrows back with careful aim.

The long arrows of the Barachans arched over the stockade and quivered upright in the earth. One struck the windowsill over which Belesa watched. Tina cried out and flinched, staring at the vibrating shaft.

The Zingarans sent their missiles in return, aiming and loosing without undue haste. The women had herded the children into their huts and now stoically awaited whatever fate the gods had in store for them.

The Barachans were famed for their furious and headlong style of battling, but they were as wary as they were ferocious and did not intend to waste their strength vainly in direct charges against the ramparts. They crept forward in their widespread formation, taking advantage of every natural depression and bit of vegetation—which was not much, for the ground had been cleared on all sides of the fort against the threat of Pictish raids.

As the Barachans got nearer to the fort, the defenders' archery became more effective. Here and there a body lay prone, its back-piece glinting in the sun and a quarrel shaft standing up from armpit or neck. Wounded men thrashed and moaned.

The pirates were quick as cats, always shifting their

position, and they were protected by their light armor. Their constant raking archery was a continual menace to the men in the stockade. Still, it was evident that as long as the battle remained an exchange of archery, the advantage must remain with the sheltered Zingarans.

Down at the boathouse on the beach, however, men were at work with axes. The count cursed sulfurously when he saw the havoc they were making among his boats, which had been built laboriously of planks sawn out of solid logs.

"They're making a mantlet, curse them!" he raged. "A sally now, before they complete it—while they are scattered—"

Galbro shook his head, glancing at the unarmored workers with their awkward pikes. "Their arrows would riddle us, and we should be no match for them in hand-to-hand fighting. We must keep behind our walls and trust to our archery."

"Well enough," growled Valenso, "if we can keep *them* outside our walls."

Time passed while the inconclusive archery duel continued. Then a group of thirty men advanced, pushing before them a great shield made of planks from the boats and the timbers of the boathouse itself. They had found an oxcart and mounted the mantlet on the wheels, which were great solid disks of oak. As they rolled it ponderously before them, it hid them from the sight of the defenders except for glimpses of their moving feet.

It rolled toward the gate, and the straggling line of archers converged toward it, shooting as they ran.

"Shoot!" yelled Valenso, going livid. "Stop them ere they reach the gate!"

A storm of arrows whistled across the palisade and feathered themselves harmlessly in the thick wood. A derisive yell answered the volley. Shafts were finding loopholes now as the rest of the pirates drew nearer; a soldier reeled and fell from the ledge, gasping and choking, with an arrow through his throat.

"Shoot at their feet!" screamed Valenso. "And forty men at the gate with pikes and axes! The rest hold the wall!"

Bolts ripped into the sand before the moving shield. A bloodthirsty howl announced that one had found its target beneath the edge. A man staggered into view, cursing and hopping as he strove to withdraw the quarrel that skewered his foot. In an instant he was feathered by a dozen arrows.

But, with a deep-throated shout, the pirates pushed the mantlet against the gate. Through an aperture in the center of the shield they thrust a heavy, iron-tipped boom, which they had made from the ridgepole of the boathouse. Driven by arms knotted with brawny muscles and backed with bloodthirsty fury, the boom began to thunder against the gate. The massive gate groaned and staggered, while from the stockade bolts poured in a steady stream; some struck home, but the wild men of the sea were afire with fighting lust.

With deep shouts they swung the ram, while from all sides the others closed in, braving the weakened arrow-storm from the walls and shooting back fast and hard.

Cursing like a madman, the count sprang from the wall and ran to the gate, drawing his sword. A clump of desperate men-at-arms closed in behind him, gripping their spears. In another moment the gate would cave in, and they must stop the gap with their bodies.

Then a new note entered the clamor: a trumpet, blaring stridently from the ship. On the crosstree, a figure waved and gesticulated wildly.

The thunder of the ram ceased, and Strombanni's bellow rose above the racket: "Wait! Wait, damn you! *Listen!*"

In the silence that followed that bull's bellow, the

blare of the trumpet was plainly heard, and a voice that shouted something that was unintelligible to the people inside the stockade. But Strombanni understood, for his voice was lifted again in profane command. The ram was released, and the mantlet began to recede from the gate as swiftly as it had advanced. Pirates who had been trading shafts with the defenders began picking up their wounded fellows and helping them hastily back to the beach.

"Look!" cried Tina at her window, jumping up and down in wild excitement, "They flee! All of them! They are running to the beach! Look! They have abandoned the shield! They leap into the longboat and pull for the ship! Oh, my lady, have we won?"

"I think not." Belesa was staring seaward. "Look!"

She threw the curtains aside and leaned from the window. Her clear young voice rose above the amazed shouts of the defenders, who turned their heads in the direction she pointed. They sent up a deep yell as they saw another ship swinging majestically around the southern point. Even as they watched, she broke out the royal flag of Zingara.

Strombanni's pirates were swarming up the sides of their carack and heaving up the anchor. Before the stranger had progressed halfway across the bay, the *Red Hand* was vanishing around the northern horn.

3. *The Dark Stranger*

The blue mist had condensed into a monstrous black figure, dimly seen and not quite definite, which filled the hither end of the cave, blotting out the still, seated figures behind. There was an impression of shagginess, pointed ears, and close-set horns.

Even as the great arms shot out like tentacles toward his throat, the Cimmerian, quick as a flash, struck at them with his Pictish ax. It was like chopping at a trunk of the ebony tree. The force of the blow broke the handle of the tomahawk and sent the copper head flying with a clank against the side of the tunnel; but, so far as the Cimmerian could tell, the blade had not bitten into the flesh of his foe at all. It took more than an ordinary edge to pierce a demon's hide. And then the great fingers closed upon his throat, to break his neck as if it were a reed. Not since he had fought Baal-pteor hand to hand in the temple of Hanuman in Zamboula had Conan felt such a grip upon him.

As the hairy fingers touched his skin, the barbarian tensed the thickly-corded muscles of his massive neck, drawing his head down between his shoulders to give his unnatural foe the least possible purchase. He dropped the knife and the broken hatchet handle, seized the huge black wrists, swung his legs upward and forward, and drove both bare heels with all his might against the chest of the thing, straightening out his long body.

The tremendous impulse of the Cimmerian's mighty back and legs tore his neck loose from that lethal grip and sent him shooting like an arrow back up the tunnel down which he had come. He landed on the stone floor on his back and flipped over in a back somersault on to his feet, ignoring the bruises and ready to flee or fight as occasion required.

As he stood there, however, glaring with bared teeth at the door to the inner cave, no black, monstrous form shambled out after him. Almost as soon as Conan had wrenched himself loose, the form had begun to dissolve into the blue mist from which it had condensed. Now it was all gone.

The man stood poised, ready to whirl and bound up the tunnel. The superstitious fears of the barbarian whirled through his mind. Although he was fearless to the point of rashness toward men and beasts, the supernatural could still throw him into terror-stricken panic.

So this was why the Picts had gone! He should have suspected some such danger. He remembered such demonological lore as he had picked up in his youth in cloudy Cimmeria and later in his wanderings over most of the civilized world. Fire and silver were said to be deadly to devils, but he had neither at the moment. Still, if such spirits took gross material form, they were in some measure subject to the limitations of that form. This lumbering monster, for instance, could run no faster than a beast of its general size and shape, and the Cimmerian thought that he could outdistance it if need be.

Plucking up his wavering courage, the man shouted with boyish braggadocio: "Ho there, ugly-face, aren't you coming out?"

No reply; the blue mist swirled in the chamber but remained in its diffused form. Fingering his bruised neck, the Cimmerian recalled a Pictish tale of a demon sent by a wizard to slay a group of strange men from the sea, but who was then confined to that cave by this same wizard lest, having once been conjured across nighted gulfs and given material form, he turn upon those who had snatched him from his native hells and rend them.

Once more, the Cimmerian turned his attention to the chests that lay ranked along the walls of the tunnel . . .

Back at the fort, the count snapped: "Out, quick!" He tore at the bars of the gate, crying: "Drag that mantlet in before these strangers can land!"

"But Strombanni has fled," expostulated Galbro, "and yonder ship is Zingaran."

"Do as I order!" roared Valenso. "My enemies are not all foreigners! Out, dogs, thirty of you, and fetch the mantlet into the stockade!"

Before the Zingaran ship had dropped anchor, about where the pirate ship had docked, Valenso's thirty stalwarts had trundled the device back to the gate and manhandled it sideways through the opening.

Up in the window of the manor house, Tina asked wonderingly: "Why does not the count open the gate and go to meet them? Is he afraid that the man he fears might be on that ship?"

"What mean you, Tina?" asked Belesa uneasily. Although no man to run from a foe, the count had never vouchsafed a reason for his self-exile. But this conviction of Tina's was disquieting, almost uncanny. Tina, however, seemed not to have heard her question.

"The men are back in the stockade," she said. "The gate is closed again and barred. The men still keep their places along the wall. If that ship was chasing Strombanni, why did it not pursue him? It is not a war galley but a carack like the other. Look, a boat is coming

35

ashore. I see a man in the bow, wrapped in a dark cloak."

When the boat had grounded, this man paced in leisurely fashion up the sands, followed by three others. He was a tall, wiry man in black silk and polished steel.

"Halt!" roared the count. "I will parley with your leader, alone!"

The tall stranger removed his helmet and made a sweeping bow. His companions halted, drawing their wide cloaks about them, and behind them the sailors leaned on their oars and stared at the flag floating over the palisade.

When the leader came within easy call of the gate, he said: "Why, surely, there should be no suspicion between gentlemen in these naked seas!"

Valenso stared at him suspiciously. The stranger was dark, with a lean, predatory face and a thin black mustache. A bunch of lace was gathered at his throat, and there was lace on his wrists.

"I know you," said Valenso slowly. "You are Black Zarono, the buccaneer."

Again the stranger bowed with stately elegance. "And none could fail to recognize the red falcon of the Korzettas!"

"It seems this coast has become a rendezvous of all the rogues of the southern seas," growled Valenso. "What do you wish?"

"Come, come, sir!" remonstrated Zarono. "This is a churlish greeting to one who has just rendered you a service. Was not that Argossean dog, Strombanni, just now thundering at your gate? And did he not take to his sea-heels when he saw me round the point?"

"True," grunted the count grudgingly, "although there is little to choose between a pirate and a renegade."

Zarono laughed without resentment and twirled his mustache. "You are blunt in speech, my lord. But I de-

36

sire only leave to anchor in your bay, to let my men hunt for meat and water in your woods, and, perhaps, to drink a glass of wine myself at your board."

"I see not how I can stop you," growled Valenso. "But understand this, Zarono: no man of your crew shall come within this palisade. If one approaches closer than thirty paces, he shall presently find an arrow through his gizzard. And I charge you to do no harm to my gardens or the cattle in the pens. One steer you may have for fresh meat, but no more. And, in case you think otherwise, we can hold this fort against your ruffians."

"You were not holding it very successfully against Strombanni," the buccaneer pointed out with a mocking smile.

"You'll find no wood to build mantlets this time, unless you fell trees or strip it from your own ship," assured the count grimly. "And your men are not Barachan archers; they're no better bowmen than mine. Besides, what little loot you'd find in this castle would not be worth the price."

"Who speaks of loot and warfare?" protested Zarono. "Nay, my men are sick to stretch their legs ashore, and nigh to scurvy from chewing salt pork. May they come ashore? I guarantee their good conduct."

Valenso grudgingly signified his consent. Zarono bowed, a shade sardonically, and retired with a tread as measured and stately as if he trod the polished crystal floor of the Kordavan royal court—where indeed, unless rumor lied, he had once been a familiar figure.

"Let no man leave the stockade," Valenso ordered Galbro. "I trust not that renegade cur. The fact that he drove Strombanni from our gate is no guarantee that he, too, would not cut our throats."

Galbro nodded. He was well aware of the enmity that existed between the pirates and the Zingaran buccaneers. The pirates were mainly Argosssean sailors turned

37

outlaw; to the ancient feud between Argos and Zingara was added, in the case of the freebooters, the rivalry of opposing interests. Both breeds preyed on the shipping and the coastal towns; and they preyed upon each other with equal rapacity.

So no one stirred from the palisade while the buccaneers came ashore, dark-faced men in flaming silk and polished steel, with scarves bound around their heads and golden hoops in their ears. They camped on the beach, a hundred and seventy-odd of them, and Valenso noticed that Zarono posted lookouts on both points. They did not molest the gardens, and the steer designated by Valenso, shouting from the palisade, was driven forth and slaughtered. Fires were kindled on the strand, and a wattled cask of ale was brought ashore and broached.

Other kegs were filled with water from the spring that rose a short distance south of the fort, and men with crossbows in their hands began to straggle toward the woods. Seeing this, Valenso was moved to shout to Zarono, striding back and forth through the camp:

"Do not let your men go into the forest! Take another steer from the pens if you lack enough meat. But if the men go tramping into the woods, they may fall foul of the Picts. Whole tribes of the painted devils live back in the forest. We beat off an attack shortly after we landed, and since then six of my men have been murdered in the forest at one time or another. There's peace between us just now, but it hangs by a thread. Do not risk stirring them up!"

Zarono shot a startled glance at the lowering woods, as if he expected to see a horde of savage figures lurking there. Then he bowed and said: "I thank you for the warning, my lord." He shouted for his men to come back, in a rasping voice that contrasted strangely with his courtly accents when addressing the count.

If Zarono's vision could have penetrated the leafy

screen, he would have been even more apprehensive. He would have seen the sinister figure that lurked there, watching the strangers with inscrutable black eyes—a hideously-painted warrior, naked but for his doeskin breechclout, with a hornbill feather drooping over his left ear.

As evening drew on, a thin skim of gray crawled up from the sea-rim and overcast the sky. The sun sank in a wallow of crimson, touching the tips of the black waves with blood. Fog crawled out of the sea and lapped at the feet of the forest, curling about the stockade in smoky wisps. The fires on the beach shone dull crimson through the mist, and the singing of the buccaneers seemed deadened and far away. They had brought old sail canvas from the carack and made shelters along the strand, where beef was still roasting and the ale granted them by their captain was doled out sparingly.

The great gate was shut and barred. Soldiers stolidly tramped the ledges of the palisade, pike on shoulder, beads of moisture glistening on their steel caps. They glanced uneasily at the fires on the beach and stared with even greater fixity toward the forest, now a vague, dark line in the crawling fog. The compound now lay empty of life—a bare, darkened space. Candles gleamed feebly through the cracks of the huts, and light streamed from the windows of the manor. There was silence except for the tread of the sentries, the drip of water from the eaves, and the distant singing of the buccaneers.

Some faint echo of this singing penetrated into the great hall, where Valenso sat at wine with his unsolicited guest.

"Your men make merry, sir," grunted the count.

"They are glad to feel the sand under their feet again," answered Zarono. "It has been a wearisome voyage—aye, a long, stern chase." He lifted his goblet gallantly to the unresponsive girl who sat on his host's right, and drank ceremoniously.

Impassive attendants ranged the walls: soldiers with pikes and helmets, servants in satin coats. Valenso's household in this wild land was a shadowy reflection of the court he had kept in Kordava.

The manor house, as he insisted on calling it, was a marvel for that remote place. A hundred men had worked night and day for months to build it. While its log-walled exterior was devoid of ornamentation, within it was as nearly a copy of Korzetta Castle as possible. The logs that composed the walls of the hall were hidden with heavy silk tapestries, worked in gold. Ship's beams, stained and polished, formed the lofty ceiling. The floor was covered with rich carpets. The broad stair that led up from the hall was likewise carpeted, and its massive balustrade had once been a galleon's rail.

A fire in the wide stone fireplace dispelled the dampness of the night. Candles in the great silver candelabrum in the center of the broad mahogany board lit the hall, throwing long shadows on the stair.

Count Valenso sat at the head of that table, presiding over a company composed of his niece, his piratical guest, Galbro, and the captain of the guard. The smallness of the company emphasized the proportions of the vast board, where fifty guests might have sat at ease.

"You followed Strombanni?" asked Valenso. "You drove him this far afield?"

"I followed Strombanni," laughed Zarono, "but he was not fleeing from me. Strombanni is not the man to flee from anyone. Nay; he came seeking for something—something I, too, desire."

"What could tempt a pirate or a buccaneer to this naked land?" muttered Valenso, staring into the sparkling contents of his goblet.

40

"What could tempt a Count of Zingara?" retorted Zarono, an avid light burning in his eyes.

"The rottenness of the royal court might sicken a man of honor," remarked Valenso.

"Korzettas of honor have endured its rottenness with tranquility for several generations," said Zarono bluntly. "My lord, indulge my curiosity: Why did you sell your lands, load your galleon with the furnishings of your castle, and sail over the horizon out of the knowledge of the regent and the nobles of Zingara? And why settle here, when your sword and your name might carve out a place for you in any civilized land?"

Valenso toyed with the golden seal-chain about his neck. "As to why I left Zingara," he said, "that is my own affair. But it was chance that left me stranded here. I had brought all my people ashore, and much of the furnishings you mentioned, intending to build a temporary habitation. But my ship, anchored out there in the bay, was driven against the cliffs of the north point and wrecked by a sudden storm out of the west. Such storms are common enough at certain times of the year. After that, there was naught to do but remain and make the best of it."

"Then you would return to civilization, if you could?"

"Not to Kordava. But perhap to some far clime—to Vendhya, or even Khitai . . ."

"Do you not find it tedious here, my lady?" asked Zarono, for the first time addressing himself directly to Belesa.

Hunger to see a new face and hear a new voice had brought the girl to the great hall that night, but now she wished that she had remained in her chamber with Tina. There was no mistaking the meaning in the glance Zarono turned on her. Although his speech was decorous and formal, his expression sober and respectful, it was

41

but a mask through which gleamed the violent and sinister spirit of the man. He could not keep the burning desire out of his eyes when he looked at the aristocratic young beauty in her low-necked satin gown and jeweled girdle.

"There is little diversity here," she answered in a low voice.

"If you had a ship," Zarono bluntly asked his host, "you would abandon this settlement?"

"Perhaps," admitted the count.

"I have a ship," said Zarono. "If we could reach an agreement—"

"What sort of an agreement?" Valenso lifted his head to stare suspiciously at his guest.

"Share and share alike," said Zarono, laying his hand on the broad with fingers spread wide, like the legs of a giant spider. The fingers quivered with nervous tension, and the buccaneer's eyes gleamed with a new light.

"Share what?" Valenso stared at him in evident bewilderment. "The gold I brought with me went down in my ship and, unlike the broken timbers, it did not wash ashore."

"Not that!" Zarono made an impatient gesture. "Let us be frank, my lord. Can you pretend it was chance that caused you to land at this particular spot, with a thousand miles of coast from which to choose?"

"There is no need to pretend," answered Valenso coldly. "My ship's master was Zingelito, formerly a buccaneer. He had sailed this coast and persuaded me to land here, telling me he had a reason he would later disclose. But this reason he never divulged because, the day after he landed, he disappeared into the woods, and his headless body was found later by a hunting party. Obviously he had been ambushed and slain by the Picts."

Zarono stared fixedly at Valenso for a space. "Sink me!" quoth he at last. "I believe you, my lord. A Korzetta has no skill at lying, regardless of his other accomplishments. And I will make you a proposal. I will admit that, when I anchored out there in the bay, I had other plans in mind. Supposing you to have already secured the treasure, I meant to take this fort by strategy and cut all your throats. But circumstances have caused me to change my mind . . ." He cast a glance at Belesa that brought color to her face and made her lift her head indignantly, and continued: "I have a ship to carry you out of exile, with your household and such of your retainers as you shall choose. The rest can fend for themselves."

The attendants along the walls shot uneasy, sidelong glances at one another. Zarono went on, too brutally cynical to conceal his attentions: "But first, you must help me secure the treasure for which I've sailed a thousand miles."

"What treasure, in Mitra's name?" demanded the count angrily. "Now you are yammering like that dog Strombanni."

"Have you ever heard of Bloody Tranicos, the greatest of the Barachan pirates?"

"Who has not? It was he who stormed the island castle of the exiled prince, Tothmekri of Stygia, put the people to the sword, and bore off the treasure the prince had brought with him when he fled from Khemi."

"Aye! And the tale of that treasure brought men of the Red Brotherhood swarming like vultures after carrion— pirates, buccaneers, and even the wild black corsairs from the South. Fearing betrayal by his captains, Tranicos fled northward with one ship and vanished from the knowledge of men. That was nearly a hundred years ago.

"But the tale persists that one man survived that last voyage and returned to the Barachans, only to be captured by a Zingaran war-galley. Before he was hanged, he told his story and drew a map in his own blood, on

43

parchment, which he somehow smuggled out of his captor's reach. This was the tale he told:

"Tranicos had sailed far beyond the paths of shipping, until he came to a bay on a lonely coast, and there he anchored. He went ashore, taking his treasure and eleven of his most trusted captains, who had accompanied him on his ship. Following his orders, the ship sailed away, to return in a week's time and pick up their admiral and his captains. In the meantime, Tranicos meant to hide the treasure somewhere in the vicinity of the bay. The ship returned at the appointed time, but there was no trace of Tranicos and his eleven captains, except for the rude dwelling they had built on the beach.

"This had been demolished, and there were tracks of naked feet about it, but no sign there had been any fighting. Nor was there any trace of the treasure, or any sign to show where it was hidden. The pirates plunged into the forest to search for their chief. Having with them a Bossonian skilled in tracking and woodcraft, they followed the signs of the missing men along old trails running some miles eastward from the shore. Becoming weary and failing to catch up with the admiral, they sent one of their number up a tree to spy, and this one reported that not far ahead a great steep-sided crag or dome rose like a tower from the forest. They started forward again, but then were attacked by a party of Picts and driven back to their ship. In despair they heaved anchor and sailed away. Before they raised the Barachas, however, a terrific storm wrecked the ship, and only that one man survived.

"That is the tale of the treasure of Tranicos, which men have sought in vain for nearly a century. That the map exists is known, but its whereabouts have remained a mystery.

"I have had one glimpse of that map. Strombanni and Zingelito were with me, and a Nemedian who sailed with

44

the Barachans. We looked upon it in Messantia, where we were skulking in disguise. Somebody knocked over the lamp, and somebody howled in the dark, and when we got the light on again, the old miser who owned the map was dead with a dirk in his heart, and the map was gone, and the night watch was clattering down the street with their pikes to investigate the clamor. We scattered, and each went his own way.

"For years thereafter, Strombanni and I watched each other, each supposing the other had the map. Well, as it turned out, neither had it; but recently word came to me that Strombanni had departed northward, so I followed him. You saw the end of that chase.

"I had but a glimpse at the map as it lay on the old miser's table and could tell nothing about it, but Strombannni's actions show that he knows this is the bay where Tranicos anchored. I believe they hid the treasure on or near that great, rocky hill the scout reported and, returning, were attacked and slain by the Picts. The Picts did not get the treasure. Men have traded up and down this coast a little, and no gold ornament or rare jewel has ever been seen in the possession of the coastal tribes.

"This is my proposal: Let us combine our forces. Strombanni is somewhere within striking distance. He fled because he feared to be pinned between us, but he will return. Allied, however, we can laugh at him. We can work out from the fort, leaving enough men here to hold it if he attacks. I believe the treasure is hidden nearby. Twelve men could not have conveyed it far. We will find it, load it in my ship, and sail for some foreign port where I can cover my past with gold. I am sick of this life. I want to go back to a civilized land and live like a noble, with riches and slaves and a castle—and a wife of noble blood."

"Well?" demanded the count, slit-eyed with suspicion.

"Give me your niece for my wife," demanded the buccaneer bluntly.

Belesa cried out sharply and started to her feet. Valenso likewise rose, livid, his fingers knotting convulsively about his goblet as if he contemplated hurling it at his guest. Zarono did not move; he sat still, one arm on the table with the fingers hooked like talons. His eyes smoldered with passion and menace.

"You dare!" ejaculated Valenso.

"You seem to forget you have fallen from your high estate, Count Valenso," growled Zarono. "We are not at the Kordavan court, my lord. On this naked coast, nobility is measured by the power of men and arms, and there I rank you. Strangers tread Korzetta Castle, and the Korzetta fortune is at the bottom of the sea. You will die here, an exile, unless I give you the use of my ship.

"You shall have no cause to regret the union of our houses. With a new name and a new fortune, you will find that Black Zarono can take his place among the aristocrats of the world and make a son-in-law of which not even a Korzetta need be ashamed."

"You are mad to think of it!" exclaimed the count violently. "You—who is that?"

A patter of soft-slippered feet distracted his attention. Tina came hurriedly into the hall, hesitated when she saw the count's eyes fixed angrily on her, curtsied deeply, and sidled around the table to thrust her small hands into Belesa's fingers. She was panting slightly, her slippers were damp, and her flaxen hair was plastered down on her head.

"Tina!" exclaimed Belesa anxiously. "Where have you been? I thought you were in your chamber hours ago."

"I was," answered the child breathlessly, "but I missed the coral necklace you gave me . . ." She held it up, a trivial trinket, but prized beyond all her other possessions because it had been Belesa's first gift to her. "I was afraid you wouldn't let me go if you knew. A soldier's wife helped me out of the stockade and back again, and please, my lady, don't make me tell who she was, because i promised not to. I found my necklace by the pool where I bathed this morning. Please punish me if I have done wrong."

"Tina!" groaned Belesa, clasping the child to her. "I'll not punish you, but you should not have gone outside the palisade, with the buccaneers camped on the beach, and always a chance of Picts skulking about. Let me take you to your chamber and change these damp clothes—"

"Yes, my lady, but first let me tell you about the black man—"

"What?" The startling interruption was a cry that burst from Valenso's lips. His goblet clattered to the floor as he caught the table with both hands. If a thunderbolt had struck him, the bearing of the lord of the castle could not have been more horrifyingly altered. His face was livid, his eyes almost starting from his head.

"What did you say?" he panted, glaring wildly at the child, who shrank back against Belesa in bewilderment. "What said you, wench?"

"A b-black man, my lord," she stammered, while Belesa, Zarono, and the attendants stared at him in amazement. "When I went down to the pool to get my necklace, I saw him. There was a strange moaning in the wind, and the sea whimpered like something afraid, and then he came. He came from the sea in a strange, black boat with blue fire playing all about it, but there was no torch. He drew his boat up on the sands below the south point and strode toward the forest, looking like a giant in the fog—a great, tall man, dark like a Kushite—"

Valenso reeled as if he had received a mortal blow. He clutched at his throat, snapping the golden chain in his violence. With the face of a madman he lurched

47

about the table and tore the child screaming from Belesa's arms.

"You little slut!" he panted. "You lie! You have heard me mumbling in my sleep and have told this lie to torment me! Say that you lie before I tear the skin from your back!"

"Uncle!" cried Belesa in outraged bewilderment, trying to free Tina from his grasp. "Are you mad? What are you about?"

With a snarl, he tore her hand from his arm and spun her staggering into the arms of Galbro, who received her with a leer he made little effort to disguise.

"Mercy, my lord!" sobbed Tina. "I did not lie!"

"I say you lied!" roared Valenso. "Gebellez!"

The stolid serving-man seized the trembling youngster and stripped her with one brutal wrench that tore her scanty garments from her body. Wheeling, he drew her slender arms over his shoulders, lifting her writhing feet clear of the floor.

"Uncle!" shrieked Belesa, writhing vainly in Galbro's lustful grasp. "You are mad! You cannot—oh, you cannot—" The voice choked in her throat as Valenso caught up a jewel-handled riding whip and brought it down across the child's frail body with a savage force that left a red weal across her naked shoulders.

Belesa moaned, sick with the anguish in Tina's shriek. The world had suddenly gone mad. As in a nightmare, she saw the stolid beast-faces of the soldiers and the servants, reflecting neither pity nor sympathy. Zarono's faintly sneering visage was part of the nightmare. Nothing in that crimson haze was real except Tina's naked white body, crisscrossed with red welts from shoulders to knees; no sound real except the child's sharp cries of agony and the panting gasps of Valenso as he lashed away with the staring eyes of a madman, shrieking:

"You lie! You lie! Curse you, you lie! Admit your guilt,

or I will flay your stubborn body! *He* could not have followed me here . . ."

"Oh, have mercy, my lord!" screamed the child, writhing vainly on the brawny servant's back and too frantic with fear and pain to have the wit to save herself by a lie. Blood trickled in crimson beads down her quivering thighs. "I saw him! I lie not! Mercy! Please! Aaah!"

"You fool! *You fool!*" screamed Belesa. "Do you not see she is telling the truth? Oh, you beast! Beast! Beast!"

Some shred of sanity seemed to return to the brain of Count Valenso of Korzetta. Dropping the whip, he reeled back against the table, clutching blindly at its edge. He shook as with an ague. His hair was plastered across his brow in dank strands, and sweat dripped from his livid countenance, which was like a carven mask of Fear. Tina, released by Gebellez, slipped to the floor in a whimpering heap. Belesa tore free from Galbro, rushed to her, sobbing, and fell on her knees. Gathering the pitiful waif in her arms, she lifted a terrible face to her uncle, to pour upon him the vials of her wrath—but he was not looking at her. He seemed to have forgotten both her and his victim. In a daze of incredulity, she heard him say to the buccaneer:

"I accept your offer, Zarono. In Mitra's name, let us find this accursed treasure and begone from this damned coast!"

At this, the fire of her fury sank to ashes. In stunned silence, she lifted the sobbing child in her arms and carried her up the stair. A glance backward showed Valenso crouching at the table, gulping wine from a huge goblet, which he gripped in both shaking hands, while Zarono towered over him like a somber predatory bird—puzzled at the turn of events but quick to take advantage of the shocking change that had come over the count. He was talking in a low, decisive voice, and Valenso nodded in mute agreement, like one who scarcely heeds what is

49

being said. Galbro stood back in the shadows, chin pinched between forefinger and thumb, and the attendants along the walls glanced furtively at one another, bewildered by their lord's collapse.

Up in her chamber, Belesa laid the half-fainting girl on the bed and set herself to wash and apply soothing ointments to the weals and cuts on her tender skin. Tina gave herself up in complete submission to her mistress's hands, moaning faintly. Belesa felt as if her world had fallen about her ears. She was sick and bewildered, overwrought, her nerves quivering from the brutal shock of what she had witnessed. Fear of and hatred for her uncle grew in her soul. She had never loved him; he was hard, grasping, and avid, apparently without natural affection. But she had considered him just and fearless. Revulsion shook her at the memory of his staring eyes and bloodless face. Some terrible fear had aroused his frenzy, and, because of this fear, Valenso had brutalized the only creature she had to love and cherish. Because of that fear he was selling her, his niece, to an infamous outlaw. What lay behind this madness? Who was the black man Tina had seen?

The child muttered in semi-delirium: "I lied not, my lady! Indeed I did not! 'Twas a black man in a black boat that burned like blue fire on the water! A tall man, almost as dark as a Kushite, wrapped in a black cloak! I was afraid when I saw him, and my blood ran cold. He left his boat on the sands and went into the forest. Why did the count whip me for seeing him?"

"Hush, Tina," soothed Belesa. "Lie quietly. The smarting will soon pass."

The door opened behind her, and she whirled, snatching up a jeweled dagger. The count stood in the door, and her flesh crawled at the sight. He looked years older; his face was gray and drawn, and his eyes stared in a way that roused fear in her bosom. She had never been close to him; now she felt as though a gulf separated them. He was not her uncle who stood there, but a stranger come to menace her.

She lifted the dagger. "If you touch her again," she whispered from dry lips, "I swear before Mitra that I will sink this blade in your breast."

He did not heed her. "I have posted a strong guard about the manor," he said. "Zarono brings his men into the stockade tomorrow. He will not sail until he has found the treasure. When he finds it, we shall sail at once for some port to be decided upon."

"And you will sell me to him?" she whispered. "In Mitra's name—"

He fixed upon her a gloomy gaze in which all considerations but his own self-interest had been crowded out. She shrank before it, seeing in it the frantic cruelty that possessed the man in his mysterious fear.

"You shall do as I command," he said presently, with no more human feeling in his voice than there is in the ring of flint on steel. And, turning, he left the chamber. Blinded by a sudden rush of horror, Belesa fell fainting beside the couch where Tina lay.

4. A *Black Drum Droning*

Belesa never knew how long she lay crushed and senseless. She was first aware of Tina's arms about her and the sobbing of the child in her ear. Mechanically she straightened herself and drew the child into her arms.

She sat there, dry-eyed, staring unseeingly at the flickering candle. There was no sound in the castle. The singing of the buccaneers on the strand had ceased. Dully, almost impersonally she reviewed her problem.

Valenso was mad, driven frantic by the story of the mysterious black man. It was to escape this stranger that he wished to abandon the settlement and flee with Zarono. That much was obvious. Equally obvious was the fact that he was ready to sacrifice her in exchange for that opportunity to escape. In the blackness of spirit which surrounded her she saw no glint of light. The serving men were dull or callous brutes, their women stupid and apathetic. They would neither dare nor care to help her. She was utterly helpless.

Tina lifted her tear-stained face as if she were listening to the prompting of some inner voice. The child's understanding of Belesa's inmost thoughts was almost uncanny, as was her recognition of the inexorable drive of Fate and the only alternative left to the weak.

"We must go, my lady!" she whispered. "Zarono shall not have you. Let us go far away into the forest. We shall go until we can go no further, and then we shall lie down and die together."

That tragic strength that is the last refuge of the weak entered Belesa's soul. It was the only escape from the shadows that had been closing in upon her since that day when they fled from Zingara.

"We will go, child."

She rose and was fumbling for a cloak, when an exclamation from Tina brought her about. The girl was on her feet, a finger pressed to her lips, her eyes wide and bright with terror.

"What is it, Tina?" The child's expression of fright induced Belesa to pitch her voice to a whisper, and a nameless apprehension crawled over her.

"Someone outside in the hall," whispered Tina, clutching her arm convulsively. "He stopped at our door, then went on toward the count's chamber at the other end."

"Your ears are keener than mine," murmured Belesa. "But there is nothing strange in that. It was the count himself, perchance, or Galbro."

She moved to open the door, but Tina threw her arms frantically about her neck, and Belesa felt the wild beating of her heart. "No, no, my lady! Open not the door! I am afraid! I do not know why, but I feel that some evil thing is skulking near us!"

Impressed, Belesa patted her reassuringly and reached a hand toward the metal disk that masked the peephole in the center of the door.

"He is coming back!" quavered Tina. "I hear him!"

Belesa heard something, too—a curious, stealthy pad, which she knew, with a chill of nameless fear, was not the step of anyone she knew. Nor was it the step of Zarono, or any booted man. Could it be the buccaneer, gliding along the hallway on bare, stealthy feet, to slay his host while he slept? She remembered the soldiers on guard below. If the buccaneer had remained in the manor for the night, a man-at-arms would be posted before his chamber door. But who was that sneaking along the corridor? None slept upstairs besides herself, Tina, the Count, and Galbro.

With a quick motion, she extinguished the candle, so that it should not shine through the peephole, and pushed aside the copper disk. All the lights in the hall—ordinarily lighted by candles—were out. Someone was moving along the darkened corridor. She sensed rather than saw a dim bulk moving past her doorway, but she could make nothing of its shape except that it was manlike. A chill wave of terror swept over her; she crouched dumb, incapable of the scream that froze behind her lips. It was not such terror as her uncle now inspired in her, or fear like her fear of Zarono, or even of the brooding forest.

It was blind, unreasoning horror that laid an icy hand on her soul and froze her tongue to her palate.

The figure passed on to the stairhead, where it was limned momentarily against the faint glow that came up from below. It was a man, but not any man such as Belesa was familiar with. She had an impression of a shaven head with aloof, aquiline features and a glossy, brown skin, darker than that of her swarthy countrymen. The head towered on broad, massive shoulders swathed in a black cloak. Then the intruder was gone.

She crouched there in the darkness, awaiting the outcry that would announce that the soldiers in the great hall had seen the intruder. But the manor remained silent. Somewhere a wind wailed shrilly; that was all.

Belesa's hands were moist with perspiration as she groped to relight the candle. She was still shaken with horror, although she could not decide just what there had been about that black figure etched against the red glow that had roused this frantic loathing in her soul. She only knew that the sight had robbed her of all her new-found resolution. She was demoralized, incapable of action.

The candle flared up, illuminating Tina's white face in the yellow glow.

"It was the black man!" whispered Tina. "I know! My blood turned cold, just as it did when I saw him on the beach. There are soldiers downstairs; why did they not see him? Shall we go and tell the count?"

Belesa shook her head. She did not care to repeat the scene that had ensued upon Tina's first mention of the black man. At any event, she dared not venture out into that darkened hallway.

"We dare not go into the forest!" shuddered Tina. "He will be lurking there."

Belesa did not ask the girl how she knew the black man would be in the forest; it was the logical hiding-place for any evil thing, man or devil. And she knew that

54

Tina was right; they dared not leave the fort now. Her determination, which had not faltered at the prospect of certain death, gave way at the thought of traversing those gloomy woods with that dark, sinister creature at large among them. Helplessly she sat down and sank her face in her hands.

Tina slept, presently, on the couch. Tears sparkled on her long lashes; she moved her smarting body uneasily in her restless slumber. Belesa watched.

Toward dawn, Belesa was aware of a stifling quality in the atmosphere; she heard a low rumble of thunder somewhere off to seaward. Extinguishing the candle, which had burned to its socket, she went to the window whence she could see both the ocean and a belt of the forest behind the fort.

The fog had disappeared, and along the eastern horizon ran a thin, pale streak that presaged dawn. But out to sea, a dusky mass was rising from the horizon. From it, lightning flickered and the low thunder growled. An answering rumble came from the black woods.

Startled, Belesa turned and stared at the forest, a brooding black rampart. A strange, rhythmic pulsing came to her ears—a droning reverberation that was not the roll of a Pictish drum.

"A drum!" sobbed Tina, spasmodically opening and closing her fingers in her sleep. "The black man—beating on black drum—in the black woods! Oh, Mitra save us!"

Belesa shuddered. The black cloud on the western horizon writhed and billowed, swelling and expanding. She stared in amazement, for the previous summer there had been no storms on this coast at this time of year, and she had never seen a cloud like that one.

It came boiling up over the world-rim in great boiling masses of blackness, veined with blue fire. It rolled and billowed with the wind in its belly. Its thundering made the air vibrate. And another sound mingled awesomely with the reverberations of the thunder—the voice of the wind, which raced before its coming. The inky horizon was torn and convulsed in the lightning-flashes. Afar to sea she saw the white-capped waves racing before the wind; she heard its droning roar, increasing in volume as it swept shoreward.

But, as yet, no wind stirred on the land. The air was hot, breathless. There was a sensation of unreality about the contrast: out there, wind and thunder and chaos sweeping inland; but here, stifling stillness. Somewhere below her a shutter slammed, startling in the tense silence, and a woman's voice was lifted, shrill with alarm. Most of the people of the fort, however, seemed to be sleeping, unaware of the oncoming hurricane.

She realized that she still heard that mysterious, droning drum-beat. She stared toward the black forest, her flesh crawling. She could see nothing, but some obscure intuition prompted her to visualize a black, hideous figure squatting under black branches and beating out a nameless incantation on a drum of exotic design.

Desperately she shook off the ghoulish conviction and looked seaward, as a blaze of lightning split the sky. Outlined against its glare, she saw the masts of Zarono's ship; she saw the tents of the buccaneers on the beach, the sandy ridges of the south point, and the rocky cliffs of the north point as plainly as by a midday sun. Louder and louder rose the roar of the wind, and now the manor was awake. Feet came pounding up the stair, and Zarono's voice yelled, edged with fright. Doors slammed, and Valenso answered, shouting to be heard above the roar of the elements.

"Why didn't you warn me of a storm from the west?" howled the buccaneer. "If the anchors hold not—"

"A storm has never come from the west before, at this time of year!" shrieked Valenso, rushing from his chamber in his nightshirt, his face livid and his hair standing stiffly on end. "This is the work of—" His words were lost as he raced madly up the ladder that led to the lookout tower, followed by the cursing buccaneer.

Belesa crouched at her window, awed and deafened. Louder and louder rose the wind, until it drowned all other sound—all except that maddening drone of a drum, which now rose like an inhuman chant of triumph. The storm roared inshore, driving before it a foaming league-long crest of white. Then all hell and destruction were loosed on that coast. Rain fell in driving torrents, sweeping the beaches with blind frenzy. The wind hit like a thunderclap, making the timbers of the fort quiver. The surf roared over the sands, drowning the coals of the fires the seamen had built.

In the glare of lightning Belesa saw, through the curtain of the slashing rain, the tents of the buccaneers whipped to ribbons and whirled away; saw the men themselves staggering toward the fort, beaten almost to the sands by the fury of the blast. And limned against the blue glare she saw Zarono's ship, ripped loose from her moorings, driven headlong against the jagged rocks that jutted up to receive her.

5. A Man from the Wilderness

The storm had spent its fury; dawn broke in a clear, blue, rain-washed sky. Bright-hued birds lifted a swelling chorus from the trees, on whose broad leaves beads of water sparkled like diamonds, quivering in the gentle morning breeze.

At a small stream that wound over the sands to join the sea, hidden beyond a fringe of trees and shrubs, a man bent to lave his hands and face. He performed his ablutions after the manner of his kind, grunting lustily and splashing like a buffalo. But in the midst of these splashings, he suddenly lifted his head, his tawny hair dripping and water running in rivulets over his brawny shoulders. For a second he crouched in a listening attitude, then was on his feet facing inland, sword in hand, all in one motion. Then he froze, glaring wide-mouthed.

A man even bigger than himself was striding toward him over the sands, making no attempt at stealth. The pirate's eyes widened as he stared at the close-fitting silk breeches, the high flaring-topped boots, the wide-skirted coat, and the headgear of a hundred years ago. There was a broad cutlass in the stranger's hand and unmistakable purpose in his approach.

The pirate went pale as recognition blazed in his eyes. "You!" he ejaculated unbelievingly. "By Mitra, you!"

Oaths streamed from his lips as he heaved up his cutlass. The birds rose in flaming showers from the trees as the clang of steel interrupted their song. Blue sparks flew from the hacking blades, and the sand grated and ground under the stamping boot heels. Then the clash of steel ended in a chopping crunch, and one man went to his knees with a choking gasp. The hilt escaped his nerveless hand; he slid full-length on the sand, which reddened with his blood. With a dying effort, he fumbled at his girdle and drew something from it, tried to lift it to his mouth, then stiffened convulsively and went limp.

The conqueror bent and ruthlessly tore the stiffening fingers from the object they crumpled in their desperate grasp.

Zarono and Valenso stood on the beach, staring at the driftwood that their men were gathering—spars, pieces of mast, broken timbers. So savagely had the storm hammered Zarono's ship against the low cliffs that most of the salvage was matchwood. A short distance behind them stood Belesa, listening to their conversation with one arm around Tina. Belesa was pale and listless, apathetic to whatever Fate held in store for her. She heard what the men said, but with little interest. She was crushed by the realization that she was but a pawn in the game, however it was to be played out—whether it was to be a wretched life, dragged out on that desolate coast, or a return effected somehow to some civilized land.

Zarono cursed venomously, but Valenso seemed dazed. "This is not the time of year for storms from the west," muttered the count, staring with haggard eyes at the men dragging the wreckage up on the beach. "It was not chance that brought that storm out of the deep to splinter the ship in which I meant to escape. Escape? I am caught like a rat in a trap, as it was meant. Nay, we are all trapped rats—"

"I know not whereof you speak," snarled Zarono, giving a vicious yank at his moustache. "I've been unable to get any sense out of you since that flaxen-haired slut upset you so last night with her tale of black men coming out of the sea. But I do know that I'll not spend my life on this cursed coast. Ten of my men went to Hell in the ship, but I have a hundred and sixty more. You have a hundred. There are tools in your fort and plenty of trees in yonder forest. We'll build a ship. I'll set men to cutting down trees as soon as they get this drift out of reach of the waves."

"It will take months," muttered Valenso.

"Well, how better to employ our time? We're here, and unless we build a ship we shall never get away. We shall have to rig up some kind of sawmill, but I've never encountered anything yet that balked me for long. I hope the storm smashed that Argossean dog Strombanni to bits! While we're building the ship, we'll hunt for old Tranicos's loot."

"We shall never complete your ship," said Valenso somberly.

Zarono turned on him angrily. "Will you talk sense? Who is this accursed black man?"

"Accursed indeed," said Valenso, staring seaward. "A shadow of mine own red-stained past, risen up to hound me to Hell. Because of him, I fled Zingara, hoping to lose my trail in the great ocean. But I should have known he would smell me out at last."

"If such a man came ashore, he must be hiding in the woods," groaned Zarono. "We'll rake the forest and hunt him out."

Valenso laughed harshly. "Seek rather for a shadow that drifts before a cloud that hides the moon; grope in the dark for an asp; follow a mist that steals out of the swamp at midnight."

Zarono cast him an uncertain look, obviously doubting

his sanity. "Who is this man? Have done with ambiguity."

"The shadow of my own mad cruelty and ambition; a horror come out of the lost ages—no man of common flesh and blood, but a—"

"Sail ho!" bawled the lookout on the northern point. Zarono wheeled, and his voice slashed the wind. "Do you know her?"

"Aye!" the reply came back faintly. "'Tis the *Red Hand!*"

Zarono cursed like a wild man. "Strombanni! The devils take care of their own! How could he ride out that blow?" The buccaneer's voice rose to a yell that carried up and down the strand. "Back to the fort, you dogs!"

Before the *Red Hand*, somewhat battered in appearance, nosed around the point, the beach was bare of human life, the palisade bristling with helmets and scarf-bound heads. The buccaneers accepted the alliance with the easy adaptability of adventurers, and the count's henchmen with the apathy of serfs.

Zarono ground his teeth as a longboat swung leisurely in to the beach, and he sighted the tawny head of his rival in the bow. The boat grounded, and Strombanni started toward the fort alone.

Some distance away, he halted and shouted in a bull's bellow that carried clearly in the still morning: "Ahoy, the fort! I would parley!"

"Well, why in Hell don't you?" snarled Zarono.

"The last time I approached under a flag of truce, an arrow broke on my brisket!" roared the pirate.

"You asked for it," said Valenso. "I gave you a fair warning to get away from us."

"Well, I want a promise that it shan't happen again!"

"You have my promise!" called Zarono with a sardonic smile.

"Damn your promise, you Zingaran dog! I want Valenso's word."

A measure of dignity remained to the count. There was an edge of authority to his voice as he answered: "Advance, but keep your men back. You shall not be shot at."

"That's enough for me," said Strombanni instantly. "Whatever a Korzetta's sins, you can trust his word."

He strode forward and halted under the gate, laughing at the hate-darkened visage Zarono thrust over at him.

"Well, Zarono," he taunted, "you are a ship shorter than you were when last I saw you! But you Zingarans were never sailors."

"How did you save your ship, you Messantian gutter-scum?" snarled the buccaneer.

"There's a cove some miles to the north, protected by a high-ridged arm of land, which broke the force of the gale," answered Strombanni. "I was anchored behind it. My anchors dragged, but they held me off the shore."

Zarono scowled blackly; Valenso said nothing. The count had not known of this cove, for he had done scant exploring of his domain. Fear of the Picts, lack of curiosity, and the need to drive his people to their work had kept him and his men near the fort.

"I come to make a trade," said Strombanni easily.

"We've naught to trade with you save sword-strokes," growled Zarono.

"I think otherwise," grinned Strombanni, thin-lipped. "You showed your intentions when you murdered Galacus, my first mate, and robbed him. Until this morning, I supposed that Valenso had Tranicos's treasure. But, if either of you had had it, you wouldn't have gone to the trouble of following me and killing my mate to get the map."

"The map?" Zarono ejaculated, stiffening.

62

"Oh, dissemble not with me!" laughed Strombanni, but anger blazed blue in his eyes. "I know you have it. Picts don't wear boots!"

"But—" began the count, nonplussed; then he fell silent as Zarono nudged him.

"And if we have the map," said Zarono, "what have you to trade that we might require?"

"Let me come into the fort," suggested Strombanni. "There we can talk."

He was not so obvious as to glance at the men peering at them from along the wall, but his listeners understood. Strombanni had a ship. That fact would figure in any bargain or battle. But, regardless of who commanded it, it would carry just so many. Whoever sailed away in it, some would be left behind. A wave of tense speculation ran along the silent throng at the palisade.

"Your men shall stay where they are," warned Zarono, indicating the boat drawn up on the beach and the ship anchored out in the bay.

"Aye. But think not to seize me and hold me for a hostage!" He laughed grimly. "I want Valenso's word that I shall be allowed to leave the fort alive and unhurt within the hour, whether we come to terms or not."

"You have my pledge," answered the count.

"All right, then. Open that gate and let's talk plainly." The gate opened and closed; the leaders vanished from sight. The common men of both parties resumed their silent surveillance of each other: the men on the palisade, the men squatting beside their boat, with a broad stretch of sand between; and, beyond a strip of blue water, the carack with steel caps glinting along her rail.

On the broad stair, above the great hall, Belesa and Tina crouched, ignored by the men below. These sat about the broad table: Valenso, Galbro, Zarono, and Strombanni. But for them, the hall was empty.

Strombanni gulped his wine and set the empty goblet on the table. The frankness suggested by his bluff countenance was belied by the dancing lights of cruelty and treachery in his wide eyes. But he spoke bluntly enough.

"We all want the treasure old Tranicos hid somewhere near this bay," he said abruptly. "Each has something the others need. Valenso has laborers, supplies, and a stockade to shelter us from the Picts. You, Zarono, have my map. I have a ship."

"What I should like to know," remarked Zarono, "is this: If you've had that map all these years, why came you not after the loot sooner?"

"I had it not. It was that dog, Zingelito, who knifed the old miser in the dark and stole the map. But he had neither ship nor crew, and it took him more than a year to get them. When he did come after the treasure, the Picts prevented his landing, and his men mutinied and made him sail back to Zingara. One of them stole the map from him and recently sold it to me."

"That was why Zingelito recognized the bay," muttered Valenso.

"Did that dog lead you here, count?" asked Strombanni. "I might have guessed it. Where is he?"

"Doubtless in Hell, since he was once a buccaneer. The Picts slew him, evidently while he was searching the woods for the treasure."

"Good!" approved Strombanni heartily. "Well, I don't know how you knew my mate was carrying the map. I trusted him, and the men trusted him more than they did me, so I let him keep it. But this morning he wandered inland with some of the others and got separated from them. We found him sworded to death near the beach, and the map gone. The men were ready to accuse me of killing him, but I showed the fools the tracks left by his slayer and proved to them that my feet wouldn't fit them. And I knew it wasn't any one of the crew, because none of them wears boots that make a track of that sort. And Picts wear no boots at all. So it had to be a Zingaran.

"Well, you have the map, but you have not the treasure. If you had it, you wouldn't have let me inside the stockade. I have you penned up in this fort. You can't get out to look for the loot, and even if you did get it you have no ship to get away in.

"Now, here's my proposal: Zarono, give me the map. And you, Valenso, give me fresh meat and other supplies. My men are nigh to scurvy after the long voyage. In return I'll take you three men, the Lady Belesa, and her girl, and set you ashore within reach of some Zingaran port—or I'll put Zarono ashore near some buccaneer rendezvous if he prefers, since doubtless a noose awaits him in Zingara. And, to clinch the bargain, I'll give each of you a handsome share in the treasure."

The buccaneer tugged meditatively at his mustache. He knew that Strombanni would not keep any such pact, if made. Nor did Zarono even consider agreeing to his proposal. To refuse bluntly, however, would be to force the issue to a clash of arms. He sought his agile brain for a plan to outwit the pirate. He wanted Strombanni's ship as avidly as he desired the lost treasure.

"What's to prevent us from holding you captive and forcing your men to give us your ship in exchange for you?" he asked.

Strombanni laughed. "Think you I'm a fool? My men have orders to heave up the anchors and sail hence if I do not appear within the hour, or if they suspect treachery. They'd not give you the ship if you skinned me alive on the beach. Besides, I have the count's word."

"My pledge is not straw," said Valenso somberly. "Have done with threats, Zarono."

65

Zarono did not reply. His mind was wholly absorbed in the problems of getting possession of Strombanni's ship and of continuing the parley without betraying the fact that he did not have the map. He wondered who in Mitra's name *did* have the map.

"Let me take my men away with me on your ship when we sail," he said. "I cannot desert my faithful followers—"

Strombanni snorted. "Why don't you ask for my cutlass to slit my gullet with? Desert your faithful—bah! You'd desert your brother to the Devil if you could gain anything by it. No! You shall not bring enough men aboard to give you a chance to mutiny and take my ship."

"Give us a day to think it over," urged Zarono, fighting for time.

Strombanni's heavy fist banged on the table, making the wine dance in the goblets. "No, by Mitra! Give me my answer now!"

Zarono was on his feet, his black rage submerging his craftiness. "You Barachan dog! I'll give you your answer —in your guts . . ."

He tore aside his cloak and caught at his sword hilt. Strombanni heaved up with a roar, his chair crashing backward to the floor. Valenso sprang up, spreading his arms between them as they faced each other across the board with jutting jaws close together, blades half drawn, and faces convulsed. "Gentlemen, have done! Zarono, he has my pledge—"

"The foul fiends gnaw your pledge!" snarled Zarono.

"Stand from between us, my lord," growled the pirate, his voice thick with lust for killing. "Your word was that I should not be treacherously entreated. It shall be considered no violation of your pledge for this dog and me to cross swords in equal play."

"Well spoken, Strom!" said a deep, powerful voice be-

66

hind them, vibrant with grim amusement. All wheeled and glared open-mouthed. Up on the stair, Belesa started up with an involuntary exclamation.

A man strode out of the hangings that masked the chamber door and advanced toward the table without haste or hesitation. Instantly he dominated the group, and all felt the situation subtly charged with a new, dynamic atmosphere.

The stranger was taller and more powerfully built than either of the freebooters, yet for all his size he moved with pantherish suppleness in his high, flaring-topped boots. His thighs were cased in close-fitting breeches of white silk. His wide-skirted, sky-blue coat was open to reveal an open-necked, white silken shirt beneath, and the scarlet sash that girded his waist. His coat was adorned with acorn-shaped silver buttons, gilt-worked cuffs and pocket flaps, and a satin collar. A lac-quered hat completed a costume obsolete by nearly a hundred years. A heavy cutlass hung at the wearer's hip.

"Conan!" ejaculated both freebooters together, and Valenso and Galbro caught their breath at that name.

"Who else?" The giant strode up to the table, laughing sardonically at their amazement.

"What—what do you here?" stuttered the senescal. "How came you here, uninvited and unannounced?"

"I climbed the palisade on the east side while you fools were arguing at the gate," Conan answered, speaking Zingaran with a barbarous accent. "Every man in the fort was craning his neck westward. I entered the manor while Strombanni was being let in at the gate. Every since, I've been in that chamber there, eavesdropping."

"I thought you were dead," said Zarono slowly. "Three years ago, the shattered hull of your ship was sighted off a reefy coast, and you were heard of on the Main no more."

"I didn't drown with my crew," answered Conan. "'Twill take a bigger ocean than that one to drown me. I swam ashore and tried a spell of mercenarying among the black kingdoms; and since then I've been soldiering for the king of Aquilonia. You might say I have become respectable," he grinned wolfishly, "or at least that I had until a recent difference with that ass Numedides. And now to business, fellow thieves."

Up on the stair, Tina was clutching Belesa in her excitement and staring through the balustrade with all her eyes. "Conan! My lady, it is Conan! Look! Oh, look!"

Belesa was looking, as though she beheld a legendary character in the flesh. Who of all the sea-folk had not heard the wild, bloody tales told of Conan, the wild rover who had once been a captain of the Barachan pirates, and one of the greatest scourges of the sea? A score of ballads celebrated his ferocious, audacious exploits. The man could not be ignored; irresistibly he had stalked into the scene, to form another, dominent element in the tangled plot. And, in the midst of her frightened fascination, Belesa's feminine instinct prompted the speculation as to Conan's attitude toward her. Would it be like Strombanni's brutal indifference or Zarono's violent desire?

Valenso was recovering from the shock of finding a stranger within his very hall. He knew that Conan was a Cimmerian, bo.n and bred in the wastes of the far north, and therefore not amenable to the physical limitations that controlled civilized men. It was not so strange that he had been able to enter the fort undetected, but Valenso flinched at the reflection that other barbarians might duplicate that feat—the dark, silent Picts, for instance.

"What would you here?" he demanded. "Did you come from the sea?"

"I came from the woods." The Cimmerian jerked his head toward the east.

"You have been living with the Picts?" Valenso asked coldly.

A momentary anger flickered in the giant's eyes. "Even a Zingaran ought to know there's never been peace between Picts and Cimmerians, and never will be," he retorted with an oath. "Our feud with them is older than the world. If you'd said that to one of my wilder brothers, you'd have found yourself with a split head. But I've lived among you civilized men long enough to understand your ignorance and lack of common courtesy—the churlishness that demands his business of a man who appears at your door out of a thousand-mile wilderness. Never mind that." He turned to the two freebooters, who stood staring glumly at him. "From what I overheard," quoth he, "I gather there is some dissension over a map."

"That is none of your affair," growled Strombanni.

"Is this it?" Conan grinned wickedly and drew from his pocket a crumpled object—a square of parchment, marked with crimson lines.

Strombanni started violently, paling. "My map!" he ejaculated. "Where did you get it?"

"From your mate, Galacus, when I killed him," answered Conan with grim enjoyment.

"You dog!" raved Strombanni, turning on Zarono. "You never had the map! You lied—"

"I never said I had it," snarled Zarono. "You deceived yourself. Be not a fool. Conan is alone; if he had a crew he'd already have cut our throats. We'll take the map from him—"

"You'll never touch it!" Conan laughed fiercely.

Both men sprang at him, cursing. Stepping back, he crumpled the parchment and cast it into the glowing coals of the fireplace. With an incoherent bellow, Strombanni lunged past him, to be met with a buffet under the ear that stretched him half-senseless on the floor. Zarono whipped out his sword, but before he could thrust, Conan's cutlass beat it out of his hand.

Zarono staggered against the table with all Hell in his eyes. Strombanni dragged himself erect with his eyes glazed and blood dripping from his bruised ear. Conan leaned slightly over the table, his outstretched cutless just touching the breast of Count Valenso.

"Don't call for your soldiers, Count," said the Cimmerian softly. "Not a sound out of you—or from you, either, dog-face!" he said to Galbro, who showed no intention of braving his wrath. "The map's burned to ashes, and it'll do no good to spill blood. Sit down, all of you."

Strombanni hesitated, made an abortive gesture toward his hilt, then shrugged his shoulders and sank sullenly into a chair. The others followed suit. Conan remained standing, towering over the table, while his enemies watched him with eyes full of bitter hate.

"You were bargaining," he said. "That's all I've come to do."

"And what have you to trade?" sneered Zarono.

"Only the treasure of Tranicos."

"*What?*" All four men were on their feet, leaning toward him.

"*Sit down!*" roared Conan, banging his broad blade on the table.

They sank back, tense and white with excitement. Conan grinned in huge enjoyment of the sensation his words had caused and continued:

"Yes! I found the treasure before I got the map. That's why I burned the map. I need it not, and nobody shall ever find it unless I show him where it is."

They stared at him with murder in their eyes.

"You're lying," said Zarono without conviction. "You've told us one lie already. You said you came from the woods, yet you say you haven't been living with the Picts. All men know this country is a wilderness, inhabited only by savages. The nearest outposts of civilization are the Aquilonian settlements on Thunder River, hundreds of miles to eastward."

"That's where I came from," replied Conan imperturbably. "I believe I'm the first white man to cross the Pictish Wilderness. When I fled from Aquilonia into Pictland, I blundered into a party of Picts and slew one, but a stone from a sling knocked me senseless during the melee and the dogs took me alive. They were Wolfmen, and they traded me to the Eagle clan in return for a chief of theirs the Eagles had captured. The Eagles carried me nearly a hundred miles westward, to burn me in their chief village; but I killed their war-chief and three or four others one night and broke away.

"I could not turn back, since they were behind me and kept herding me westward. A few days ago, I shook them off; and, by Crom, the place where I took refuge turned out to be the treasure trove of old Tranicos! I found it all: chests of garments and weapons—that's where I got these clothes and this blade—heaps of coins and gems and golden ornaments, and—in the midst of all—the jewels of Tothmekri gleaming like frozen starlight! And old Tranicos and his eleven captains sitting about an ebon table and staring at the hoard, as they've stared for a hundred years!"

"What?"

"Aye!" he laughed. "Tranicos died in the midst of his treasure, and all with him! Their bodies had not rotted or shriveled. They sit there in their high boots and skirted coats and lacquered hats, with their wineglasses in their stiff hands, just as they have sat for a century!"

71

"That's an unchancy thing!" muttered Strombanni uneasily, but Zarono snarled:

"What boots it? 'Tis the treasure we want. Go on, Conan."

Conan seated himself at the board, filled a goblet, and quaffed it before he answered.

"The first wine I've drunk since I left Aquilonia, by Crom! Those cursed Eagles hunted me so closely through the forest that I had hardly time to munch the nuts and roots I found. Sometimes I caught frogs and ate them raw because I dared not light a fire."

His impatient hearers informed him profanely that they were not interested in his dietary adventures prior to finding the treasure.

He grinned insolently and resumed: "Well, after I stumbled on to the trove, I lay up and rested a few days, and made snares to catch rabbits, and let my wounds heal. I saw smoke against the western sky but thought it some Pictish village on the beach. I lay close, but as it happens the loot's hidden in a place the Picts shun. If any spied on me, they didn't show themselves.

"Last night I started westward, intending to strike the beach some miles north of the spot where I'd seen the smoke. I wasn't far from the shore when that storm hit. I took shelter under a lee of rock and waited until it had blown itself out. Then I climbed a tree to look for Picts, and from it I saw Strom's carack at anchor and his men coming in to shore. I was making my way toward his camp on the beach when I met Galacus. I shoved a sword through him, because there was an old feud between us."

"What had he done to you?" asked Strombanni.

"Oh, stole a wench of mine years ago. I shouldn't have known he had a map, had he not tried to eat it ere he died.

"I recognized it for what it was, of course, and was considering what use I could make of it, when the rest of you dogs came up and found the body. I was lying in a thicket not a dozen yards from you while you were arguing with your men over the matter. I judged the time wasn't ripe for me to show myself!" He laughed at the rage and chagrin displayed in Strombanni's face. "Well, while I lay there listening to your talk, I got the drift of the situation and learned, from things you let fall, that Zorono and Valenso were a few miles south on the beach. So when I heard you say that Zarono must have done the killing and taken the map, and that you meant to go and parley with him, seeking an opportunity to murder him and get it back—"

"Dog!" snarled Zarono.

Although livid, Strombanni laughed mirthlessly. "Do you think I'd play fair with a treacherous cur like you? Go on, Conan."

The Cimmerian grinned. It was evident that he was deliberately fanning the fires of hate between the two men.

"Nothing much, then. I came straight through the woods while you tacked along the coast and raised the fort before you did. Your guess that the storm had destroyed Zarono's ship was a good one—but then, you knew the configuration of this bay.

"Well, there's the story. I have the treasure, Strom has a ship, Valenso has supplies. By Crom, Zarono, I see not where you fit into the scheme, but to avoid strife I'll include you. My proposal is simple enough.

"We'll split the treasure four ways. Strom and I shall sail away with our shares aboard the *Red Hand*. You and Valenso take yours and remain lords of the wilderness, or build a ship out of tree trunks, as you wish."

Valenso branched and Zarono swore, while Strombanni grinned quietly.

"Are you fool enough to go aboard the *Red Hand*

73

alone with Strombanni?" snarled Zarono. "He'll cut your throat before you're out of sight of land!"

Conan laughed with genuine enjoyment. "This is like the problem of the wolf, the sheep, and the cabbage," he admitted. "How to get them across the river without their devouring one another!"

"And that appeals to your Cimmerian sense of humor!" complained Zarono.

"I will not stay here!" cried Valenso, a wild gleam in his dark eyes. "Treasure or no treasure, I must go!"

Conan gave him a slit-eyed glance of speculation. "Well then," said he, "how about this plan: We divide the loot as I suggested. Then Strombanni sails away with Zarono, Valenso, and such members of the count's household as he may select, leaving me in command of the fort, and the rest of Valenso's men, and all of Zarono's. I'll build my own ship."

Zarono looked sick. "I have the choice of remaining here in exile, or abandoning my crew and going alone on the *Red Hand* to have my throat cut?"

Conan's laughter rang gustily through the hall, and he smote Zarono jovially on the back, ignoring the black murder in the buccaneer's glare. "That's it, Zarono!" quoth he. "Stay here while Strom and I sail away, or sail away with Strombanni, leaving your men with me."

"I'd rather have Zarono," said Strombanni frankly. "You'd turn my own men against me, Conan, and cut my throat before I raised the Barachans."

Sweat dripped from Zarono's livid face. "Neither I, nor the count, nor his niece will ever reach the land alive if we ship with that devil," said he. "You are both in my power in this hall. My men surround it. What's to prevent my cutting you both down?"

"Not a thing," Conan admitted cheerfully, "except the fact that if you do, Strombanni's men will sail away and

74

leave you stranded on this coast, where the Picts will presently cut all your throats; and the fact that with me dead you'd never find the treasure; and the fact that I'll split your skull down to your chin if you try to summon your men."

Conan laughed as he spoke, as if at some whimsical situation; but even Belesa sensed that he meant what he said. His naked cutlass lay across his knees, and Zarono's sword was under the table, out of the buccaneer's reach. Galbro was not a fighting man, and Valenso seemed incapable of decision or action.

"Aye!" said Strombanni with an oath. "You'd find the two of us no easy prey. I'm agreeable to Conan's proposal. What say you, Valenso?"

"I must leave this coast!" whispered Valenso, staring blankly. "I must hasten—I must go—go far—quickly!"

Strombanni frowned, puzzled at the count's strange manner, and turned to Zarono, grinning wickedly. "And you, Zarono?"

"What can I say?" snarled Zarono. "Let me take my three officers and forty men aboard the *Red Hand*, and the bargain's made."

"The officers and thirty men!"

"Very well."

"Done!"

There was no shaking of hands or ceremonial drinking of wine to seal the pact. The two captains glared at each other like hungry wolves. The count plucked his mustache with a trembling hand, rapt in his own somber thoughts. Conan stretched like a great cat, drank wine, and grinned on the assemblage, but it was the sinister grin of a stalking tiger.

Belesa sensed the murderous purposes that reigned there, the treacherous intent that dominated each man's mind. Not one had any intention of keeping his part of the pact, Valenso possibly excluded. Each of the free-booters intended to possess both the ship and the entire treasure. None would be satisfied with less.

But how? What was going on in each crafty mind? Belesa felt oppressed and stifled by the atmosphere of hatred and treachery. The Cimmerian, for all his ferocious frankness, was no less subtle than the others—and even fiercer. His domination of the situation was not physical alone, although his gigantic shoulders and massive limbs seemed too big for even the great hall. There was an iron vitality about the man that overshadowed even the hard vigor of the other freebooters.

"Lead us to the treasure!" Zarono demanded.

"Wait a bit," answered Conan. "We must keep our power evenly balanced, so that one cannot take advantage of the others. We'll work it thus: Strom's men shall come ashore, all but a half-dozen or so, and camp on the beach. Zarono's men shall come out of the fort and likewise camp on the strand, within easy sight of them. Then each crew can watch the other, to see that nobody slips after us who go for the treasure, to ambush either of us. Those left aboard the *Red Hand* shall take her out into the bay, out of reach of either party. Valenso's men shall stay in the fort but leave the gate open. Will you come with us, Count?"

"Go into that forest?" Valenso shuddered and drew his cloak about his shoulders. "Not for all the gold of Tranicos!"

"All right. 'Twill take about thirty men to carry the loot. We'll take fifteen from each crew and start as soon as we can."

Belesa, keenly alert to every angle of the drama being played out beneath her, saw Zarono and Strombanni shoot furtive glances at each other, then quickly lower their gaze as they lifted their glasses, to hide the murky intent in their eyes. She perceived the fatal weakness in

Conan's plan and wondered how he could have over-looked it. Perhaps he was too arrogantly confident in his personal prowess. But she knew that he would never come out of that forest alive. Once the treasure was in their grasp, the others would form a rogue's alliance long enough to rid themselves of the man both hated. She shuddered, staring morbidly at the man she knew to be doomed. Strange to see that powerful fighting man sitting there, laughing and swilling wine, in full prime and power, and to know that he was already doomed to a bloody death.

The whole situation was pregnant with dark and bloody portents. Zarono would trick and kill Strombanni if he could, and she knew that Strombanni had already marked Zarono for death and, doubtless, her uncle and herself also. If Zarono won the final battle of cruel wits, their lives were safe—but, looking at the buccaneer as he sat there chewing his mustache, with all the stark evil of his nature showing naked in his dark face, she could not decide which was more abhorrent—death or Zarono.

"How far is it?" demanded Strombanni.

"If we start within the hour, we can be back before midnight," answered Conan. He emptied his goblet, rose, adjusted his girdle, and glanced at the count. "Valenso," he said, "are you mad, to kill a Pict in his hunting paint?"

Valenso started. "What do you mean?"

"Do you mean to say you don't know that your men killed a Pict hunter in the woods last night?"

The count shook his head. "None of my men was in the woods last night."

"Well, somebody was," grunted the Cimmerian, fumbling in a pocket. "I saw his head nailed to a tree near the edge of the forest. He wasn't painted for war. I found no boot tracks, from which I judged that it had been nailed up there before the storm. But there were plenty of other signs—moccasin tracks on the wet ground. Picts have been there and seen that head. They were men of some other clan, or they'd have taken it down. If they happen to be at peace with the clan the dead man belonged to, they'll make tracks to his village to tell his tribe."

"Perhaps they slew him," suggested Valenso.

"No, they didn't. But they know who did, for the same reason that I know. This chain was knotted about the stump of the severed neck. You must have been utterly mad, to identify your handiwork like that."

He drew forth something and tossed it on the table before the count, who lurched up, choking, as his hand flew to his throat. It was the gold seal-chain that he had habitually worn about his neck.

"I recognized the Korzetta seal," said Conan. "The presence of that chain alone would tell any Pict it was the work of a foreigner."

Valenso did not reply. He sat staring at the chain as if at a venomous serpent.

Conan scowled at him and glanced questioningly at the others. Zarono made a quick gesture to indicate that the count was not quite right in the head. Conan sheathed his cutlass and donned his lacquered hat.

"All right; let's go," he said.

The captains gulped down their wine and rose, hitching at their sword belts. Zarono laid a hand on Valenso's arm and shook him slightly. The count started and stared about him, then followed the others out like a man in a daze, the chain dangling from his fingers. But not all left the hall.

Forgotten on the stair, Belesa and Tina, peeping between the balusters, saw Galbro fall behind the others, loitering until the heavy door closed after them. Then he hurried to the fireplace and raked carefully at the smouldering coals. He sank to his knees and peered closely at something for a long space. Then he straight-

78

ened and, with a furtive air, stole out of the hall by another door.

Tina whispered: "What did Galbro find in the fire?"

Belesa shook her head; then, obeying the promptings of her curiosity, rose and went down to the empty hall. An instant later, she was kneeling where the seneschal had knelt, and she saw what he had seen.

It was the charred remnant of the map that Conan had thrown into the fire. It was ready to crumble at a touch, but faint lines and bits of writing were still discernible upon it. She could not read the writing, but she could trace the outlines of what seemed to be the picture of a hill or crag, surrounded by marks evidently representing dense trees. She could make nothing of it; but, from Galbro's actions, she believed that he recognized it as portraying some scene or topographical feature familiar to him. She knew the seneschal had penetrated inland further than any other man of the settlement.

6. The Plunder of the Dead

The fortress stood strangely quiet in the noonday heat that had followed the storm of the dawn. Voices of people within the stockade sounded subdued, muffled. The same drowsy stillness reigned on the beach outside, where the rival crews lay in armed suspicion, separated by a few hundred yards of bare sand. Far out in the bay, the *Red Hand* lay at anchor with a handful of men aboard her, ready to snatch her out of reach at the slightest indication of treachery. The carack was Strombanni's trump card, his best guaranty against the trickery of his associates.

Belesa came down the stair and paused at the sight of Count Valenso seated at the table, turning the broken chain about in his hands. She looked at him without love and with more than a little fear. The change that had come over him was appalling; he seemed to be locked up in a grim world all his own, with a fear that flogged all human characteristics out of him.

Conan had plotted shrewdly to eliminate the chances of an ambush in the forest by either party. But, as far as Belesa could see, he had failed utterly to safeguard himself against the treachery of his companions. He had disappeared into the woods, leading the two captains and their thirty men, and the Zingaran girl was positive that she would never see him alive again.

Presently she spoke, and her voice was strained and harsh to her own ear: "The barbarian has led the captains into the forest. When they have the gold in their hands, they'll slay him. But when they return with the treasure, what then? Are we to go aboard the ship? Can we trust Strombanni?"

Valenso shook his head absently. "Strombanni would murder us all for our shares of the loot. But Zarono secretly whispered his intentions to me. We will not go aboard the *Red Hand* save as her masters. Zarono will see that night overtakes the treasure party, so they shall be forced to camp in the forest. He will find a way to kill Strombanni and his men in their sleep. Then the buccaneers will come on stealthily to the beach. Just before dawn, I will send some of my fishermen secretly from the fort, to swim out to the ship and seize her. Strombanni never thought of that, and neither did Conan. Zarono and his men will come out of the forest and, together with the buccaneers encamped on the beach, fall upon

80

the pirates in the dark, while I lead my men-at-arms from the fort to complete the rout Without their captain, they will be demoralized and, outnumbered, fall easy prey to Zarono and me. Then we shall sail in Strombanni's ship with all the treasure."

"But what of me?" she asked with dry lips.

"I have promised you to Zarono," he answered harshly. "But for my promise, he would not take us off."

"I will never marry him," she said helplessly.

"You shall," he responded gloomily, without the slightest touch of sympathy. He lifted the chain so that it caught the gleam of the sun, slanting through a window. "I must have dropped it on the sand," he muttered. "*He* has been that near—on the beach . . ."

"You did not drop it on the strand," said Belesa, in a voice as devoid of mercy as his own; her soul seemed turned to stone. "You tore it from your throat, by accident, last night in this hall, when you flogged Tina. I saw it gleaming on the floor before I left the hall."

He looked up, his face gray with a terrible fear; she laughed bitterly, sensing the mute question in his dilated eyes. "Yes! The black man! He was here! In this hall! He must have found the chain on the floor. The guardsmen did not see him, but he was at your door last night. I saw him, padding along the upper hallway."

For an instant she thought he would drop dead of sheer terror. He sank back in his chair, the chain slipping from his nerveless fingers and clinking on the table.

"In the manor!" he whispered. "I thought bolts and bars and armed guards could keep him out, fool that I was! I can no more guard against him than I can escape him! At my door! At my door!" The thought overwhelmed him with horror. "Why did he not enter?" he shrieked, tearing at the lace upon his collar as though it strangled him. "Why did he not end it? I have dreamed of waking in my darkened chamber to see him squatting

81

above me, with the blue hell-fire playing about his head! Why—"

The paroxysm passed, leaving him faint and trembling.

"I understand!" he panted. "He is playing with me, as a cat with a mouse. To have slain me last night in my chamber were too easy, too merciful. So he destroyed the ship in which I might have escaped him, and he slew that wretched Pict and left my chain upon him, so that the savages might believe I had slain him. They have seen that chain upon my neck many a time.

"But why? What subtle deviltry has he in mind, what devious purpose no human mind can grasp or understand?"

"Who is this black man?" asked Belesa, a chill of fear crawling along her spine.

"A demon loosed by my greed and lust to plague me throughout eternity!" he whispered. He spread his long, thin fingers on the table before him and stared at her with hollow, weirdly luminous eyes, which seemed to see her not at all but to look through her and far beyond to some dim doom.

"In my youth, I had an enemy at court," he said, as if speaking more to himself than to her. "A powerful man who stood between me and my ambition. In my lust for wealth and power, I sought aid from the people of the black arts—a sorcerer who, at my desire, raised up a fiend from the outer gulfs of existence. It crushed and slew mine enemy; I grew great and wealthy, and none could stand before me. But I thought to cheat the wizard of the price a mortal must pay who calls the black folk to do his bidding.

"He was Thoth-Amon of the Ring, in exile from his native Stygia. He had fled in the reign of King Mentupherra, and when Mentupherra died and Ctesphon ascended the ivory throne of Luxur, Thoth-Amon lingered in Kordava though he might have returned home, dunning me for the debt I owed him. But, instead of paying him the moiety of my gains as I had promised, I denounced him to my own monarch, so that Thoth-Amon must needs willy-nilly return to Stygia in haste and stealth. There he found favor and waxed in wealth and magical might until he was the virtual ruler of the land.

"Two years ago in Kordava, word came to me that Thoth-Amon had vanished from his accustomed haunts in Stygia. And then one night I saw his brown devil's face leering at me from the shadows in my castle hall.

"It was not his material body, but his spirit sent to plague me. This time I had no king to protect me, for upon the death of Ferdrugo and the setting up of the regency, the land, as you know, had fallen into factional strife. Before Thoth-Amon could reach Kordava in the flesh, I sailed to put broad seas between me and him. He has his limitations; to follow me across the seas he must remain in his human, fleshly body. But now this field has tracked me down by his uncanny powers even here in this vast wilderness.

"He is too crafty to be trapped or slain as one would do with a common man. When he hides, no man can find him. He steals like a shadow in the night, making naught of bolts and bars. He blinds the eyes of guardsmen with sleep. He can command the spirits of the air, the serpents of the deep, and the fiends of the night; he can raise storms to sink ships and throw down castles. I hoped to drown my trail in the blue, rolling waves—but he has tracked me down to claim his grim forfeit . . ."

The weird eyes lit palely as Valenso gazed beyond the tapestried walls to far, invisible horizons. "I'll trick him yet," he whispered. "Let him delay to strike this night, and dawn shall find me with a ship under my heels, and again I will cast an ocean between me and his vengeance."

'Hell's fire!"

Conan stopped short, glaring upward. Behind him, the seamen halted—two compact clumps of them, bows in their hands and suspicion in their attitude. They were following an old path made by Pictish hunters, which led due east. Although they had progressed only some thirty yards, the beach was no longer visible.

"What is it?" demanded Strombanni suspiciously. "Why are you stopping?"

"Are you blind? Look there!"

From the thick limb of a tree that overhung the trail, a head grinned down at them: a dark, painted face, framed in thick black hair, in which a hornbill feather drooped over the left ear.

"I took that head down and hid it in the bushes," growled Conan, scanning the woods about them narrowly. "What fool could have stuck it back up there? It looks as if somebody were trying his damnedest to bring the Picts down on the settlement."

Men glanced at one another darkly, a new element of suspicion added to the already seething cauldron. Conan climbed the tree, secured the head, and carried it into the bushes, where he tossed it into a stream and watched it sink.

"The Picts whose tracks are about this tree weren't Hornbills," he growled, returning through the thicket. "I've sailed these coasts enough to know something about the sea-land tribes. If I read the prints of their moccasins aright, they were Cormorants. I hope they're having a war with the Hornbills. If they're at peace, they'll head straight for the Hornbill village, and there'll be trouble. I don't know how far away that village is—but, as soon as they learn of this murder, they'll come through the forest like starving wolves. That's the worst insult possible to a Pict—to kill a man not in war-paint and stick his head up in a tree for the vultures to eat. Damned peculiar things going on along this coast. But that's always the way when civilized men come into the wilderness; they're all crazy as Hell. Come on."

Men loosened blades in their scabbards and shafts in their quivers as they strode deeper into the forest. Men of the sea, accustomed to rolling expanses of gray water, they were ill at ease with mysterious, green walls of trees and vines hemming them in. The path wound and twisted until most of them quickly lost their sense of direction and did not even know in which direction the beach lay.

Conan was uneasy for another reason. He kept scanning the trail and finally grunted: "Somebody's passed along here recently—not more than an hour ahead of us. Somebody in boots, with no woodcraft. Was he the fool who found that Pict's head and stuck it back up in that tree? No, it couldn't have been he. I didn't find his tracks under the tree. But who was it? I found no tracks there, except those of the Picts I'd already seen. And who's this fellow hurrying ahead of us? Did either of you bastards send a man ahead of us for any reason?"

Both Strombanni and Zarono loudly disclaimed any such act, glaring at each other with mutual disbelief. Neither man could see the signs Conan pointed out; the faint prints that he saw on the grassless, hard-beaten trail were invisible to their untrained eyes.

Conan quickened his pace, and they hurried after him, fresh coals of suspicion added to the smoldering fire of distrust. Presently the path veered northward, and Conan left it and began threading his way through the trees in a southeasterly direction. The afternoon wore on as the sweating men plowed through bushes and climbed over logs. Strambanni, momentarily falling behind with Zarono, murmured:

"Think you he's leading us into an ambush?"

"He might," retorted the buccaneer. "In any case, we shall never find our way back to the sea without him to

85

guide us." Zarono gave Strombanni a meaningful look.

"I see your point," said the latter. "This may force a change in our plans."

Suspicion grew as they advanced and had almost reached panic proportions when they emerged from the thick woods and saw, just ahead of them, a gaunt crag that jutted up from the forest floor. A dim path, leading out of the woods from the east, ran along a cluster of boulders and wound up the crag on a ladder of stony shelves to a flat ledge near the summit.

Conan halted, a bizarre figure in his piratical finery. "That trail is the one I followed, when I was running from the Eagle Picts," he said. "It leads up to a cave behind that ledge. In that cave are the bodies of Tranicos and his captains, and the treasure he plundered from Tothmekri. But a word before we go up after it: If you kill me here, you'll never find your way back to the trail we followed from the beach. I know you seafaring men; you're helpless in the deep woods. Of course, the beach lies due west; but, if you have to make your way through the tangled woods, burdened with the plunder, it'll take you, not hours, but days. And I don't think these woods will be very safe for white men, when the Hornbills learn about their hunter."

He laughed at the ghastly, mirthless smiles with which they greeted his recognition of their intentions toward him. And he also comprehended the thought that sprang in the mind of each: Let the barbarian secure the loot for them and lead them back to the beach trail before they killed him.

"All of you stay here except Strombanni and Zarono," said Conan. "We three are enough to pack the treasure down from the cave."

Strombanni grinned mirthlessly. "Go up there alone with you and Zarono? Do you take me for a fool? One man at least comes with me!"

And he designated his boatswain, a brawny, hard-faced giant, naked to his broad leather belt, with gold hoops in his ears and a crimson scarf around his head.

"And my executioner comes with me!" growled Zarono. He beckoned to a lean sea-thief with a face like a parchment-covered skull, who carried a two-handed scimitar naked over his bony shoulder.

Conan shrugged his shoulders. "Very well. Follow me."

They were close on his heels as he strode up the winding path and mounted the ledge. They crowded him close as he passed through the cleft in the wall behind it, and their breath sucked greedily between their teeth as he called their attention to the iron-bound chests on either side of the short, tunnel-like cavern.

"A rich cargo here," he said carelessly. "Silks, laces, garments, ornaments, weapons—the loot of the southern seas. But the real treasure lies beyond that door.

The massive door stood partly open. Conan frowned. He remembered closing that door before he left the cavern. But he said nothing of the matter to his eager companions as he drew aside to let them through.

They looked into a wide cavern, lit by a strange, blue glow that glimmered through a smoky, mistlike haze. A great ebon table stood in the midst of the cavern, and, in a carved chair with a high back and broad arms, which might once have stood in the castle of some Zingaran baron, sat a giant figure, fabulous and fantastic. There sat Bloody Tranicos, his great head sunk on his bosom, one hand still gripping a jeweled goblet—Tranicos, in his lacquered hat, his gilt-embroidered coat with jeweled buttons that winked in the blue flame, his flaring boots and gold-worked baldric, which upheld a jewel-hilted sword in a golden sheath.

And ranging the board, each with his chin resting on his lace-bedecked breast, sat the eleven captains. The blue fire played weirdly on them and on their giant admiral, as it flowed from the enormous jewel on the tiny ivory pedestal, striking glints of frozen fire from the heaps of fantastically-cut gems that shone before the place of Tranicos—the plunder of Khemi, the jewels of Tothmekri! The stones whose value was greater than that of all the rest of the known jewels in the world put together!

The faces of Zarono and Strombanni showed pallid in the blue glow. Over their shoulders, their men gaped stupidly.

"Go in and take them," invited Conan, drawing aside.

Zarono and Strombanni crowded avidly past him, jostling each other in their haste. Their followers were treading on their heels. Zarono kicked the door wide open—and halted, with one foot on the threshold, at the sight of a figure on the floor, previously hidden from view by the partly-closed door. It was a man, prone and contorted, with his head drawn back between his shoulders and his white face twisted in a grin of mortal agony.

"Galbro!" exclaimed Zarono. "Dead! What—" With sudden suspicion, he thrust his head over the threshold. Then he jerked back and screamed: "There's death in the cavern!"

Even as he screamed, the blue mist swirled and condensed. At the same time, Conan hurled his weight against the four men bunched in the doorway, sending them staggering—but not headlong into the misty cavern as he had planned. Suspecting a trap, they were recoiling from the sight of the dead man and the materializing demon. Hence his violent push, while it threw them off their feet, yet failed of the result he desired. Strombanni and Zarono sprawled half over the threshold on their knees, the boatswain tumbled over their legs, and the executioner caromed against the wall.

Before Conan could follow up his ruthless intention of kicking the fallen men into the cavern and holding the

88

door against them until the supernatural horror within had done its deadly work, he had to turn and defend himself against the frothing onslaught of the executioner, who was the first to regain his balance and his wits.

The buccaneer missed a tremendous swipe with his headsman's sword as the Cimmerian ducked, and the great blade banged against the stone wall, spattering blue sparks. The next instant, the executioner's skull-faced head rolled on the cavern floor under the bite of Conan's cutlass.

In the split seconds this swift action consumed, the boatswain regained his feet and fell on the Cimmerian, raining blows with a cutlass that would have overwhelmed a lesser man. Cutlass met cutlass with a ring of steel that was deafening in the narrow cavern.

Meanwhile the two captains, terrified of they knew not what in the cavern, scuttled back out of the doorway so quickly that the demon had not fully materialized before they were over the magical boundary and out of its reach. By the time they rose to their feet, reaching for their swords, the monster had diffused again into blue mist.

Hotly engaged with the boatswain, Conan redoubled his efforts to dispose of his antagonist before help could come to him. The boatswain dripped blood at each step as he was driven back before the ferocious onslaught, bellowing for his companions. Before Conan could deal the finishing stroke, the two chiefs came at him with swords in their hands, shouting for their men.

The Cimmerian bounded back and leaped out on to the ledge. Although he felt himself a match for all three men—each a famed swordsman—he did not wish to be trapped by the crews, which would come charging up the path at the sound of the battle.

These were not coming with as much celerity as he expected, however. They were bewildered by the sounds and the muffled shouts issuing from the cavern above them, but no man dared start up the path for fear of a sword in the back. Each band faced the other tensely, grasping their weapons but incapable of decision. When they saw the Cimmerian bound out on the ledge, they still hesitated. While they stood with their arrows nocked, he ran up the ladder of handholds niched in the crag near the cleft and threw himself prone on the summit of the crag, out of their sight.

The captains stormed out on the ledge, raving and brandishing their swords. Their men, seeing that their leaders were not at sword-strokes, ceased menacing each other and gaped in bewilderment.

"Dog!" screamed Zarono. "You planned to trap and murder us! Traitor!"

Conan mocked them from above. "Well, what did you expect? You two were planning to cut my throat as soon as I got the plunder for you. If it hadn't been for that fool Galbro, I should have trapped the four of you and explained to your men how you rushed in heedless to your doom."

"And with us both dead, you'd have taken my ship and all the loot, too!" frothed Strombanni.

"Aye! And the pick of each crew! I've been thinking of coming back to the Main for months, and this was a good opportunity!

"It was Galbro's footprints I saw on the trail, although I know not how the fool learned of this cave, or how he expected to lug the loot away by himself."

"But for the sight of his body, we should have walked into that death-trap," muttered Zarono, his swarthy face still ashy.

"What was it," said Strombanni. "Some poisonous mist?"

"Nay, it writhed like a live thing and came together

in some fiendish form ere we backed out. It is some devil bound to the cave by a spell."

"Well, what are you going to do?" their unseen tormentor yelled sardonically.

"What *shall* we do?" Zarono asked Strombanni. "The treasure cavern cannot be entered."

"You can't get the treasure," Conan assured them from his eyrie. "The demon will strangle you. It nearly got me, when I stepped in there. Listen, and I'll tell you a tale the Picts tell in their huts when the fires burn low!

"Once, long ago, twelve strange men came out of the sea. They fell upon a Pictish village and put all the folk to the sword, except a few who fled in time. Then they found a cave and heaped it with gold and jewels. But a shaman of the slaughtered Picts—one of those who escaped—made magic and evoked a demon from one of the lower hells. By his sorcerous powers, he forced this demon to enter the cavern and strangle the men as they sat at wine. And, lest this demon thereafter roam abroad and molest the Picts themselves, the shaman confined it by his magic to the inner cavern. The tale was told from tribe to tribe, and all the clans shun the accursed spot.

"When I crawled in there to escape the Eagle Picts, I realized that the old legend was true and referred to Tranicos and his men. Death guards old Tranicos's treasure!"

"Bring up the men!" frothed Strombanni. "We'll climb up and hew him down!"

"Don't be a fool!" snarled Zarano. "Think you any man on earth could climb those hand-holds in the teeth of his sword? We'll have the men up here, right enough, to feather him with shafts if he dares show himself. But we'll get those gems yet. He has some plan of obtaining the loot, or he'd not have brought thirty men to bear it back. If he could get it, so can we. We'll bend a cutlass blade to make a hook, tie it to a rope, and cast it about the leg of that table, then drag it to the door."

"Well thought, Zarono!" came down Conan's mocking voice. "Exactly what I had in mind. But how will you find your way back to the beach path? It'll be dark long before you reach the beach, if you have to feel your way through the woods, and I'll follow you and kill you one by one in the dark."

"It's no empty boast," muttered Strombanni. "He can move and strike in the dark as subtly and silently as a ghost. If he hunts us back through the forest, few of us will live to see the beach."

"Then we'll kill him here," gritted Zarono. "Some of us will shoot at him, while the rest climb the crag. If he is not struck by arrows, some of us will reach him with our swords. Listen! Why does he laugh?"

"To hear dead men making plots," came Conan's grimly amused voice.

"Heed him not," scowled Zarono. Lifting his voice, he shouted for the men below to join him and Strombanni on the ledge.

The sailors started up the slanting trail, and one started to shout a question. Simultaneously there sounded a hum like that of an angry bee, ending with a sharp thud. The buccaneer gasped, and blood gushed from his open mouth. He sank to his knees, a black shaft protruding from his back. A yell of alarm went up from his companions.

"What's the matter?" shouted Strombanni.

"Picts!" bawled a pirate, lifting his bow and loosing blindly. At his side, a man moaned and went down with an arrow through his throat.

"Take cover, you fools!" shrieked Zarono. From his vantage point, he glimpsed painted figures moving in the bushes. One of the men on the winding path fell back dying. The rest scrambled hastily down among the rocks about the foot of the crag. They took cover clumsily, not being used to fighting of this kind. Arrows flickered from the bushes, splintering on the boulders. The men on the ledge lay prone.

"We're trapped!" said Strombanni, his face pale. Bold enough with a deck under his feet, this silent, savage warfare shook his ruthless nerves.

"Conan said they feared this crag," said Zarono. "When night falls, the men must climb up here. We'll hold this crag; the Picts won't rush us."

"Aye!" mocked Conan above them. "They won't climb the crag to get at you, that's true. They'll merely surround it and keep you here until you all die of thirst and starvation."

"He speaks truth," said Zarono helplessly. "What shall we do?"

"Make a truce with him," muttered Strombanni. "If any man can get us out of this jam, he can. Time enough to cut his throat later." Lifting his voice, he called: "Conan, let's forget our feud for the time being. You're in this fix as much as we are. Come down and help us out of it."

"How do you figure that?" retorted the Cimmerian. "I have but to wait until dark, climb down the other side of this crag, and melt into the forest. I can crawl through the line the Picts have thrown around this hill, return to the fort, and report you all slain by the savages—which will shortly be the truth!"

Zarono and Strombanni stared at each other in pallid silence.

"But I'll not do that!" Conan roared. "Not because I have any love for you dogs, but because I don't leave white men, even my enemies, to be butchered by Picts."

The Cimmerian's touseled black head appeared over the crest of the crag. "Now listen closely: That's only a small band down there. I saw them sneaking through the brush when I laughed, a while ago. Anyway, if there had been many of them, every man at the foot of the crag would be dead already. I think that's a band of fleet-footed young bucks sent ahead of the main war party to cut us off from the beach. I'm certain a big war band is heading in our direction from somewhere.

"They've thrown a cordon around the west side of the crag, but I don't think there are any on the east side. I'm going down on that side, to get into the forest and work around behind them. Meanwhile, you crawl down the path and join your men among the rocks. Tell them to unstring their bows and draw their swords. When you hear me yell, rush the trees on the west side of the clearing."

"What of the treasure?"

"To Hell with the treasure! We shall be lucky if we get out of here with our heads on our shoulders."

The black-maned head vanished. They listened for sounds to indicate that Conan had crawled to the almost sheer eastern wall and was working his way down, but they heard nothing. Nor was there any sound in the est. No more arrows broke against the rocks where the sailors were hidden. But all knew that fierce, black eyes were watching with murderous patience.

Gingerly, Strombanni, Zarono, and the boatswain started down the winding path. They were halfway down when black shafts began to whisper around them. The boatswain groaned and toppled limply down the slope, shot throuth the heart. Arrows shivered on the helmets and breastplates of the chiefs as they tumbled in frantic haste down the steep trail. They reached the foot in a scrambling rush and lay panting among the boulders, swearing breathlessly.

"Is this more of Conan's trickery?" wondered Zarono profanely.

"We can trust him in this matter," asserted Strombanni. "These barbarians live by their own particular code of honor, and Conan would never desert men of his own complexion to be slaughtered by people of another race. He'll help us against the Picts, even though he plans to murder us himself—*hark!*"

A blood-freezing yell knifed the silence. It came from the woods to the west, and simultaneously an object arched out of the trees, struck the ground, and rolled bouncingly toward the rocks—a severed human head, the hideously painted face frozen in a snarl of death.

"Conan's signal!" roared Strombanni, and the desperate freebooters rose like a wave from the rocks and rushed headlong toward the woods.

Arrows whirred out of the bushes, but their flight was hurried and erratic; only three men fell. Then the wild men of the sea plunged through the fringe of foliage and fell on the naked painted figures that rose out of the gloom before them. There was a murderous instant of panting, ferocious, hand-to-hand effort. Cutlasses beat down war-axes, booted feet trampled naked bodies, and then bare feet were rattling through the bushes in headlong flight as the survivors of that brief carnage quit the fray, leaving seven still, painted figures stretched on the bloodstained leaves that littered the earth. Farther back in the thickets sounded a thrashing and heaving; then it ceased, and Conan strode into view, his lacquered hat gone, his coat torn, his cutlass dripping in his hand.

"What now?" panted Zarono. He knew the charge had succeeded only because Conan's unexpected attack on the rear of the Picts had demoralized the painted men and prevented them from falling back before the rush. But he exploded into curses as Conan passed his cutlass through a buccaneer who writhed on the ground with a shattered hip.

"We cannot carry him with us," grunted Conan. "It wouldn't be any kindness to leave him to be taken alive by the Picts. Come on!"

They crowded close at his heels as he trotted through the trees. Alone, they would have sweated and blundered among the thickets for hours before they found the beach trail—if they had ever found it. The Cimmerian led them as unerringly as if he had been following a blazed path, and the rovers shouted with hysterical relief as they burst suddenly upon the trail that ran westward.

"Fool!" Conan clapped a hand on the shoulder of a pirate who started to break into a run and hurled him back among his companions. "You'll burst your heart and fall within a thousand yards. We're miles from the beach. Take an easy gait. We may have to sprint the last mile; save some of your wind for it. Come on, now!"

He set off down the trail at a steady jog-trot. The seamen followed him, suiting their pace to his.

The sun was touching the waves of the western ocean. Tina stood at the window from which Belesa had watched the storm.

"The setting sun turns the ocean to blood," she said. "The carack's sail is a white fleck on the crimson waters. The woods are already darkened with clustering shadows."

"What of the seamen on the beach?" asked Belesa languidly. She reclined on a couch, her eyes closed, her hands clasped behind her head.

"Both camps are preparing their supper," said Tina. "They gather driftwood and build fires. I can hear them shouting to one another—*what is that?*"

The sudden tenseness in the girl's tone brought Belesa upright on the couch. Tina grasped the windowsill, her face white.

"Listen! A howling, far off, like many wolves!"

"Wolves?" Belesa sprang up, fear clutching her heart. "Wolves do not hunt in packs at this time of year—"

"Oh, look!" shrilled the girl, pointing. "Men are running out of the forest!"

In an instant, Belesa was beside her, staring wide-eyed at the figures small in the distance, streaming out of the woods.

"The sailors!" she gasped. "Empty-handed! I see Zarono—Strombanni—"

"Where is Conan?" whispered the child. Belesa shook her head.

"Listen! Oh, listen!" whimpered Tina, clinging to her. "The Picts!"

All in the fort could hear it now—a vast ululation of mad exultation and blood lust, from the depths of the dark forest. The sound spurred on the panting men, reeling toward the palisade.

"Hasten!" gasped Strombanni, his face a drawn mask of exhausted effort. "They are almost at our heels. My ship—"

"She is too far for us to reach," panted Zarono. "Make for the stockade. See, the men camped on the beach have seen us!"

He waved his arms in breathless pantomime, but the men on the strand understood and recognized the significance of that wild howling, rising to a triumphant crescendo. The sailors abandoned their fires and cooking pots and fled for the stockade gate. They were pouring through it as the fugitives from the forest rounded the south angle and reeled into the gate, a heaving, frantic mob, half dead from exhaustion. The gate was slammed with frenzied haste, and sailors began to climb to the footwalk to join the men-at-arms already there.

Belesa, who had hurried down from the manor, confronted Zarono. "Where is Conan?"

The buccaneer jerked a thumb toward the blackening woods. His chest heaved; sweat poured down his face.

"Their scouts were at our heels ere we gained the beach. He paused to slay a few and give us time to get away."

He staggered away to take his place on the footwalk, whither Strombanni had already mounted. Valenso stood there, a somber, cloak-wrapped figure, strangely silent and aloof. He was like a man bewitched.

"Look!" yelped a pirate, above the deafening howling of the yet unseen horde. A man emerged from the forest and raced fleetly across the open belt.

"Conan!" Zarono grinned wolfishly. "We're safe in the stockade; we know where the treasure is. No reason why we shouldn't feather him with arrows now."

"Nay!" Strombanni caught his arm. "We shall need his sword. Look!"

Behind the fleet-footed Cimmerian, a wild horde burst from the forest, howling as they ran—naked Picts, hundred and hundreds of them. Their arrows rained about the Cimmerian. A few strides more, and Conan reached the eastern wall of the stockade, bounded high, seized the points of the logs, and heaved himself up and over, his cutlass in his teeth. Arrows thudded venomously into the logs where his body had just been. His resplendent coat was gone, his white shirt torn and blood-stained.

"Stop them!" he roared as his feet hit the ledge inside. "If they get on the wall, we're done for!"

Pirates, buccaneers, and men-at-arms responded instantly, and a storm of arrows and quarrels tore into the oncoming horde. Conan saw Belesa with Tina clinging to her hand, and his language was picturesque.

"Get into the manor," he commanded in conclusion. "Their shafts will arch over the wall—what did I tell you?" A black shaft cut into the earth at Belesa's feet and quivered like a serpent's head. Conan caught up a longbow and leaped to the footwalk. "Some of you fellows prepare torches!" he roared, above the clamor of battle. "We can't find them in the dark!"

The sun had sunk in a welter of blood. Out in the bay, the men aboard the carack had cut the anchor chain, and the *Red Hand* was rapidly receding on the crimson horizon.

7. *Men of the Woods*

Night had fallen, but torches streamed across the strand, casting the mad scene into lurid revealment. Naked men in paint swarmed the beach; like waves they came against the palisade, bared teeth and blazing eyes gleaming in the glare of the torches thrust over the wall. Hornbill feathers waved in black manes, and the feathers of the cormorant and the sea-falcon. A few warriors, the wildest and most barbaric of them all, wore sharks' teeth woven in their tangled locks. The sea-land tribes had gathered from up and down the coast in all directions to rid their country of the white-skinned invaders.

They surged against the palisade, driving a storm of arrows before them, fighting into the teeth of the shafts and bolts that tore into their masses from the stockade. Sometimes they came so close to the wall that they were hewing at the gate with their war-axes and thrusting their spears through the loopholes. But each time the tide ebbed back without flowing over the palisade, leaving its drift of dead. At this kind of fighting, the freebooters of the sea were at their stoutest. Their arrows and bolts tore holes in the charging horde; their cutlasses hewed the wild men from the palisades they strove to scale.

Yet again and again, the men of the woods returned to the onslaught with all the stubborn ferocity that had been roused in their fierce hearts.

"They are like mad dogs!" gasped Zarono, hacking downward at the dark hands that grasped the palisade points and the dark faces that snarled up at him.

"If we can hold the fort until dawn, they'll lose heart," grunted Conan, splitting a feathered skull with professional precision. "They won't maintain a long siege. Look, they're falling back."

The charge rolled back. The men on the wall shook the sweat out of their eyes, counted their dead, and took a fresh grip on the blood-slippery hilts of their swords. Like blood-hungry wolves, grudgingly driven from a cornered prey, the Picts skulked back beyond the ring of torches. Only the bodies of the slain lay before the palisade.

"Have they gone?" Strombanni shook back his wet, tawny locks. The cutlass in his fist was notched and red; his brawny arm was splashed with blood.

"They're still out there." Conan nodded toward the outer darkness that ringed the circle of torches, made more intense by their light. He glimpsed movements in the shadows, the glitter of eyes and the red glint of copper weapons.

"They've drawn off for a bit, though," he said. "Put sentries on the wall and let the rest eat and drink. 'Tis past midnight, and we've been fighting for hours without respite. Ha, Valenso, how goes the battle with you?"

The count, in dented, blood-splashed helmet and cuirass, moved somberly up to where Conan and the captains stood. For answer, he muttered something inaudible under his breath. And then out of the darkness a voice spoke: a loud, clear voice that rang through the entire fort.

"Count Valenso! Count Valenso of Korzetta! Do you hear me?" It spoke with a Stygian accent.

Conan heard the count gasp as if he had been stricken with a mortal wound. Valenso reeled and grasped the tops of the logs of the stockade, his face pale in the torch-light. The voice resumed:

"It is I, Thoth-Amon of the Ring! Did you think to flee me once more? It is too late for that! All your schemes shall avail you naught, for tonight I shall send a messenger to you. It is the demon that guarded the treasure of Tranicos, whom I have released from his cave and bound to my service. He will inflict upon you the doom that you, you dog, have earned: a death at once slow, hard, and disgraceful. Let us see you mulct your way out of that!"

The speech ended in a peal of musical laughter. Valenso gave a scream of terror, jumped down from the footwalk, and ran staggering up the slope toward the manor.

When the lull came in the fighting, Tina had crept to their window, from which they had been driven by the danger of flying arrows. Silently she watched the men gather about the fire. Belesa was reading a letter that had been delivered by a serving-woman to her door. It read:

Count Valenso of Korzetta to his niece Belesa, greeting:

My doom has come upon me at last. Now that I am resigned if not reconciled to it, I would have you know that I am not insensible of the fact that I have used you in a manner not consistent with the honor of the Korzettas. I did so because circumstances left me no other choice. Although it is late

101

for apologies, I ask that you think not too hardly of me; and, if you can bring yourself to do so, and by some chance you survive this night of doom, that you pray to Mitra for the soiled soul of your father's brother. Meanwhile, I advise that you remain away from the great hall, lest the same fate that awaits me encompass you also. Farewell.

Belesa's hands shook as she read. Although she could never love her uncle, this was still the most human action she had ever known him to take.

At the window, Tina said: "There ought to be more men on the walls. Suppose the black man came back?"

Belesa, going over beside her to look out, shuddered at the thought.

"I am afraid," murmured Tina. "I hope Strombanni and Zarono are killed."

"And not Conan?" asked Belesa curiously.

"Conan would not harm us," said the child confidently. "He lives up to his barbaric code of honor, but they are men who have lost all honor."

"You are wise beyond your years, Tina," said Belesa, with the vague uneasiness that the precocity of the child often aroused in her.

"Look!" Tina stiffened. "The sentry is gone from the south wall! I saw him on the ledge a moment ago; now he has vanished."

From their window, the palisade points of the south wall were just visible over the slanting roofs of a row of huts which paralleled that wall for almost its entire length. A sort of open-topped corridor, three or four yards wide, was formed by the stockade and the back of the huts, which were built in a solid row. These huts were occupied by the serfs.

"Where could the sentry have gone?" whispered Tina uneasily.

Belesa was watching one end of the hut row, which was not far from a side door of the manor. She could have sworn she saw a shadowy figure glide from behind the huts and disappear at the door. Was that the vanished sentry? Why had he left the wall, and why should he steal so subtly into the manor? She did not believe it was the sentry she had seen, and a nameless fear congealed her blood.

"Where is the count, Tina?" she asked.

"In the great hall, my lady. He sits alone at the table, wrapped in his cloak and drinking wine, with a face as gray as death."

"Go and tell him what we have seen. I will keep watch from this window, lest the Picts steal over the unguarded wall."

Tina scampered away. Suddenly remembering the warning in the count's letter about staying out of the main hall, Belesa rose, hearing Tina's slippered feet pattering along the corridor, receding down the stair.

Then abruptly, terribly, there rang out a scream of such poignant fear that Belesa's heart almost stopped with the shock of it. She was out of the chamber and flying down the corridor before she was aware that her limbs were in motion. She ran down the stairs—and halted as if turned to stone.

She did not scream as Tina had screamed. She was incapable of sound or motion. She saw Tina, was aware of the reality of small hands frantically grasping her. But these were the only sane realities in a scene of black nightmare and lunacy and death, dominated by the monstrous, anthropomorphic shadow that spread awful arms against a lurid, hell-fire glare.

Out in the stockade, Strombanni shook his head at Conan's question. "I heard nothing."

"I did!" Conan's wild instincts were roused; he was

103

tensed, his eyes blazing. "It came from the south wall, behind those huts!"

Drawing his cutlass, he strode toward the palisade. From the compound, the wall on the south and the sentry posted there were not visible, being hidden behind the huts. Strombanni followed, impressed by the Cimmerian's manner.

At the mouth of the open space between the huts and the wall, Conan halted warily. The space was dimly lighted by torches flaring at either corner of the stockade. And, about midway of that corridor, a crumpled shape sprawled on the ground.

"Bracus!" swore Strombanni, running forward and dropping on one knee beside the figure. "By Mitra, his throat's been cut from eat to ear!"

Conan swept the space with a quick glance, finding it empty save for himself, Strombanni, and the dead man. He peered through a loophole. No living man moved within the ring of torchlight outside the fort.

"Who could have done this?" he wondered.

"Zarono!" Strombanni sprang up, spitting fury like a wildcat, his hair bristling, his face convulsed. "He has set his thieves to stabbing my men in the back! He plans to wipe me out by treachery! Devils! I am leagued within and without!"

"Wait!" Conan reached a restraining hand. "I don't believe Zarono—"

But the maddened pirate jerked away and rushed around the end of the hut row, breathing blasphemies. Conan ran after him, swearing. Strombanni made straight toward the fire by which Zarono's tall, lean form was visible as the buccaneer chief quaffed a jack of ale.

His amazement was supreme when the jack was dashed violently from his hand, spattering his breastplate with foam, and he was jerked around to confront the passion-distorted face of the pirate captain.

"You murdering dog!" roared Strombanni. "Will you slay my men behind my back while they fight for your filthy hide as well as for mine?"

Conan was hurrying toward them, and on all sides men ceased eating and drinking to stare in amazement.

"What do you mean?" sputtered Zarono.

"You've set your men to stabbing mine at their posts!" screamed the maddened Barachan.

"You lie!" Smoldering hate burst into sudden flame.

With an incoherent howl, Strombanni heaved up his cutlass and cut at the buccaneer's head. Zarono caught the blow on his armored left arm, and sparks flew as he staggered back, ripping out his own sword.

In an instant, the captains were fighting like madmen, their blades flaming and flashing in the firelight. Their crews reacted instantly and blindly. A deep roar went up as pirates and buccaneers drew their swords and fell upon one another. The men left on the walls abandoned their posts and leaped down into the stockade, blades in hand. In an instant the compound was a battleground, where knotting, writhing groups of men smote and slew in a blind frenzy. Some of the men-at-arms and serfs were drawn into the mêlée, and the soldiers at the gate turned and stared down in amazement, forgetting the enemy that lurked outside.

It all happened so quickly—smoldering passions exploding into sudden battle—that men were fighting all over the compound before Conan could reach the maddened chiefs. Ignoring their swords, he tore them apart with such violence that they staggered backward, and Zarono tripped and fell flat.

"You cursed fools, will you throw away all our lives?"

Strombanni was frothing mad and Zarono was bawling for assistance. A buccaneer ran at Conan from behind and cut at his head. The Cimmerian half turned and caught his arm, checking the stroke in midair.

105

"Look, you fools!" he roared, pointing with his sword.

Something in his tone caught the attention of the battle-crazed mob. Men froze in their places and twisted their heads to stare. Conan was pointing to a soldier on the footwalk. The man was reeling, clawing the air, and choking as he tried to shout. He pitched headlong to the ground, and all saw the black arrow standing out from between his shoulders.

A cry of alarm arose from the compound. On the heels of the shout came a clamor of blood-freezing screams and the shattering impact of axes on the gate. Flaming arrows arched over the wall and stuck in logs, and thin wisps of blue smoke curled upward. Then, from behind the huts that ranged the south wall, came swift and furtive figures racing across the compound.

"The Picts are in!" roared Conan.

Bedlam followed his shout. The freebooters ceased their feud. Some turned to meet the savages; some sprang to the wall. Savages were pouring from behind the huts and streaming over the compound; their axes clashed against the cutlasses of the sailors.

Zarono was still struggling to his feet when a painted savage rushed upon him from behind and brained him with a war-axe.

Conan, with a clump of sailors behind him, was battling with the Picts inside the stockade; Strombanni, with most of his men, was climbing up on the stockade, slashing at the dark figures already swarming over the wall. The Picts, who had crept up unobserved and surrounded the fort while the defenders were fighting among themselves, were attacking from all sides. Valenso's soldiers were clustered at the gate, trying to hold it against a howling swarm of exultant demons who thundered against it from the outside with a tree trunk.

More and more savages streamed from behind the huts, having scaled the undefended south wall. Strombanni and his pirates were beaten back from the other sides of the palisade, and in an instant the compound was swarming with naked warriors. They dragged down the defenders like wolves; the battle resolved into swirling whirlpools of painted figures surging about small groups of desperate white men. Picts, sailors, and men-at-arms littered the earth, stamped underfoot by the heedless feet.

Blood-smeared braves dived howling into huts, and shrieks rose above the din of battle as women and children died beneath the red axes. When they heard those pitiful cries, the men-at-arms abandoned the gate, and in an instant the Picts had burst it and were pouring into the palisade at that point also. Huts began to go up in flames.

"Make for the manor!" roared Conan, and a dozen men surged in behind him as he hewed an inexorable way through the snarling pack.

Strombanni was at his side, wielding his red cutlass like a flail. "We can't hold the manor," grunted the pirate.

"Why not?" Conan was too busy with his crimson work to spare a glance.

"Because—uh!" a knife in a dark hand sank deep in the Barachan's back. "Devil eat you, bastard!" Strombanni turned staggeringly and split the savage's skull to his teeth. The pirate reeled and fell to his knees, blood starting from his lips.

"The manor's burning!" he croaked, and slumped over in the dust.

Conan cast a swift look about him. The men who had followed him were all down in their blood. The Pict gasping out his life under the Cimmerian's feet was the last of the group that had barred his way. All about him, battle was swirling and surging, but for the moment he stood alone.

He was not far from the south wall. A few strides and he could leap to the ledge, swing over, and be gone through the night. But he remembered the helpless girls in the manor—from which, now, smoke was rolling in billowing masses. He ran toward the manor.

A feathered chief wheeled from the door, lifting a war-axe, and, behind the racing Cimmerian, lines of fleet-footed braves were converging upon him. He did not check his stride. His downward-sweeping cutlass met and deflected the axe and split the skull of the wielder. An instant later, Conan was through the door and had slammed and bolted it against the axes that thudded into the wood.

The great hall was full of drifting wisps of smoke, through which he groped, half blinded. Somewhere a woman was whimpering little, catchy, hysterical sobs of nerve-shattering horror. He emerged from a whorl of smoke and stopped dead in his tracks, glaring down the hall.

The hall was dim and shadowy with drifting smoke. The great silver candelabrum was overturned, the candles extinguished; the only illumination was a lurid glow from the great fireplace and the wall in which it was set, where the flames licked from burning floor to smoking roof beams. And limned against that lurid glare, Conan saw a human worm swinging slowly at the end of a rope. The dead face, distorted beyond recognition, turned toward him as the body swung; but Conan knew it was Count Valenso, hanged to his own roof beam.

But there was something else in the hall. Conan saw it through the drifting smoke: a monstrous black figure, outlined against the hell-fire glare. That outline was vaguely human, although the shadow thrown on the burning wall was not human at all.

"Crom!" muttered Conan aghast, paralyzed by the

realization that he was confronted by a being against whom his sword was useless. He saw Belesa and Tina, clutched in each other's arms, crouching at the bottom of the stair.

The black monster reared up, looming gigantic against the flame, great arms spread wide. A dim face leered through the drifting smoke—semi-human, demoniac, altogether terrible. Conan glimpsed the close-set horns, the gaping mouth, the peaked ears. It was lumbering toward him through the smoke, and an old memory woke with desperation.

Near the Cimmerian lay the great overturned candelabrum, once the pride of Korzetta Castle: fifty pounds of massy silver, intricately worked with figures of gods and heroes. Conan grasped it and heaved it high above his head.

"Silver and fire!" he roared in a voice like a clap of wind, and hurled the candelabrum with all the power of his iron muscles. Full on the great black breast it crashed, fifty pounds of silver winged with terrific velocity. Not even the black one could stand before such a missile. The demon was carried off its feet—hurled back into the open fireplace, which was a roaring mouth of flame. A horrible scream shook the hall, the cry of an unearthly thing gripped suddenly by earthly death. The mantel cracked, and stones fell from the great chimney, half hiding the black, writhing limbs at which the flames ate in elemental fury. Burning beams crashed down from the roof and thundered on the stones, and the whole heap was enveloped in a roaring burst of fire.

Flames were creeping down the stair when Conan reached it. He caught up the fainting child under one arm and dragged Belesa to her feet. Through the crackle and snap of the fire sounded the splintering of the front door under the war-axes.

He glared about, sighted a door opposite the stair landing, and hurried through it, carrying Tina and dragging Belesa, who seemed dazed. As they came into the chamber beyond, a crash behind them announced that the roof was falling in the hall. Through a strangling wall of smoke, Conan saw an open, outer door on the other side of the chamber. As he lugged his charges through it, he saw that it sagged on broken hinges, lock and bolt snapped and splintered as if by some terrific force.

"The devil came in by this door!" Belesa sobbed hysterically. "I saw him—but I did not know—"

They emerged into the firelit compound a few feet from the row of huts that lined the south wall. A Pict was skulking toward the door, eyes red in the firelight and axe lifted. Dropping Tina and swinging Belesa away from the blow, Conan snatched out his cutlass and drove it through the savage's breast. Then, sweeping both girls off their feet, he ran, carrying them, toward the south wall.

The compound was full of billowing smoke-clouds that half hid the red work going on there, but the fugitives had been seen. Naked figures, black against the dull glare, pranced out of the smoke, brandishing gleaming axes. They were still yards behind him when Conan ducked into the space between the huts and the wall. At the other end of the corridor, he saw other howling shapes, running to cut him off.

Halting short, he tossed Belesa bodily to the footwalk, then Tina, and then leaped up after them. Swinging Belesa over the palisade, he dropped her into the sand outside, and dropped Tina after her. A thrown axe crashed into a log by his shoulder, and then he, too, was over the wall and gathering up his dazed and helpless charges. When the Picts reached the wall, the space before the palisade was empty of all except the dead.

110

8. *Swords of Aquilonia*

Dawn was tinging the dim waters an old-rose hue. Far out across the tinted waters, a fleck of white grew out of the mist—a sail that seemed to hang suspended in the pearly sky. On a bushy headland, Conan the Cimmerian held a ragged cloak over a fire of green wood. As he manipulated the cloak, puffs of smoke rose upward, quivered against the dawn, and vanished.

Belesa crouched near him, one arm about Tina. She asked: "Do you think they'll see it and understand?"

"They'll see it, right enough," he assured her. "They've been hanging off this coast all night, hoping to sight some survivors. They're scared stiff; there's only half a dozen of them, and not one can navigate well enough to sail from here to the Barachan Isles. They'll understand my signals; 'tis the pirate code. They'll be glad to ship under me, since I'm the only captain left."

"But suppose the Picts see the smoke?" She shuddered, glancing back over the misty sands and bushes to where, miles to the north, a column of smoke stood up in the still air.

"They're not likely to see it. After I hid you in the woods, I crept back and saw them dragging barrels of wine and ale out of the storehouses. Already most of them were reeling. By this time, they'll all be lying around, too drunk to move. If I had a hundred men, I could wipe out the whole horde—Crom and Mitra!" he cried suddenly. "That's not the *Red Hand* after all, but a war galley! What civilized state would send a unit of its fleet hither? Unless somebody would have words with your uncle, in which case they'll need a spaewoman to raise his ghost."

He scowled out to sea in an effort to make out the details of the craft through the mist. The approaching ship was bow-on, so that all he could see was a gilded bow ornament, a small sail bellying in the faint onshore breeze, and the bank of oars on each side rising and falling like a single pair.

"Well," said Conan, "at least they're coming to take us off. It would be a long walk back to Zingara. Until we find out who they are and whether they're friendly, say naught of who I am. I'll think of a proper tale by the time they get here."

Conan stamped out the fire, handed the cloak back to Belesa, and stretched like a great, lazy cat. Belesa watched him in wonder. His unperturbed manner was not assumed; the night of fire and blood and slaughter, and the flight through the black woods afterward, had left his nerves untouched. He was as calm as if he had spent the night in feasting and revel. Bandages torn from the hem of Belesa's gown covered a few minor wounds that he had received in fighting without armor.

Belesa did not fear him; she felt safer than she had felt since she landed on that wild coast. He was not like the freebooters, civilized men who had repudiated all standards of honor and lived without any. Conan, on the other hand, lived according to the code of his people, which was barbaric and bloody but at least upheld its own peculiar standards of honor.

"Think you he is dead?" she asked.

He did not ask her to whom she referred. "I believe so," he replied. "Silver and fire are both deadly to evil spirits, and he got a bellyfull of both."

"How about his master?"

"Thoth-Amon? Gone back to lurk in some Stygian tomb, I suppose. These wizards are a queer lot."

Neither spoke of that subject again; Belesa's mind shrank from the task of conjuring up the scene when a black figure skulked into the great hall, and a long-delayed vengeance was horribly consummated.

The ship was larger, but some time would yet elapse before it made shore. Belesa asked:

"When you first came to the manor, you said something of having been a general in Aquilonia and then having to flee. What is the tale on that?"

Conan grinned. "Put it down to my own folly in trusting that quince-faced Numedides. They made me general because of some small successes against the Picts; and then, when I'd scattered five times my own number of savages in a battle at Velitrium and broken their confederacy, I was called back to Tarantia for an official triumph. All very tickling to the vanity, riding beside the king while girls scatter rose petals before you; but then at the banquet the bastard plied me with drugged wine. I woke up in chains in the Iron Tower, awaiting execution."

"Whatever for?"

He shrugged. "How know I what goes on in what that numb-wit calls his brain? Perhaps some of the other Aquilonian generals, resentful of the sudden rise of an outland barbarian into their sacred ranks, had worked upon his suspicions. Or perhaps he took offense at some of my frank remarks about his policy of spending the royal treasury to adorn Tarantia with golden statues of himself instead of for the defense of his frontiers.

"The philosopher Alcemides confided to me, just before I quaffed the drugged draught, that he hoped to write a book on the use of ingratitude as a principle of statecraft, using the king as a model. Heigh-ho! I was too drunk to realize he was trying to warn me.

113

"I had, however, friends with whose aid I was smuggled out of the Iron Tower, given a horse and a sword, and turned loose. I rode back to Bossonia with the idea of raising a revolt, beginning with my own troops. But, when I got there, I found my sturdy Bossonians gone, sent to another province, and in their place a brigade of ox-eyed yokels from the Tauran, most of whom had never heard of me. They insisted on trying to arrest me, so I had to split a few skulls in cutting my way out. I swam Thunder River with arrows whizzing about my ears . . . and here I am."

He frowned out toward the approaching ship again. "By Crom, I'd swear yonder ensign bore the leopard of Poitain, did I did not know it were a thing impossible. Come."

He led the girls down to the beach as the chant of the coxswain became audible. With a final heave on the oars, the crew drove the galley's bow with a rush up the sand. As men tumbled off the bow, Conan yelled:

"Prospero! Trocero! What in the name of all the gods are you doing . . ."

"Conan!" they roared, and closed in on him, pounding his back and wringing his hands. All spoke at once, but Belesa did not understand the speech, which was that of Aquilonia. The one referred to as "Trocero" must be the Count of Poitain, a broad-shouldered, slim-hipped man who moved with the grace of a panther despite the gray in his black hair.

"What do you here?" persisted Conan.

"We came for you," said Prospero, the slim, elegantly-clad one.

"How did you know where I was?"

The stout, bald man addressed as "Publius" gestured toward another man in the black robe of a priest of Mitra. "Dexitheus found you by his occult arts. He swore you still lived and promised to lead us to you."

114

The black-robed man bowed gravely. "Your destiny is linked with that of Aquilonia, Conan of Cimmeria," he said. "I am but one small link in the chain of your fate."

"Well, what's this all about?" said Conan. "Crom knows I'm glad to be rescued from this forsaken sand-spit, but why came you after me?"

Trocero spoke: "We have broken with Numedides, being unable longer to endure his follies and oppressions, and we seek a general to lead the forces of revolt. You're our man!"

Conan laughed gustily and stuck his thumbs in his girdle. "It's good to find some who understand true merit. Lead me to the fray, my friends!" He glanced around and his eyes caught Belesa, standing timidly apart from the group. He gestured her forward with rough gallantry. "Gentlemen, the Lady Belesa of Korzetta." Then he spoke to the girl in her own language again. "We can take you back to Zingara, but what will you do then?"

She shook her head helplessly. "I know not. I have neither money nor friends, and I am not trained to earn my living. Perhaps it would have been better had one of those arrows struck my heart."

"Do not say that, my lady!" begged Tina. "I will work for us both!"

Conan drew a small leather bag from his girdle. "I didn't get Tothmekri's jewels," he rumbled, "but here are some baubles I found in the chest where I got the clothes I'm wearing." He spilled a handful of flaming rubies into his palm. "They're worth a fortune, themselves." He dumped them back into the bag and handed it to her.

"But I can't take these—" she began.

"Of course you shall take them! I might as well leave you for the Picts to scalp as to take you back to Zingara to starve," said he. "I know what it is to be penniless in a Hyborian land. Now, in my country, sometimes there are famines; but people go hungry only when there's no

115

food in the land at all. But in civilized countries I've seen people sick of gluttony while others were starving. Aye, I've seen men fall and die of hunger against the walls of shops and storehouses crammed with food.

"Sometimes I was hungry, too, but then I took what I wanted at sword's point. But you can't do that. So you take these rubies. You can sell them and buy a castle, and slaves, and fine clothes, and with them it won't be hard to get a husband, because civilized men all desire wives with these possessions."

"But what of you?"

Conan grinned and indicated the circle of Aquilonians. "Here's my fortune. With these true friends, I shall have all the wealth in Aquilonia at my feet."

The stout Publius spoke up: "Your generosity does you credit, Conan, but I wish you had consulted with me first. For revolutions are made not only by wrongs, but also by gold; and Numedides' publicans have so beggared Aquilonia that we shall be hard put to find the money to hire mercenaries."

"Ha!" laughed Conan. "I'll get you gold enough to set every blade in Aquilonia swinging!" In a few words he told of the treasure of Tranicos and of the destruction of Valenso's settlement. "Now the demon's gone from the cave; the Picts will be scattering to their villages. With a detail of well-armed men, we can make a quick march to the cavern and back before they realize we're in Pictland. Are you with me?"

They cheered until Belesa feared that their noise would draw the attention of the Picts. Conan cast her a sly grin and muttered in Zingaran, under cover of the racket:

"How d'you like 'King Conan'? Sounds not bad, eh?"

Wolves Beyond the Border

The revolution progresses with hurricane speed.
While knights and sergeants in gleaming mail clash
in charge and counter-charge on the Aquilonian
plains, civil war rages along the Pictish frontier between the partisans of Conan and those of Numedides. The Picts, naturally, see their opportunity.
Here is the tale of some of the events of that strife-
torn land, as told by one of the survivors of the conflict; for the Hyborian Age was a time of stirring
events in many times and places, not merely those
in which Conan was present.

1.

I⊤ was the mutter of a drum that awakened me. I lay
still amidst the bushes where I had taken refuge, straining my ears to locate it, for such sounds are illusive in the
deep forest. In the dense woods about me, there was
no sound. Above me, the tangled vines and brambles bent
close to form a massed roof, and above them loomed the
higher, gloomier arch of the branches of the great trees.
Not a star shone through that leafy vault. Low-hanging
clouds seemed to press down upon the very treetops.
There was no moon; the night was as dark as a witch's
hate.

The better for me. If I could not see my enemies,
neither could they see me. But the whisper of that omi-
nous drum stole through the night: thrum! thrum! thrum!
—a steady monotone that grunted and growled of nameless secrets. I could not mistake the sound. Only one drum
in the world makes just that deep, menacing, sullen thunder: a Pictish war-drum, in the hands of those wild painted
savages who haunt the wilderness beyond the border of
the Westermarck.

And I was beyond that border, alone, and concealed
in a brambly covert in the midst of the great forest, where
those naked fiends have reigned since Time's earliest
dawn.

Now I located the sound; the drum was beating westward of my position and, I believed, at no great distance.

Quickly I girt my belt more firmly, settled war-axe and knife in their beaded sheaths, strung my heavy bow, and made sure that my quiver was in place at my left hip—groping with my fingers in the utter darkness—and then I crawled from the thicket and went warily toward the sound of the drum.

That it personally concerned me I did not believe. If the forest men had discovered me, their discovery would have been announced by a sudden knife in my throat, not by a drum beating in the distance. But the throb of the war-drum had a significance no forest-runner could ignore. It was a warning and a threat, a promise of doom for those invaders whose lonely cabins and axe-marked clearings menaced the immemorial solitude of the wilderness. It meant fire and torture, flaming arrows dropping like falling stars through the darkness, and the red axes crunching through skulls of men and women and children.

So through the blackness of the nighted forest I went, feeling my way delicately among the mighty boles, sometimes creeping on hands and knees, and now and then my heart in my throat when a creeper brushed across my face or groping hand. For there are huge serpents in that forest, which sometimes hang by their tails from branches and so snare their prey. But the creatures I sought were more terrible than any serpent, and as the drum grew louder I went as cautiously as if I trod on naked swords. And presently I glimpsed a red gleam among the trees and heard a mutter of barbaric voices mingling with the snarl of the drum.

Whatever weird ceremony might be taking place yonder under the black trees, it was likely that they had outposts scattered about the place; and I knew how silent and motionless a Pict could stand, merging with the natural forest even in dim light, and unsuspected until his blade was through his victim's heart. My flesh crawled at the thought of colliding with one such grim sentry in the darkness, and I drew my knife and held it extended before me. But I knew not even a Pict could see me in that blackness of tangled forest-roof and cloud-massed sky.

The light revealed itself as a fire, before which silhouettes moved like black devils against the red fires of Hell. And presently I crouched close among the dense tamarack and looked into a black-walled glade and the figures that moved therein.

There were forty or fifty Picts, naked but for loincloths and hideously painted, who squatted in a wide semicircle, facing the fire, with their backs to me. By the hawk feathers in their thick black manes, I knew them to be of the Hawk Clan, or Onayaga. In the midst of the glade there was a crude altar made of rough stones heaped together, and at the sight of this my flesh crawled anew. For I had seen these Pictish altars before, all charred with fire and stained with blood, in empty forest glades. And, though I had never witnessed the rituals wherein these things were used, I had heard the tales told about them by men who had been captives among the Picts, or spied upon them even as I was spying.

A feathered shaman was dancing between the fire and the altar, a slow, shuffling dance indescribably grotesque, which caused his plumes to swing and sway about him. And his features were hidden by a grinning scarlet mask that looked like a forest-devil's face.

In the midst of the semicircle of warriors squatted one with the great drum between his knees, and as he smote it with his clenched fist it gave forth that low, growling rumble which is like the mutter of distant thunder.

Between the warriors and the dancing shaman stood one who was no Pict. For he was as tall as I, and his skin, light in the play of the fire. But he was clad only in doeskin loinclout and moccasins, and his body was painted, and there was a hawk feather in his hair. So I knew he must be a Ligurean, one of those light-skinned savages who dwell in small clans in the great forest, generally at war with the Picts but sometimes at peace and allied with them. Their skins are white as an Aquilonian's. The Picts are a white race, too, in that they are not black or brown or yellow; but they are black-eyed and black-haired and dark of skin. Neither they nor the Ligureans are spoken of as "white" by the people of Westermarck, who only designate thus a man of Hyborian blood.

Now, as I watched, I saw three warriors drag a man into the ring of the firelight—another Pict, naked and bloodstained, who still wore in his tangled mane a feather that identified him as a member of the Raven Clan, with whom the Hawkmen were ever at war. His captors cast him down upon the altar, bound hand and foot, and I saw his muscles swell and writhe in the firelight as he sought in vain to break the rawhide thongs which prisoned him.

Then the shaman began dancing again, weaving intricate patterns about the altar and the man upon it; and he who beat the drum wrought himself into a fine frenzy, thundering away like one possessed of a devil. And suddenly, down from an overhanging branch dropped one of those great serpents of which I have spoken. The firelight glistened on its scales as it writhed toward the altar, its beady eyes glittering and its forked tongue darting in and out; but the warriors showed no fear, though it passed within a few feet of some of them. And that was strange, for ordinarily those serpents are the only living creatures a Pict fears.

The monster reared its head up on arched neck above the altar, and it and the shaman faced one another across the prone body of the prisoner. The shaman danced with a writhing of body and arms, scarcely moving his feet, and as he danced, the great serpent danced with him, weaving and swaying as though spellbound, and from the mask of the shaman rose a weird wailing that shuddered like the wind through the dry reeds along the sea-marshes. And slowly the great reptile reared higher and higher and began looping itself about the altar and the man upon it, until his body was hidden by its shimmering folds, and only his head was visible, with that other terrible head swaying close above it.

The shrilling of the shaman rose to a crescendo of infernal triumph, and he cast something into the fire. A great green cloud of smoke billowed up and rolled about the altar, so that it almost hid the pair upon it, making their outlines indistinct and illusive. But in the midst of that cloud I saw a hideous writhing and *changing*—those outlines melted and flowed together horribly, and for a moment I could not tell which was the serpent and which the man. A shuddering sigh swept over the assembled Picts like a wind moaning through nighted branches.

Then the smoke cleared away and the snake lay limply on the altar, and I thought both were dead. But the shaman seized the neck of the serpent and unlooped the limp trunk from about the altar and let the great reptile ooze to the ground, and he tumbled the body of the man from the stones to fall beside the monster, and cut the rawhide thongs that bound wrist and ankle.

Then he began a weaving dance about them, chanting as he danced and swaying his arms in mad gestures. And presently the man moved. But he did not rise. His head swayed from side to side, and I saw his tongue dart out and in again. And, Mitra! he began to *wriggle* away from the fire, squirming along on his belly, as a snake crawls!

And the serpent was suddenly shaken with convulsions and arched its neck and reared up almost its full length, and then fell back, loop on loop, and reared up again vainly, horribly like a man trying to rise and stand and walk upright, after being deprived of his limbs.

The wild howling of the Picts shook the night, and I was sick where I crouched among the bushes, and fought an urge to retch. I understood the meaning of this ghastly ceremony now. I had heard tales of it. By black, primordial sorcery that spawned and throve in this primal forest, that painted shaman had transferred the soul of a captured enemy into the foul body of a serpent. It was the revenge of a fiend. And the screaming of the blood-mad Picts was like the yelling of all Hell's demons.

And the victims writhed and agonized side by side, the man and the serpent, until a sword flashed in the hand of the shaman and both heads fell together—and, gods! it was the serpent's trunk which but quivered and jerked a little and then lay still, and the man's body which rolled and knotted and thrashed like a beheaded snake. A deathly faintness and weakness took hold of me, for what civilized man could watch such black diabolism unmoved? And these savages, smeared with war-paint, howling and posturing and triumphing over the ghastly doom of a foe, seemed not human beings at all to me, but foul fiends of the black night whom it were a duty and an obligation to slay.

The shaman sprang up and faced the ring of warriors and, ripping off his mask, threw up his head and howled like a wolf. And as the firelight fell full on his face, I recognized him, and with that recognition all horror and revulsion gave way to red rage, and all thought of personal peril and the recollection of my mission, which was my first obligation, was swept away. For that shaman was old Teyanoga of the South Hawks, he who burned alive my friend Jon Galter's son.

In the lust of my hate I acted almost instinctively— whipped up my bow, notched an arrow, and loosed, all in an instant. The firelight was uncertain, but the range was not great, and we of the Westermarck live by the twang of the bow. Old Teyanoga yowled like a cat and reeled back, and his warriors howled with amaze to see a shaft quivering suddenly in his breast. The tall, light-skinned warrior wheeled, and for the first time I saw his face—and, Mitra! he was a Hyborian.

The horrid shock of that surprise held me paralyzed for a moment and had almost undone me. For the Picts instantly sprang up and rushed into the forest like panthers, seeking the foe who shot that arrow. They had reached the first fringe of bushes when I jerked out of my spell of amaze and horror. I sprang up and raced away in the darkness, ducking and dodging among the trees, which I avoided more by instinct than otherwise, for it was dark as ever. I knew the Picts could not strike my trail, but must hunt as blindly as I fled. And presently, as I ran northward, I heard behind me a hideous howling, whose blood-mad fury was enough to freeze the blood even of a forest-runner. And I believed that they had plucked my arrow from the shaman's breast and discovered it to be a Hyborian's shaft. That would bring them after me with fiercer blood-lust than ever.

I fled on, my heart pounding from fear and excitement, and the horror of the nightmare I had witnessed. And that a Hyborian should have stood there as a welcome and evidently honored guest—for he was armed; I had seen knife and hatchet at his belt—was so monstrous that I wondered if, after all, the whole thing had been a nightmare. For never before had a Hyborian observed the Dance of the Changing Serpent save as a prisoner, or as a spy, as I had. And what monstrous thing it portended I knew not, but I was shaken with foreboding and horror at the thought.

And because of my horror I went more carelessly than is my wont, seeking haste at the expense of stealth, and occasionally blundering into a tree I could have avoided had I taken more care. And I doubt not it was the noise of this blundering progress which brought the Pict upon me, for he could not have seen me in that pitch-darkness.

Behind me sounded no more yells, but I knew that the Picts were ranging like fire-eyed wolves through the forest, spreading in a vast semicircle and combing it as they ran. That they had picked up my trail was evidenced by their silence, for they never yell except when they believe that only a short dash is ahead of them, and feel sure of their prey.

The warrior who heard the sounds of my flight could not have been one of that party, for he was too far ahead of them. He must have been a scout, ranging the forest to guard against his comrades' being surprised from the north.

At any rate, he heard me running close to him, and came like a devil of the black night. I knew of him first only by the swift pad of his naked feet, and when I wheeled I could not even make out the dim bulk of him, but only heard the soft thudding of those inexorable feet, coming at me unseen in the darkness.

They see like cats in the dark, and I knew he saw well enough to locate me, though doubtless I was only a dim blur in the darkness. But my blindly upswung hatchet met his falling knife, and he impaled himself on my knife as he lunged in, his death-yell ringing like a peal of doom under the forest-roof. And it was answered by a ferocious clamor to the south, only a few hundred yards away; and then they were racing through the bushes, giving tongue like wolves certain of their quarry.

I ran for it in good earnest now, abandoning stealth entirely for the sake of speed and trusting to luck that I should not dash out my brains against a tree trunk in the darkness.

125

But here the forest opened up somewhat; there was no underbrush, and something almost like light filtered in through the branches, for the clouds were clearing a little. And through this forest I fled like a damned soul pursued by demons, hearing the yells at first rising higher and higher in bloodthirsty triumph, then edged with anger and rage as they grew fainter and fell away behind me; for in a straightaway race no Pict can match the long legs of a forest-runner. The desperate risk was that there were other scouts or war-parties ahead of me who, hearing my flight, could easily cut me off; but it was a risk I had to take. But no painted figures started up like phantoms out of the shadows ahead of me; and presently, through the thickening growth that betokened the nearness of a creek, I saw a glimmer far ahead of me and knew it was the light of Fort Kwanyara, the southernmost outpost of Schohira.

2.

Perhaps, before continuing with this chronicle of the bloody years, it might be well were I to give an account of myself, and the reason why I traversed the Pictish wilderness, by night and alone.

My name is Gault Hagar's son. I was born in the province of Conajohara. But two years before this tale, the Picts broke over the Black River and stormed Fort Tuscelan and slew all within save one man, and drove all the settlers of the province east of Thunder River.

Conajohara became again part of the wilderness, haunted only by wild beasts and wild men. The people of Conajohara scattered throughout the Westermarck, in Schohira, Conawaga, or Oriskonie; but many of them—my family among them—went southward and settled near Fort Thandara, an isolated outpost on the Warhorse River. There they were later joined by other settlers for whom the older provinces were too thickly inhabited, and presently there grew up the district known as the Free Province of Thandara, because it was not like the other provinces, which were royal grants to great lords east of the marches and settled by them, but cut out of the wilderness by the pioneers themselves without aid of the Aquilonian nobility. We paid no taxes to any baron. Our governor was not appointed by any lord, but we elected him ourselves, from our own people, and he was responsible only to the king. We manned and built our forts ourselves, and sustained ourselves in war as in peace. And Mitra knows war was a constant state of affairs, for there was never peace between us and our savage neighbors, the wild Panther, Alligator, and Otter tribes of Picts.

But we throve, and seldom questioned what went on east of the marches in the kingdom whence our grandsires had come. Scarcely had we become settled, however, when events in Aquilonia did touch upon us in the wilderness. Word came of civil war, and a fighting man risen to wrest the throne from the ancient dynasty. And sparks from that conflagration set the frontier ablaze, and turned neighbor against neighbor and brother against brother. And it was because knights in their gleaming steel were fighting and dying on the plains of Aquilonia that I was hastening alone through the stretch of wilderness that separated Thandara from Schohira, with news that might well change the destiny of all the Westermarck.

Fort Kwanyara was a small outpost, a square blockhouse of hewn logs with a palisade, on the bank of Knife Creek. I saw its banner streaming against the pale rose of the morning sky and noted that only the ensign of the province floated there. The royal standard that should have risen above it, flaunting the golden serpent, was not in evidence. That might mean much or nothing. We of the frontier are careless about the delicate punctilios of custom and etiquette, which mean so much to the knights beyond the marches.

I crossed Knife Creek in the early dawn, wading through the shallows, and was challenged by a picket on the other bank, a tall man in the buckskins of a ranger. When he knew I was from Thandara: "By Mitra!" quoth he, "your business must be urgent, that you cross the wilderness instead of taking the longer road."

For Thandara was separated from the other provinces, as I have said, and the Little Wilderness lay between it and the Bossonian Marches. A safe road ran around it into the Marches and thence to the other provinces, but it was a long and tedious road.

Then he asked for news from Thandara, but I told him I knew little of the latest events, having just returned from a long scout into the country of the Ottermen. This was a lie, but I had no way of knowing Schohira's political color and was not inclined to betray my own until I knew. Then I asked him if Hakon Strom's son was in Fort Kwanyara, and he told me that the man I sought was not in the fort, but was at the town of Schondara, which lay a few miles east of the fort.

"I hope Thandara declares for Conan," said he with an oath, "for I tell you plainly it is our political complection. And it is my cursed luck which keeps me here with the handful of rangers who watch the border for raiding Picts. I would give my bow and hunting shirt to be with our army, which lies even now at Thenitea on Ogaha

Creek, waiting for the onslaught of Brocas of Torh with his damned renegades."

I said naught but was astounded. This was news indeed. For the Baron of Torh was lord of Conawaga, not Schohira, whose patron was Lord Thasperas of Kormon.

"Where is Thasperas?" I asked, and the ranger answered, a thought shortly: "Away in Aquilonia, fighting for Conan." And he looked at me narrowly as if he had begun to wonder if I were a spy.

"Is there a man in Schohira," I began, "who has such connections with the Picts that he dwells, naked and painted, among them, and attends their ceremonies of blood-feast and—"

I checked myself at the fury that contorted the Schohiran's features.

"Damn you," says he, choking with passion, "what is your purpose in coming here to insult us thus?"

And indeed, to call a man a renegade was the direst insult that could be offered along the Westermarck, though I had not meant it that way. But I saw the man was ignorant of any knowledge concerning the renegade I had seen, and not wishing to give out information, I merely told him that he misunderstood my meaning.

"I understand it well enough," said he, shaking with passion. "But for your dark skin and southern accent, I would deem you a spy from Conawaga. But spy or no, you cannot insult the men of Schohira in such a manner. Were I not on military duty, I would lay down my weapon-belt and show you what manner of men we breed in Schohira."

"I want no quarrel," said I. "But I am going to Schondara, where it will not be hard for you to find me, if you so desire. I am Gault Hagar's son."

"I will be there anon," quoth he grimly. "I am Otho Gorm's son, and they know me in Schohira."

I left him striding his post along the bank and fingering his knife hilt and hatchet as if he itched to try their edges on my head, and I swung wide of the small fort to avoid other scouts or pickets. For in these troublous times, suspicion might fall on me as a spy very easily. Nay, this Otho Gorm's son was beginning to turn such thoughts in his thick noodle when they were swept away by his personal resentment at what he mistook for a slur. And having quarreled with me, his sense of personal honor would not allow him to arrest me on suspicion of being a spy—even had he thought of it. In ordinary times, none would think of halting or questioning a Hyborian crossing the border—but everything was in a mad whirl now; it must be, if the patron of Conawaga was invading the domain of his neighbors.

The forest had been cleared about the fort for a few hundred yards in each direction, forming a solid green wall. I kept within this wall as I skirted the clearing, and met no one, even when I crossed several paths leading from the fort. I headed eastward, avoiding clearings and farms, and the sun was not high in the heavens when I sighted the roofs of Schondara.

The forest ran to within less than half a mile of the town, which was a handsome one for a frontier village, with neat houses mostly of squared logs, some painted, but also some fine frame buildings, which is something we have not in Thandara. But there was not so much as a ditch or a palisade about the village, which was strange to me. For we of Thandara build our dwelling places for defense as much as shelter, and while there was not then a village in the width and breadth of the province —the land being but newly settled—yet every cabin was like a tiny fortress.

Off to the right of the village stood a fort, in the midst of a meadow, with palisade and ditch, and a ballista pivot-mounted on a raised platform. This structure was somewhat larger than Fort Kwanyara, but I saw few heads moving above the parapet, either helmeted or capped. And only the spreading-winged hawk of Schohira flapped on the standard. And I wondered why, if Schohira were for Conan, they did not fly the banner he had chosen—the golden lion on a black field, the standard of the regiment he commanded as a mercenary general of Aquilonia.

Away to the left, at the edge of the forest, I saw a large house of stone set amidst gardens and orchards, and knew it for the estate of Lord Valerian, the richest landowner in western Schohira. I had never seen the man, yet knew he was wealthy and powerful. But now the Hall, as it was called, seemed deserted.

The town seemed curiously deserted, likewise; at least of men, though there were women and children in plenty, and it seemed to me that the men had assembled their families here for safety. I saw few able-bodied men. As I went up the street, many eyes followed me suspiciously, but none spoke except to reply briefly to my questions.

At the tavern only a few old men and cripples huddled about the ale-stained tables and conversed in low tones. All conversation ceased as I loomed in the doorway in my worn buckskins, and all turned to stare at me silently.

More significant silence when I asked for Hakon Strom's son, and the host told me that Hakon was ridden to Thenitea shortly after sun-up, where the militia-army lay encamped, but would reuurn shortly. So, being hungry and weary, I ate a meal in the taproom, aware of those questioning eyes fixed upon me, and then lay down in a corner on a bearskin the host fetched for me, and slept. And was so slumbering when Hakon Strom's son returned, close upon sunset.

He was a tall man, rangy and broad-shouldered like most Westlanders, and clad in buckskin hunting shirt and fringed leggings and moccasins like myself. Half a dozen rangers were with him, and they sat them down at a board close to the door and watched him and me over the rims of their ale jacks.

When I named myself and told him I had a word for him, he looked at me closely and bade me sit with him at a table in the corner where mine host brought us ale foaming in leathern jacks.

"Has no word come through of the state of affairs in Thandara?" I asked.

"No sure word; only rumors."

"Very well," said I. "I bring you word from Brant Drago's son, governor of Thandara, and the council of captains, and by this sign you shall know me for a true man." And so saying I dipped my finger in the foamy ale and with it drew a symbol on the table, and instantly erased it. He nodded, his eyes blazing with interest.

"This is the word I bring you," quoth I: "Thandara has declared for Conan and stands ready to aid his friends and defy his enemies."

At that he smiled joyfully and grasped my brown hand warmly with his own rugged fingers.

"Good!" he exclaimed. "But it is no more than I expected."

"What man of Thandara could forget Conan?" said I. "Nay, I was but a stripling in Conajohara, but I remember him when he was a forest-runner and a scout there. When his rider came into Thandara, telling us that Poitain was in revolt, with Conan striking for the throne, and asking our support—he asked no volunteers for his army, merely our loyalty—we sent him one word: 'We have not forgotten Conajohara.' Then came Baron Attelius over the marshes against us, but we ambushed him in the Little Wilderness and cut his army to pieces.

And now I think we need fear no invasion in Thandara."

"I wish I could say the same for Schohira," he said grimly. "Baron Thasperas sent us word that we could do as we chose—he has declared for Conan and joined the rebel army. But he did not demand western levies. Nay, both he and Conan know the Westermarck needs every man it has to guard the border.

"He removed his troops from the forts, however, and we manned them with our own foresters. There was some little skirmishing among ourselves, especially in the towns like Coyaga, where dwell the landholders, for some of them held to Numedides—well, these loyalists either fled away to Conawaga with their retainers, or else surrendered and gave their pledge to remain neutral in their castles, like Lord Valerian of Schondara. The loyalists who fled swore to return and cut all our throats. And presently Lord Brocas marched over the border.

"In Conawaga the landowners and Brocas are for Numedides, and we have heard pitiful tales of their treatment of the common people who favor Conan."

I nodded, not surprised. Conawaga was the largest, richest, and most thickly settled province in all the Westermarck, and it had a comparatively large and very powerful class of titled landholders—which we have not in Thandara and by the favor of Mitra never shall.

"It is an open invasion for conquest," said Hakon. "Brocas commanded us to swear loyalty to Numedides —the dog! I think the black-jowled fool plots to subdue all the Westermarck and rule it as Numedides' viceroy. With an army of Aquilonian men-at-arms, Bossonian archers, Conawaga loyalists, and Schohira renegades, he lies at Coyaga, ten miles beyond Ogaha Creek. Thenitea is full of refugees from the eastern country he has devastated.

"We do not fear him, though we are outnumbered. He must cross Ogaha Creek to strike us, and we have fortified the west bank and blocked the road against his cavalry."

"That touches upon my mission," I said. "I am authorized to offer the services of a hundred and fifty Thandaran rangers. We are all of one mind in Thandara and fight no internal wars; and we can spare that many men from our war with the Panther Picts."

"That will be good news for the commandant of Fort Kwanyara!"

"What?" quoth I. "Are *you* not the commandant?"

"Nay," said he, "it is my brother, Dirk Strom's son."

"Had I known that, I would have given my message to him," I said. "Brant Drago's son thought you commanded Kwanyara. However, it does not matter."

"Another jack of ale," quoth Hakon, "and we'll start for the fort so that Dirk shall hear your news first-hand. A plague on commanding a fort! A party of scouts is good enough for me."

And in truth Hakon was not the man to command an outpost or any large body of men, for he was too reckless and hasty, though a brave man and a gay rogue.

"You have but a skeleton force left to watch the border," I said. "What of the Picts?"

"They keep the peace to which they swore," answered he. "For some months there has been peace along the border, except for the usual skirmishing between individuals of both races."

"Valerian Hall seemed deserted."

"Lord Valerian dwells there alone alone except for a few servants. Where his fighting men have gone, none knows. But he has sent them off. If he had not given his pledge, we should have felt it necessary to place him under guard, for he is one of the few Hyborians to whom the Picts give heed. If it had entered his head to stir

134

them up against our borders, we might be hard put to it to defend ourselves against them on one side and Brocas on the other.

"The Hawks, Wildcats, and Turtles listen when Valerian speaks, and he has even visited the towns of the Wolf Picts and come away alive."

If that were true, it were strange indeed, for all men knew the ferocity of the great confederacy of allied clans known as the Wolf Tribe, which dwelt in the west beyond the hunting grounds of the three lesser tribes he had named. Mostly they held aloof from the frontier, but the threat of their hatred was ever a menace along the borders of Schohira.

Hakon looked up as a tall man in trunk-hose, boots, and scarlet cloak entered the taproom.

"There is Lord Valerian now," he said.

I stared, started, and was on my feet instantly.

"That man?" I ejaculated. "I saw that man last night beyond the border, in a camp of the Hawks, watching the Dance of the Changing Snake!"

Valerian heard me and whirled, going pale. His eyes blazed like those of a panther.

Hakon sprang up, too. "What are you saying?" he cried. "Lord Valerian gave his pledge—"

"I care not!" I exclaied fiercely, striding forward to confront the tall noble. "I saw him where I lay hidden among the tamarack. I could not mistake that hawklike face. I tell you he was there, naked and painted like a Pict—"

"You lie, damn you!" cried Valerian, and whipping aside his cloak he caught at the hilt of his sword. But before he could draw it I closed with him and bore him to the floor, where he caught at my throat with both hands, blaspheming like a madman. Then there was a swift stamp of feet, and men were dragging us apart, grasping my lord firmly, who stood white and panting with

135

fury, still clutching my neckcloth, which had been torn away from my throat in the struggle.

"Loose me, you dogs!" he raved. "Take your peasant hands from me! I'll cleave this liar to the chin—"

"Here is no lie," I said more calmly. "I lay in the tamarack last night and watched while old Teyanoga dragged a Raven chief's soul from his body and forced it into that of a tree-serpent. It was my arrow which struck down the shaman. And I saw you there—you, a Hyborian, naked and painted, accepted as one of the clan."

"If this be true—" began Hakon.

"It is true, and there is your proof!" I exclaimed. "Look there! On his bosom!"

His doublet and shirt had been torn open in the scuffle; and there, dim on his naked breast, showed the outline of the white skull which the Picts paint only when they mean war against the Hyborians. He had sought to wash it off his skin, but Pictish paint stains strongly.

"Disarm him," said Hakon, white to the lips.

"Give me my neckcloth," I demanded, but his lordship spat at me, and thrust the cloth inside his shirt.

"When it is returned to you it shall be knotted in a hangman's noose about your rebel neck," he snarled.

Hakon seemed undecided.

"Let us take him to the fort," I said. "Give him in custody of the commander. It was for no good purpose that he took part in the Dance of the Snake. Those Picts were painted for battle. That symbol on his breast means he intended to take part in the war for which they danced."

"But, great Mitra, this is incredible!" exclaimed Hakon. "A Hyborian, loosing those painted devils on his friends and neighbors?"

My lord said naught. He stood there between the men who grasped his arms, livid, his thin lips drawn back in a snarl that bared his teeth, but all hell burned like yellow fire in his eyes, where I seemed to sense lights of madness.

But Hakon was uncertain. He dared not release Valerian, and he feared what the effect might be on the people if they saw the lord being led to a captive to the fort.

"They will demand the reason," he argued, "and when they learn he has been dealing with the Picts in their war-paint, a panic might well ensue. Let us lock him into the gaol until we can bring Dirk here to question him."

"It is dangerous to compromise with a situation like this," I answered bluntly. "But it is for you to decide. You are in command here."

So we took his lordship out the back door, secretly. It being dusk by that time, we reached the gaol without being noticed by the people, who indeed stayed indoors mostly. The gaol was a small affair of logs, somewhat apart from the town, with four cells, and one only occupied, that by a fat rogue who had been imprisoned overnight for drunkenness and fighting in the street. He stared to see our prisoner. Not a word said Lord Valerian as Hakon locked the grilled door upon him and detailed one of the men to stand guard. But a demon fire burned in his dark eyes as if behind the mask of his pale face he were laughing at us with fiendish triumph.

"You place only one man on guard?" I asked Hakon.

"Why more?" said he. "Valerian cannot break out, and there is no one to rescue him."

It seemed to me that Hakon was prone to take too much for granted; but after all, it was none of my affair, so I said no more.

Then Hakon and I went to the fort, and there I talked with Dirk Strom's son, the commander, who was in command of the town in the absence of Jon Marko's son, the governor appointed by Lord Thasperas. Jon Marko's son was now in command of the militia-army, which lay

137

at Thenitea. Dirk looked sober indeed when he heard my tale, and said he would come to the gaol and question Lord Valerian as soon as his duties permitted, though he had little belief that my lord would talk, for he came of a stubborn and haughty breed. He was glad to hear of the men Thandara offered him, and told me that he could find a man to return to Thandara accepting the offer, if I wished to remain in Schohira a while, which I did.

Then I returned to the tavern with Hakon, for it was our purpose to sleep there that night, and set out for Thenitea in the morning. Scouts kept the Schohirans posted on the movements of Brocas, and Hakon, who had been in their camp that day, said Brocas showed no signs of moving against us, which made me believe that he was waiting for Valerian to lead his Picts against the border. But Hakon still doubted, in spite of all I had told him, believing Valerian had but visited the Picts through friendliness as he often did. But I pointed out that no Hyborian, however friendly to the Picts, was ever allowed to witness such a ceremony as the Dance of the Snake; he would have to be a blood-member of the clan.

3.

I awakened suddenly and sat up in bed. My window was open, both shutters and pane, for coolness, for it was an upstairs room, and there was no tree nigh by which a thief might gain access. But some noise had awakened me, and now, as I stared at the window, I saw the starlit sky blotted out by a bulky, misshapen figure. I swung my legs off the bed, demanding to know who it was, and groped for my hatchet; but the thing was on me with frightful speed. And before I could even rise, something was around my neck, choking and strangling me. Thrust almost against my face was a dim, frightful visage, but all I could make out in the darkness was a pair of flaming red eyes and a peaked head. My nostrils were filled with a bestial reek.

I caught one of the thing's wrists, and it was hairy as an ape's and thick with iron muscles. But then I had found the haft of my hatchet, and I lifted it and split that misshapen skull with one blow. It fell clear of me, and I sprang up, gagging and quivering in every limb. I found flint, steel, and tinder and struck a light and lit a candle, and glared wildly at the creature lying on the floor.

In form it was like a man, gnarled and misshapen, covered with thick hair. Its nails were long and black, like the talons of a beast, and its chinless, low-browed head was like that of an ape. The thing was a *chaken*, one of those semi-human beings which dwell deep in the forests.

There came a knocking on my door, and Hakon's voice called to know what the trouble was, so I bade him enter. He rushed in, ax in hand; his eyes widened at the sight of the thing on the floor.

"A chakan!" he whispered. "I have seen them, far to the west, smelling out trails through the forests—the damned bloodhounds! What is that in his fingers?"

A chill of horror crept along my spine as I saw the creature still clutched a neckcloth in his fingers—the cloth which he had tried to knot like a hangman's noose about my neck.

"I have heard that Pictish shamans catch these creatures and tame them and use them to smell out their enemies," he said slowly. "But how could Lord Valerian so use one?"

"I know not," I answered. "But that neckcloth was given to the beast, and according to its nature it smelled my trail out and sought to break my neck. Let us go to the gaol, and quickly."

Hakon roused his six rangers, and we hurried there and found the guard lying before the open door of Valerian's empty cell with his throat cut. Hakon stood like one turned to stone, and then a faint call made us turn, and we saw the white face of the drunkard peering at us from the next cell.

"He's gone," quoth he. "Lord Valerian's gone. Hark'ee: an hour agone while I lay on my bunk, I was awakened by a sound outside, and saw a strange dark woman come out of the shadows and walk up to the guard. He lifted his bow and bade her halt, but she laughed at him, staring into his eyes, and he became as one in a trance. He stood staring stupidly—and, Mitra! she took his own knife from his girdle and cut his throat, and he fell down and died. Then she took the keys from his belt and opened the door, and Valerian came out, and laughed like a devil out of Hell, and kissed the wench, and she laughed with him. And she was not alone, for *something* lurked in the shadows behind her—some vague, monstrous being that never came into the light of the lanthorn hanging over the door.

"I heard her say best to kill the fat drunkard in the next cell, and by Mitra I was so nigh dead of fright I knew not if I were even alive. But Valerian said I was dead drunk, and I could have kissed him for that word. So they went away, and as they went he said he would send her companion on a mission, and then they would go to the cabin on Lynx Creek, and there meet his retainers, who had been hiding in the forest ever since he sent them from Valerian Hall. He said that Teyanoga would come to them there and they would cross the border and go among the Picts and bring them back to cut all our throats."

Hakon looked livid in the lanthorn light.

"Who is this woman?" I asked curiously.

"His half-breed Pictish mistress," he said. "Half Hawk Pict and half Ligurean. They call her the Witch of Skandaga. I have never seen her, never before credited the tales whispered of her and Lord Valerian. But it is the truth."

"I thought I had slain old Teyanoga," I muttered. "The old fiend must bear a charmed life—I saw my shaft quivering in his breast. What now?"

"We must go to the hut on Lynx Creek and slay them all," said Hakon. "If they loose the Picts on the border, there will be the devil to pay. We can spare no more men from the fort or the town. We are enough. I know not how many men there will be on Lynx Creek, and I do not care. We will take them by surprise."

He released the drunkard to carry word to the fort of what had befallen, and we set out at once through the starlight. The land lay silent, lights twinkling dimly in the houses. To the westward loomed the black forest, silent, primordial, a brooding threat to the people who dared it.

We went in single file, bows strung and held in our left hands, hatchets swinging in our right hands. Our moccasins made no sound in the dew-wet grass. We melted into the woods and struck a trail that wound among oaks and alders. Here we strung out with some fifteen feet between each man and the next, Hakon leading; and presently we dipped down into a grassy hollow and saw light streaming faintly from the cracks of shutters that covered a cabin's windows.

Hakon halted us and whispered for the men to wait,

while we crept forward and spied upon them. We stole up and surprised the sentry—a Schohiran renegade, who must have heard our stealthy approach but for the wine which staled his breath. I shall never forget the fierce hiss of satisfaction that breathed between Hakon's clenched teeth as he drove his knife into the villain's heart. We left the body hidden in the tall, rank grass and stole up to the very wall of the cabin and dared to peer in at a crack.

There were Valerian, with his fierce eyes blazing, and a dark, wildly beautiful girl in doeskin loinclout and beaded moccasins, and her blackly burnished hair bound back by a gold band, curiously wrought. And there were half a dozen Schohiran renegades—sullen rogues in the woolen breeches and jerkins of farmers, with cutlasses at their belts; three forest-runners in buckskins, wild-looking men; and half a dozen Gunderman guards, compactly-built men with yellow hair cut square and confined under steel caps, corselets of chain mail, and polished leg-pieces. They were girt with swords and daggers—fair-skinned men with steely eyes and an accent differing greatly from that of the Westermarck. They were sturdy fighters, ruthless and well-disciplined, and very popular as guardsmen among the landowners of the frontier.

Listening there, we heard them all laughing and conversing. Valerian was boastful of his escape; the renegades, sullen and full of oaths and curses for their former friends; the forest-runners, silent and attentive; the Gundermen, careless and jovial, which joviality thinly masked their utterly ruthless natures. And the half-breed girl, whom they called Kwarada, laughed and plagued Valerian, who seemed grimly amused. And Hakon trembled with fury as we listened to the boasting of Valerian:

". . . getting out was as easy as cracking an egg. But, by Mitra, I've sent a visitor to that cursed Thandaran traitor that shall do his proper business for him! And when I shall have roused the Picts and led them across the border to smite the rebels from the west, while Brocas attacks from Coyaga, all his kind shall get their just deserts."

Then we heard a light patter of feet and hugged the wall close. The door opened, and seven Picts entered, horrific figures in paint and feathers. They were led by old Teyanoga, whose breast was bandaged, whereby I knew my shaft had but fleshed itself in those massive muscles. And wondered if the old demon were really a werewolf which could not be killed by mortal weapons as he boasted and many believed.

We lay close there, Hakon and I, and heard Teyanoga say in broken Aquilonian: "You want Hawks, Wildcats, Turtles strike across border. If we strike now, Wolfmen ravage our land while we fight in Schohira. Wolfmen very strong, very many. Hawks, Wildcats, Turtles must clasp hands with Wolfmen."

"Well," said Valerian, "when will you make this treaty with the Wolfmen?"

"Chiefs of all four tribes meet tonight on edge of Ghost Swamp. Make talk-talk with Wizard of Swamp. All do what Wizard say."

"Hm," said Valerian, "'tis not yet midnight. If we step lively, we can reach Ghost Swamp in two hours. We shall go forthwith, to see if I cannot persuade the Wizard to induce the Wolves to join the other tribes."

Hakon whispered into my ear: "Crawl back and fetch the others, quickly! Tell them to surround the hut and to kindle a fire!"

I saw that it was in his mind that we should attack, outnumbered as we were; but so fired was I by the infamous plot to which we had listened that I was as eager as he. I stole back and brought the others. We clustered about the windows in pairs, one man with his bow drawn and another with his axe raised to beat in the shutters. One man was told off to kindle a fire wherewith to burn the hut. As I rejoined Hakon at the front door, I heard the voice of Valerian from within:

"Come on, men! We must be on our way at once."

Then came the sound of men rising to their feet and securing their weapons and gear. Hakon, aflame with eagerness, fidgeted in the dark while the man who was kindling the flame fiddled with flint and steel and tinder and twigs. At last the ranger had a neat little blaze going, and others thrust branches into it for torches.

Then Hakon ran at the door and beat it in with his axe, which was no light hatchet of Pictish style but a real battle-chopper, such as armored knights use to smash open each other's crayfish-shells. At the same instant, others of us burst in the shutters and poured arrows into the room, striking down some. And others applied their torches to the roof, to set the cabin on fire. But the roof was made of overlapping slabs of bark, which was damp from recent rains and so did not kindle in so lively a fashion as we should have liked.

Thrown into confusion, those inside made no attempt to hold the cabin. The candles were upset and went out, but the fire lent a dim glow, by which the rangers continued to shoot into the room.

Valerian and his pack then rushed the door, colliding head-on with Hakon and a knot of rangers, including myself, as we burst in. Some we struck down at the outset; but in an instant they were mingled with us in a grunting, snarling grapple, inside the cabin and out.

I found myself in close embrace with a burly, bareheaded Gunderman in a mail shirt. No doubt he had doffed his helmet against the heat of the cabin and had forgotten to put it on again in his haste. In his right hand he held a short sword; I, in mine, a war-axe. Each grasped the other's right wrist with his left hand. We

144

strained and sweated and grunted, reeling and stamping about as each strove to wrest his weapon-arm loose for a fatal blow. At last I hooked my leg behind his and sent him sprawling, with me on top of him. In the fall he lost his grip on my wrist but somehow got his hand on the half of my hatchet and wrenched it loose when my grip was momentarily loosened.

The Gunderman's first blow with the hatchet glanced from my shoulder, his aim having been disturbed by the foot of one of the battlers, who unwittingly trod on some lower part of his frame. My own free hand happened upon a half-buried stone, about the size of an apple. And I tore it out of the ground and smote my man on the forehead even as he was striking up at me again with my own hatchet. Feeling his muscles slacken, I took the stone in both hands and brought it down with all my strength upon his skull. I heard the bone crunch, and the man gave one jerk and lay still.

I scrambled to my feet to plunge back into the fray —and lo, there was no more fray. Bodies lay here and there—some of theirs and some of ours—but the surviving Gundermen, renegades, and Picts were all fleeing into the woods. I saw the backs of several as they fled and heard the whistle of an arrow that one of the surviving rangers sent after them, but what of the haste of the archer and the uncertainty of the light, I do not think the shaft found its mark.

The rascals still much outnumbered us and, had they tried, could have wiped out Hakon's party; but the surprise and their lack of organization prevented this. Had Hakon been a craftier war-leader, he would have had us bar the door against the foe's escape, while fire and arrows did our work for us, instead of helping their flight by breaking it open. But it was ever his way to come to grips with his foe as quickly as might be, without giving much thought to the long-term strategy of the case.

Those rangers who were still on their feet stood panting until someone shouted: "The cabin! Valerian is there!"

I whirled to see, framed in the doorway no more than a spear's length away, Lord Valerian and his leman. Even as hands leaped to weapons, Kwarada laughed a shrill witch-laugh and hurled something on the ground. It burst with a bright flame that, going out, left our vision so full of colored spots that we could discern naught in the darkness. And it gave out a foul smoke that veiled the door of the cabin and sent us reeling back, coughing and sputtering as if we had been ducked in Lynx Creek. By the time we could see and breathe again, the pair had vanished.

Hakon moved among his men, taking stock. Two had been slain and two wounded, one in the arm and one in the leg. We had brought down seven of the foe—mostly with our arrows through the windows at the outset—and of these several were still alive, but not for long. Some of Valerian's men, too, carried wounds away with them. The ranger with the wounded leg was obliged to stay where he was, with his wound bound up, until friends came to carry him back to the village.

When the arm of the other wounded ranger had been tied up, Hakon told him: "Hasten back to Schondara and warn Dirk that the invasion is coming. Tell him to get the people and their movable goods into the fort and to send a squad hither to fetch Karlus home. We are for Ghost Swamp to do what we can. If we return not to Schondara, let them prepare for the worst."

The ranger nodded and set off at a jog-trot. And Hakon, the two unwounded rangers, and I prepared to follow Valerian and his people. I would have waited for reinforcements; but Hakon, lashed on by the feeling that he had caused Valerian's escape from the gaol, would brook no delay. We made sure each was well armed; I took the sword of the Gunderman I had slain and replaced the bow I had lost in my flight from the Picts by one that had belonged to a fallen ranger.

Luckily, Hakon and one of the rangers knew the way, having scouted as far as the swamp before; and the stars gave us enough light to keep from falling into holes or getting lost. Soon the roof of leaves again closed over our heads, and we crossed Lynx Creek and plunged into the wilderness.

4.

We walked single file, making no noise other than the occasional snap of a twig or rustle of a branch, such as even a Pict will make when moving at night. A trail of sorts led southwest from the hut, but it had become overgrown until it could scarcely be told from a deer trail.

We went soberly, each absorbed in his own thoughts; for it was no holiday jaunt that we were undertaking. Pictland is a fearsome country at best, full of savage men and equally savage beasts, such as wolves, panthers, and the giant serpents of which I have spoken. And there are said to be other beasts, too, that have vanished from other parts of the earth, such as the great saber-toothed cat, and a beast of the elephant kind. I had never seen an elephant, but my brother once visited Tarantia and beheld such a beast in the menagerie of King Numedides, on a day when the king let the common people walk through his gardens. Now and then, the Picts would bring an ivory tusk from one of these beasts to some trader in the Westermarck.

Even less pleasant neighbors are the swamp-demons, or forest-devils as some call them. These cluster in places like Ghost Swamp. In the daytime they vanished—no man knows whither—but at night they appear, thick as bats, and howl like damned souls in Hell. Nor is howling all they do; more than one borderer has had his throat slashed from ear to ear by the sweep of a swamp-demon's claws, when he ventured too near one of their infernal assemblies. It was a measure of the power of the Wizard of the Swamp that he dwelt in the midst of one of their favorite haunts.

After a while, we came to Tullian's Creek, named for a Schohiran settler who lost his head to a Pictish war-party. Tullian's Creek forms the boundary between Schohira and the Pictish lands. At least, so said the last treaty between the savages and the governor of Schohira, though little heed to the treaty any man of either race paid when he thought that something he desired lay beyond the border.

We crossed Tullian's Creek, hopping from rock to rock. Beyond the creek, Hakon halted to confer in whispers with the ranger who knew the way. And after some peering about and pushing branches aside, they found a fork in the trail and took the left-hand path, bearing further to the south and hence toward Ghost Swamp. Hakon cautioned us to move more silently, yet at the same time urged us to greater speed.

"We are fain not to be caught near the Pictish camp by the coming of dawn," he whispered.

Even to the canniest woodsman, speed and silence are opposed qualities; the more a man strives for one, the less he can achieve of the other. Nonetheless, we jogged along that trail at a good pace, dodging branches and avoiding dead sticks as best we could.

And we followed the trail for perhaps two hours. Where the woods thinned, I cast anxious glances to the left, to see if the sky—whereof small patches could be discerned among the leaves—had yet begun to lighten in the east. The sky, however, showed naught but the slowly wheeling fields of stars, and since the moon was new we should not see it more that night. Besides the breathing of the men and the occasional swish of a leaf or crack of a twig, the only sounds were the buzz and click of night insects, and sometimes the rustle of some small wild beast, fleeing through the brush.

Once we all halted and froze at a distant coughing sound. After a time, one of the rangers said: "Panther!" We moved on, as if panthers were of no concern to us. And in truth they were not, for a panther hunts singly and would never attack four grown men. Picts are something else.

Presently Hakon signaled us to halt. And as we stood listening, faint sounds—not those of wild beasts—came to our ears. There was a meager mutter or murmur, barely audible, like the first sounds of an approaching thunderstorm, which a man feels with his bones as much as with his ears. And by straining our eyes, now sharpened to more than their usual keenness by our long immersion in darkness, we could see faint ruddy glows through the tree-trunks.

Now we left the trail and stalked through the woods to the left of it, moving with more stealth than speed. We went bent double, slipping from the cover of a bush to the shadow of a tree and then to a bush again.

Soon we heard the guttural voices of Picts, and Hakon again held up his hand for caution. Then we saw them. Three Picts stood or sat in a group on the trail. They had been posted as sentinels but were not taking their duties much to heart. They were playing a game with chips of wood, tossing them into the air to see which chips fell bark side up. The Picts murmured, laughed, and now and then cast playful boasts and threats at each other, much as other men would do to relieve boredom.

I wormed to where Hakon lay and breathed: "Shall we attack?"

"Nay," he replied. "They'd whoop and bring the whole encampment about our ears. I will listen to see if I can pick up news, and then we will go on."

He remained where he was, one ear cocked toward the Picts. And I listened, too; but my knowledge of the Pictish tongue is a mere smattering. While I could catch an occasional word, there were not enough of these to string together in a meaningful statement. I thought, however, that I caught the name "Valerian," at least what I took to be our renegade lord's name as mangled by a Pictish tongue.

Hakon listened for a while longer, then nodded to himself in a satisfied way and signed us to follow him. And we began to move again toward the glow of the campfires, when an appalling sound made us start back. Coming from our left, it was a hoarse, screaming roar, as if some giant blew a trumpet fouled with spittle.

Then came a great crashing as the source of the sound made off. And I caught a glimpse of it—one of those beasts of the elephant kind whereof I have spoken, as tall as two tall men, one atop the other. Its two long tusks, nearly straight, reached almost to the ground, and I think it bore a coat of short hair, but that was impossible to determine by starlight in so short a glimpse. I am told that they sleep standing up, as horses often do, and no doubt this one had been awakened from its midnight slumber by our sound and scent. I have never heard of one of these beasts straying so far east, near the borders of the Westermarck; and thus Hakon and I are the only men in the Westermarck to claim to have seen a Pictish elephant alive.

The results of the encounter were, however, disastrous to us. In his surprise, Hakon backed into the ranger behind him, who in turn leaped back and bumped the second ranger with such force that the latter went sprawling. I escaped a similar overthrow only by an agile bound. All this leaping and bumping and falling aroused the Picts, and the next thing I knew was the twang of Hakon's bow as he loosed at the first one.

I turned to see the three of them bounding toward us, leaping the bushes like deer, flourishing their weapons, and barking commands and exhortations. Hakon's shaft caught one fairly in the throat, but the other two were instantly upon us. One hurled a short javelin and reached for his hatchet.

I snatched at my quiver but, ere I could notch an arrow, one of the Picts was already too close. So I swung my bow in both hands against the side of the Pict's head. As the savage reeled from the blow, I dropped the bow and went for the Gunderman's sword. And as I closed with the Pict, I blocked a blow of his hatchet with my left arm while sinking the short blade into his vitals with a long, low thrust. Still the fellow fought. When another thrust failed to bring him down, I aimed a cut at his neck that half severed it. And down he went at last.

Panting, I looked about to see that only Hakon and I remained on our feet. Hakon was wrenching his heavy axe out of the skull of the other Pict. Of our rangers, one lay dead with his skull split by the Pict's hatchet, while the other sat with his back against a tree, gripping the shaft of the javelin, the head of which was buried in his belly.

Hakon cursed under his breath. The whole fight had taken scarce a dozen heartbeats, yet three Picts and two rangers were dead or mortally wounded. Our only bit of good fortune was that the Picts had attacked so suddenly that none had given a war-whoop. There had been some guttural exclamations; but the Picts in the camp had doubtless heard the scream of the elephant, known it for what it was, and attributed the subsequent sounds of fight to the crashing retreat of the beast. At any rate, none came to investigate.

Hakon whispered: "There are only two of us left, and each must do what he can though it cost him his life. We must slay Valerian and the Wizard. The Picts said that Valerian had gone to Ghost Swamp to consult with the Wizard of the Swamp and the chiefs of the various tribes. He has left most of his men in camp with the Picts. Let us circle the encampment and strike the trail that leads thence to the swamp. You shall lie in wait beside the trail and, if Valerian comes along it, slay him. I will go into the swamp itself and seek to slay the Wizard, and Valerian, too, if I catch him."

"Friend Hakon," I protested, "you are taking most of the peril upon yourself. As an officer, your life is worth more to our people than mine. I am no more cowardly than most men; let me invade the swamp while you watch by the trail." For to enter the swamp was plainly the more perilous of the two tasks, since a man faced not only the hazard of the Picts but also those of swamp-demons, alligators, and unseen bog-holes.

"Nay," said Hakon. "I have seen this swamp before, and you have not." And when I would have argued, he silenced me by reminding me that he was in command.

Then quoth the wounded ranger in a weak, gasping voice: "Leave me not to fall into the hands of the Picts! When they find these bodies, they will be in a fury for revenge."

"We cannot carry you—" began Hakon, but the ranger said:

"Nay, I meant that not. I am done for, with this spear in my guts. Give me a quick death ere you go!"

So Hakon drew his knife and quickly cut his comrade's throat, while I turned my eyes away. The hard necessities of warfare sometimes go against the grain; but it had been no mercy to leave the man for the savages to torture.

5.

It soon appeared that the Picts had planned to go directly from the council at Ghost Swamp to the attack on Schondara. In the camp, hundreds of warriors lay snoring on rude beds of boughs or under hastily built huts and lean-tos, while dying campfires sent up lazy coils of blue smoke. No women or children were in sight, showing that this was a war party and not a simple tribal assembly.

There were in fact four separate camps, one each for the Hawk, Wildcat, and Turtle tribes and a larger one for the Wolfmen. These camps were scattered irregularly, so that in trying to skirt one we nearly ran into another. But at last we had threaded our way past all of them and picked up the trail to the swamp. As before, we scouted beside the trail instead of on it. The camps proved farther from Ghost Swamp than we had expected. Doubtless the Pictish warriors, fearless though they were, had not cared to sleep any closer to the haunts of the swamp-demons than they had to.

But at last we found a place where a clump of young pines grew beside the trail, and around their bases a great mass of ferns. This, we decided, would be the site for the ambuscade. And so I stretched myself out on my belly, with bow strung and arrow notched on the ground before me, while Hakon went away down the gentle slope toward Ghost Swamp. And as I looked that way, I could see patches of brightness through the trees that told of open water.

The night was now far spent, and I feared lest dawn come upon us ere we had accomplished our tasks. Did this happen, I planned to crawl back away from the trail to some thicker covert, lie up there during the day, and then try again, if the Picts were still encamped here. Thirst would become a problem before the day was out, but I should cope with that when I came to it.

Time crawled. I strained my eyes and ears, hoping for Valerian and his escort to appear out of the gloom along the trail; but all was silent save for the hum of gnats and the grunt of a bull alligator from the direction of the swamp. Even the swamp-demons chose not to howl this night.

A man cannot, however, keep his attention screwed up to the sticking-point forever. I had been up nearly all the night, and had hiked ten or fifteen miles, and had fought two skirmishes, slaying a man in each one. For all my good intentions, nature had its way with me. It seemed to me that I let my heavy eyelids droop but an instant, when a heavy, muscular form landed on top of me and a chorus of hideous yells made the forest ring about me.

I started awake, too mazed with sleep to struggle with much effect. Several Picts had pounced upon me, four of them seizing my four limbs while another crouched on my back. And before I could do more than curse them by Mitra and Ishtar, they had stripped me of weapons and bound my wrists and ankles, giving me a few cuffs and kicks for good measure. I became aware that the sky was much lighter than when I had dozed off, showing that some little time had passed.

There were sounds of chopping, and presently a Pict appeared with a pole he had just cut from a sapling. This was thrust between my arms and between my legs. Two brawny Picts hoisted the ends of the pole to their shoulders and set out briskly toward the swamp, with Gault Hagar's son dangling from the pole between them like a huntsman's quarry. The rest followed, speaking in deep, grunting tones. Some even laughed, a thing Picts rarely do, since they deem open mirth undignified and reserve it for such worthy occasions as the torture of a captive.

At first I was too cast down by the shame of letting myself be surprised, and by my apprehensions of the fate awaiting me, to heed much save my own misery. But then I recollected that I was not dead yet, and that last-minute changes of fortune were not unknown in the world. And so I began to watch about me for any thing or circumstance that might provide a means of escape.

Dawn was breaking when we reached the borders of Ghost Swamp. By craning my neck, I saw the vast, stagnant waters of the swamp, broken by clumps of reeds and other water plants. Wisps of mist rose ghostlike from the still waters, which reflected the cloud-flecked blue of the dawning sky. Here and there, trunks of dead trees stood up like petrified witches.

We jogged out on a tongue of land that extended into the water. From the end of this point, my bearers splashed into the water. They followed a line of stepping stones, placed so that their tops were just below the surface of the water. We crossed another stretch of boggy land, and more stepping stones, and so at last we came to the place of the Wizard of the Swamp.

The Wizard dwelt on an isle, which rose a little higher above the level of the waters than does most of the land

155

in that malevolent marsh. On this small elevation, among the trees that crowned it, rose a circle of huts, like those the Picts build in their villages. As we approached the hillock, one of the Picts of my party ran ahead, so that by the time I arrived, all those present had turned out to greet me. The ground was littered with gourds; no doubt the chiefs had spent the night in guzzling weak Pictish beer as well as in talk.

Those on the isle were the Wizard himself, Valerian and a few of his retainers, Kwarada, Teyanoga, and a score of Picts. Feathers and paint identified the Picts as the chiefs of the Turtles, Hawks, Wildcats, and Wolves, all of them yawning and bleary-eyed from their night-long session. Valerian grinned like a Pictish idol when he saw me.

"The rebel from Thandara!" he cried. "By Mitra, you are a persistent devil; would all those on the side of His lawful Majesty were as firm in their virtue as you are in your villainy! Do but wait, my fine friend; we shall have rare sport with you and your fellow traitor. You shall learn the price of treason to your natural lords."

The Picts who were carrying me slipped the pole from their shoulders and dropped me heavily to the dank ground. As I rolled over, I saw that the stake had been driven into the earth in the center of the circle of huts. And to this, Hakon Strom's son was bound.

Valerian, still looking at me, jerked his head toward Hakon. "He thought he could slink past the Wizard's guard of swamp-demons," he said.

Hakon and I exchanged glances but saw naught to be gained by speech at that moment. The Wizard gave orders in Pictish, and some Picts went back over the causeway of stepping stones. Others began digging a hole in the earth near the stake to which Hakon was tied.

The Wizard was a strange-looking being: aged, bent, and scrawny, with a brown skin almost as dark as that

156

of a Kushite, a mop of white hair, and a long, silky white beard. His features were unlike those of any man I had ever seen. His nose was broad and flat, his forehead and chin sloped back, and his eyes were hidden beneath brows of such pronounced beetle that they seemed to look out of black caverns. He could have been a hybrid of man and chakan. Now I understood the tales repeated in the Westermarck, that the Wizard was neither Pict nor Ligurean, but the last survivor of a race that had dwelt in the land before the Picts overran it. Truly, the Pictish wilderness harbors many strange survivors from bygone times.

Like the Picts, the Wizard was naked but for a deer-skin clout. Instead of painted designs such as the Picts wore, he bore on his chest and back a design of small scars, arranged in lines and circles. He said something to the Picts, who took away the pole whereby they had borne me and jerked me to my feet. And he came close and stared up into my face, his little black eyes sparkling out of the depths of those cavernous eye-sockets. Then he turned away for more talk with the Picts.

Presently the Picts that had left the isle returned with a length of tree trunk, which they trimmed with their axes to a suitable length. The other Picts had meanwhile dug the hole to more than knee-deep. They placed one end of the log in this hole and shoveled the earth back in, holding the log upright. They stamped the earth and pounded it with war-clubs and the handles of their spades to make it firm, and soon had a twin of Hakon's stake.

At a word from the Wizard, they dragged me to the stake. While a couple of brawny savages held my arms, another one cut my bonds with his knife. Then they stripped me to my loincloth, slammed me against the stake, and began binding me with long rawhide thongs. I pretended not to resist, but while they were tying me I stiffened my body and tensed my muscles. The Picts did not seem to notice; mayhap they thought I was showing my white man's pride. Soon they had me bound to the stake, with my arms hanging at my sides, as rigidly as a Stygian mummy.

The chiefs and Valerian and his mistress were clustered about the Wizard, talking. One small Turtle chief, however, approached me with an evil smirk. And he suddenly whipped his hatchet from his belt and hurled it, turning over and over, right at my face.

I gave myself up for gone, but the copper blade thudded into the wood just above my head, so that the handle touched my forehead.

The Turtle chief and some other Picts broke into cries of triumph, vaunting their pleasure at having made me flinch. One of the early stages of Pictish torture is to shoot arrows and throw axes and knives at the prisoner, missing him as closely as possible. If he winces, that scores a point for his tormentors; if he withstands the missiles without flinching, that scores a point for him. It is a foolish sort of game, but I would have resisted the temptation to flinch, rather than give them the satisfaction, had I had any warning of the fellow's intentions.

But this deed started a great argument among the Picts. And two or three of them sided with the chief who had thrown the hatchet, while the others opposed. The thrower and his friends kept repeating the Pictish word for "now," while the others said "anon." One Pict was busily whittling small wooden spikes or splinters, a hand's breadth long, for the evident purpose of sticking them into the captives' hides and igniting them.

At last the Wizard sided with those saying "anon." I turned my head toward Hakon's stake and asked:

"What is their dispute? The question of when we shall be put to the torment?"

158

"Aye," said Hakon. "That little Turtle and his friends wish to practice their art upon us now, while the others prefer to save us until after the sack of Schondara. The Wizard says we are his, to do with as he pleases, and he will tell them when they may have us."

"If he has anything worse than Pictish tortures in mind—" I said, shuddering as I remembered the Dance of the Changing Serpent.

And now the Wizard and all the chiefs disappeared into the huts; Valerian and Kwarada entered one. Two common Picts were left to stand guard over us, while the rest jogged off toward the encampment.

"They will catch some sleep ere setting forth on the attack," quoth Hakon. "From what I heard, they mean to move out around noon and reach Schondara just after dark."

"They would naturally prefer not to attack in daylight, with darts from the ballista whizzing about their ears," I said.

"From the hints I picked up," said Hakon. "They have some other weapon in mind—something the wizard has readied for them." He turned to one of the sentries. "Ho there, you!" he said, still speaking Aquilonian. "How about a little of that beer your chiefs were making so free with last night?"

Both Picts looked blankly at him and turned back to each other. When Hakon repeated his question in Pictish, their eyes lighted with understanding if not with friendly feelings. One of the twain growled a surly "Nay," while the other spat on the ground.

"At least I think they understand us not," said Hakon, speaking our own tongue again. "Have you any thoughts for getting us out of here?"

"Not yet, but I feel one coming," I said. "It will have to wait until the chiefs have departed. And let us not talk too much, lest these scoundrels become suspicious."

We spent a weary morning, bound to those accursed stakes and tormented by thirst, flies, and the cutting pressure of our bonds. Hakon suffered no little from sunburn, though I being naturally swarthy was less affected. Both of us bore many wicked bruises from the fights we had fought.

The chiefs snored in their huts. From the direction of the encampment came the murmur of voices as the warriors awoke.

At last, when the sun stood high overhead, the Wizard emerged from his hut and blew a whistle, made from what appeared to be a length of human arm-bone. Soon Valerian and all the Picts reappeared, yawning and stretching. There was much hustle and bustle. While some ate a quick repast, others thumbed and whetted the edges of their weapons.

At length the Wizard called them all together. From his hut he dragged out a huge leathern sack with its mouth lashed tightly closed and several long leather thongs trailing from it. And something distended the sack to its greatest size, but we could not tell what this something was. It could not be heavy, since the old sorcerer dragged the sack by himself, unaided. The sack was like a bladder blown full of air and then tied to keep the air from escaping, but on a vastly larger scale.

The Wizard gave directions while the Picts manipulated the sack. They tied it by the thongs to the end of a forked pole, twelve or fourteen feet long.

At last the whole lot of them trailed off, a couple of the common Picts bearing the pole with the mysterious bag on their shoulders. The same two who had guarded us during the morning were left behind to guard us some more. Their glowering faces and muttered curses showed how much they liked missing the assault on Schondara and the killing, raping, and looting to which they had looked fondly forward.

When the last of the chiefs' party had vanished into the trees that walled Ghost Swamp, the Wizard shuffled close to Hakon, peered into his face, and tested his bonds. And he did the same with me. We returned stare for stare, and the Wizard walked away and sat down cross-legged between two of the huts. And he worked some form of divination with little flat pieces of bone. He would toss a fistful of them into the air and study the pattern they made as they fell, then sweep them up and try over. He began to croon some chant in his cracked old voice, in a tongue that I did not recognize but that was certainly not Pictish.

Of the two Picts left behind to guard us, one sat with his back to a hut and fell asleep. The other paced up and down impatiently, betimes practicing thrusts with his knife and blows with his stone-headed war-club at the empty air. He leaped and whirled, crouching, feinting, and striking. When he tired of this, he sat down beside his comrade and tried to start a conversation; but the other Pict only grunted.

Then the active Pict poked the other in the ribs and said softly: "Look yonder!"

He indicated the Wizard, who still sat cross-legged before his strips of bone. But now he no longer picked them up and tossed them; he sat immobile, gazing out across the swamp.

The two Picts rose lithely and padded over to the Wizard. And they peered into his face, and one of them whistled and snapped his fingers. No slightest movement made the Wizard. He had gone into a trance, sending his soul across nighted gulfs to seek out arcane knowledge.

The Picts conversed earnestly in low tones, glancing first at the Wizard and then at us. From the occasional word I caught, I judged the drift of their speech to be that, since the Wizard was now insensible, they should

161

abandon their post to race after their fellow tribesmen, arriving at Schondara in time for the massacre.

Presently the taller of the two—the active one—strode purposefully toward Hakon and me, swinging his war-club. Evidently he meant to brain us ere leaving, lest we escape in his absence. Meeting his glittering gaze, I filled my lungs and opened my mouth to shout to the Wizard, who if he bore us no tender feelings at least did not wish us slain just yet. I knew not whether my shout would rouse him from his trance, but it was the only course of resistance open to me.

As I did so, the shorter Pict called out, and the taller one halted. After more argument, both turned their backs on the Wizard's isle and splashed off across the causeway.

"We are rid of them, at least," muttered Hakon, "but how in the seven hells shall we get out of these bonds? Those who tied us up were no tenderfeet."

"Watch and see," I murmured.

I had relaxed all my muscles, so that the loops of rawhide embraced me a shade less firmly. And now I began moving my arms and hands up and down inside their bonds, striving to work the loops down toward my hips.

The sun declined toward the west, the flies buzzed, the Wizard sat still as a statue; and still I worked at the loops, sweat pouring down my face and my mouth a cavity full of desert dust. And at last one loop shifted down to where I could engage it with the nail of my right little finger. This was not much, but with further shrugging motions I managed to get the nails of the first and third fingers over it, and then at last that of the middle finger.

No longer having to go round my right hand, the loop relaxed a trifle, and soon I was able to work it down below my left hand as well.

The afternoon wore on; a flight of hundreds of ducks soared over the swamp; but still I chafed and worried at my bonds. And then I found one forearm free, and then another. With my freed hands I worked the loops that bound my upper arms up over my shoulders . . . And then I was free!

I stood for an instant, rubbing my limbs and wincing at the prickly pains. I looked toward the Wizard, but he moved not.

A faltering stride took me to the side of Hakon. His bindings were even more complete than mine had been. Having been stripped, I had no knife wherewith to cut him loose. As I worked at his thongs, he muttered:

"We shall be all night at this rate, Gault. See if you cannot find a blade of some sort."

I gnawed at his bonds, but progress seemed as slow that way as trying to slide them off him. Then I took his advice and searched the huts, one after another. But the Wizard's guests had taken all their gear with them. In the Wizard's own hut I found simple cooking utensils and a lot of magical paraphernalia; but naught with a real cutting edge. The only weapon was a bow of curious design and a quiver full of arrows. When I examined the arrows, I saw that they would be of no use. They had chisel-shaped heads of stone and were evidently meant for fowling, not for bringing down bigger game like men.

I remembered that the Wizard wore a knife at his girdle. This, it seemed, was the only real weapon left in the Wizard's isle. There was nothing to do but try to take it from him.

As I stole up, the Wizard still sat in his trance. Moving stealthily, I snatched a handful of his white hair, jerked his head around, and dealt him a mighty buffet on the jaw with the fist of my free hand.

The blow knocked the old man over. For an instant his body twitched and thrashed, like that of a beheaded serpent; but then it began to move with purpose. By this time I had clamped my hands upon his throat and

163

squeezed with all my might. But the Wizard struggled up, with more strength than one would have believed his skinny frame could hold. He punched and clawed and kicked, seeming to be made of steel wires and rawhide thongs. His dirty thumbnail groped for my eyes until I sank my teeth into his thumb.

For an instant his deep-set eyes met mine, and suddenly I felt my soul being drawn out of my body. Something within me told me that I was on the wrong side. It told me to release my hold and do whatever the Wizard asked, for he was my rightful master. But I closed my eyes and continued to squeeze.

We were up, then down, then up again, rolling over and over. He fumbled for his knife and got it out, but by that time he was fast weakening and only succeeded in giving me a scratch along the ribs. Then I got my knee on his knife hand and forced it into the dirt. All this while I continued to squeeze his windpipe, lest he utter some frightful spell and damn my soul to hells everlasting.

Little by little the thrashings of the Wizard died away. Even after his body lay limply in the dirt, I continued to press my thumbs into his throat, not wishing him to come to life of a sudden after I released him.

When I could no longer detect any heartbeat or other sign of life, I took the Wizard's knife and cut his throat. Then I hastened to free Hakon. He stood for a moment, rubbing his limbs and cursing.

"What was in that bag?" I asked.

"The Wizard put all the demons of the swamp in it," he said. "When the Picts rush the fort, they will thrust that long pole over the stockade. Then one of them will pull one of those trailing thongs, and the bag will open. The swamp-demons will swarm out and slay every human being they see who is on his feet."

164

"Why will they not also slay Valerian and his savages?"

"The Wizard has also put a spell on the demons, so they will attack only those who are upright. Therefore, as soon as the bag is opened, the Picts will throw themselves flat on the ground, until the massacre is over and the demons have departed for their swampy home."

"We must still try to stop them," I said. "But Mitra curse it, there is not a weapon in the place, save the old man's knife here. I do not count a bow with a set of birding arrows in the Wizard's hut."

"Those were better than naught," said he grimly. "Even a fowling shaft can inflict a nasty wound, if driven hard from close range. You must carry the bow, though. The Picts twisted my arm when they captured me so that I could not draw a steady shaft just now."

And so Hakon and I, naked but for our loincloths and moccasins, set out across the causeway in pursuit of Valerian's savage army. I bore the Wizard's bow, and Hakon his knife.

6.

When we crossed Tullian's Creek we went cautiously, lest the Picts should have left a rear guard to watch. Across Lynx Creek we went more carefully yet, but no Picts did we come upon. There was no sign of Karlus at the hut, so he had evidently been rescued. We saw indications of the Picts' passage—here a feather fallen from some brave's topknot; there a moccasin whose thong had broken—but of the savages themselves there was no sign.

We did not come upon them until after sunset, when we reached the fields surrounding Schondara. The Picts were strung out in a great crescent around these clearings. Lying behind clumps of ferns, scarcely daring to breathe, we saw Valerian, his mistress, and other chiefs, together with the bag and its pole, in the center of the array. All were lying or squatting just inside the cover of the trees that fringed the fields.

In the distance, Schondara showed no lights; it seemed that the village had received its warning and was aware of the lurking foes. The fort showed lights, and from it came a buzz of sound: the speech of crowded people and the complaints of their animals. At least, in the fort, the villagers could put up a fight; but the Picts still outnumbered them many times over and should be able to carry the fort by force of numbers even if the Wizard's spells did not work.

Behind us, faintly visible through the trees, a silvery crescent moon sank toward the horizon, above which the departing sun had left bands of orange and yellow and apple-green. Overhead the stars were coming out.

Hakon whispered: "If they will hold the attack until it is a little darker, do you think you can get within easy bowshot of that bag?"

"Why?" I asked. "What good will that do?"

"Try it and see."

Then I understood Hakon's plan and was astonished by the daring of it. And presently we wriggled forward like serpents until we were behind a huge old oak. I rose slowly, holding my breath lest I draw the attention of the nearest Picts, who were a mere twenty paces in front of me, lying behind cover even as we had been doing.

Slowly I drew a fowler's arrow and notched it. As the darkness deepened by imperceptible degrees, a drum began to boom nearby. And from the fort came the clang of the alarm gong. I thought I could even hear the clicking sound of the ballistas being cocked.

With a rustling sound, the Picts rose to their feet and gathered in clumps behind their war-chiefs. A murmur of guttural talk ran up and down the crescent, despite the barking demands of the chiefs for silence.

Then the drum changed its beat to a quick one-two. Two Picts raised the pole with the bag, so that it towered, swaying, over their heads.

"Now!" breathed Hakon.

I sighted on the bag and breathed a prayer to Mitra. I had never shot this bow; the light was poor; the bag wobbled from side to side.

The drum beat changed again. Whistles and rattles sounded; sharp commands ran down the line. With a frightful ululation of whoops, hundreds of Picts streamed out of the forest toward the village and the fort, yelling like fiends.

I shot. As soon as I released my shaft, I knew I had shot awry and snatched at the quiver for a second. But the bag, swaying back and forth on its pole, chose to wobble into the path of my arrow. The shaft struck home with a sound like a bursting drumhead.

The Picts holding the pole started forward with the rest, then paused, gazing fearfully upward. A rending sound came from the bag, whence swirled a great smoky mass.

"Down flat!" yelled Hakon in my ear, pulling my arm as he threw himself down. I needed no second reminder, but joined him prone on the forest floor.

The bag sagged and drooped, losing all its plumpness. The cloud that had issued from it spread out over the far-flung Pictish force, which was now racing across fields, trampling crops, toward Schondara. And as the cloud spread, it took on a lumpy appearance, as if solidifying into solid masses. The dark masses condensed into living creatures—tall, thin beings with birdlike legs and lower parts and half-human heads and upper portions. Each had long, skinny arms ending in hands armed with huge, curved claws. As tall as a man, each demon was accompanied by a weird, flickering glow, as if the being were bathed in the cold flames of marsh fire.

I have no idea how many of the things there were. I hid my face, lest my eye meet that of a demon and he draw nigh. There may have been a hundred or five hundred.

Shrieking and howling, the demons raced hither and yon, at every stride striking down a Pict with a sweep of those talons. Shrieking even louder than the swamp-demons, the Picts ran for their lives in all directions; but the demons were faster. Near us one Pict, his head shorn clean off by a sweep of demoniac claws, took two steps without it ere he fell into the brush.

A few Picts remembered to throw themselves flat. But the great majority, taken by surprise and not having received the expected command to drop to earth, panicked and fled. That was fatal; after them bounded the furious demons on their long birds' legs, swifter than any man could run.

One by one the flickering nimbi that veiled the swamp-demons faded away, as the devils vanished into the forest. At last there was no living creature in sight.

Hakon and I arose, stretched our stiff muscles, and headed for Schondara. A Pict popped up in front of us, like a startled rabbit. Instead of coming for us with a whoop and a flourish of his war-axe, he turned his head away, pretending not to see us, and jogged off into the forest. I blame him not. The thing we had just seen was enough to blast the courage of even so fierce and warlike a folk as the Picts.

We found Valerian's head and left arm, and then the rest of him, lying beside the pole with the leathern bag. The head we took with us for proof of our tale. Kwarada we did not see.

A ranger met us at the edge of Schondara; Dirk Strom's son, puzzled by the scattering of the Pictish host, had sent the man out to scout. When he heard our tale, he ran back to the fort, shouting the good news. Presently we were being carried on the shoulders of a yelling, cheering throng into the fort and around the crowded courtyard.

But the picture I best remember is the face of Otho Gorm's son, standing with his back to the outer stockade in the torchlight. He had come to Schondara after all, to pursue his quarrel with me. And now he stood with utter dumfoundment writ on his foolish face, watching Hakon and me being hailed as the saviors of the province! I would have twitted him about it, but he slipped out and went back to Fort Kwanyara that night, rather than have to eat his hasty words.

And then came the news that the wretched Numedides was dead, and Conan was king. Since then the border has been more peaceful than ever within living memory; for all know, on both sides of the boundary, that King Conan means what he says and will stand for no trifling with treaties, either by the savages or by us. Thandara now has thriving towns and villages.

But I must admit that life was more exciting in the old days, when there was no law save as each borderer could make his own.

The Phoenix on the Sword

Storming the capital city and slaying King Numedides on the steps of his throne—which he promptly
takes for his own—Conan, now in his early or mid-
forties, finds himself the king of the greatest of the
Hyborian nations.

A king's life, however, proves no bed of houris.
Within the year, the minstrel Rinaldo is chanting
defiant ballads in praise of the "martyred" Numedides. Ascalante, Count of Thune, is gathering a
group of plotters to topple the barbarian from his
throne. Conan finds that people have short memo-
ries, and that he, too, suffers from the uneasiness of
head that goes with a crown.

1.

Over shadowy spires and gleaming towers lay the ghostly darkness and silence that runs before dawn. Into a dim alley, one of a veritable labyrinth of mysterious winding ways, four masked figures came hurriedly from a door which a dusky hand furtively opened. They spoke not but went swiftly into the gloom, cloaks wrapped closely about them; as silently as the ghosts of murdered men they disappeared in the darkness. Behind them a sardonic countenance was framed in the partly opened door; a pair of evil eyes glittered malevolently in the gloom.

"Go into the night, creatures of the night," a voice mocked. "O fools, your doom hounds your heels like a blind dog, and you know it not."

The speaker closed the door and bolted it, then turned and went up the corridor, candle in hand. He was a somber giant, whose dusky skin revealed his Stygian blood. He came into an inner chamber, where a tall, lean man in worn velvet lounged like a great, lazy cat on a silken couch, sipping wine from a huge golden goblet.

"Well, Ascalante," said the Stygian, setting down the candle, "your dupes have slunk into the streets like rats from their burrows. You work with strange tools."

"Tools?" replied Ascalante. "Why, they consider *me* that. For months now, ever since the Rebel Four summoned me from the southern desert, I have been living

172

in the very heart of my enemies, hiding by day in this obscure house, skulking through dark alleys and darker corridors at night. And I have accomplished what those rebellious nobles could not. Working through them, and through other agents, many of whom have never seen my face, I have honeycombed the empire with sedition and unrest. In short I, working in the shadows, have paved the downfall of the king who sits throned in the sun. By Mitra, I was a statesman before I was an outlaw."

"And these dupes who deem themselves your masters?"

"They will continue to think that I serve them, until our present task is completed. Who are they to match wits with Ascalante? Volmana, the dwarfish count of Karaban; Gromel, the giant commander of the Black Legion; Dion, the fat baron of Attalus; Rinaldo, the hare-brained minstrel. I am the force which has welded together the steel in each, and by the clay in each, I will crush them when the time comes. But that lies in the future; tonight the king dies."

"Days ago I saw the impeiial squadrons ride from the city," said the Stygian.

"They rode to the frontier which the heathen Picts assail—thanks to the strong liquor which I've smuggled over the borders to madden them. Dion's great wealth made *that* possible. And Volmana made it possible to dispose of the rest of the imperial troops which remained in the city. Through his princely kin in Nemedia, it was easy to persuade King Numa to request the presence of Count Trocero of Poitain, seneschal of Aquilonia; and, of course, to do him honor, he'll be accompanied by an imperial escort, as well as his own troops, and Prospero, King Conan's right-hand man. That leaves only the king's personal bodyguard in the city—besides the Black Legion. Through Gromel, I've corrupted a spend-

173

thirfty officer of that guard and bribed him to lead his men away from the king's door at midnight.

"Then, with sixteen desperate rogues of mine, we enter the palace by a secret tunnel. After the deed is done, even if the people do not rise to welcome us, Gromel's Black Legion will be sufficient to hold the city and the crown."

"And Dion thinks that crown will be given to him?"

"Yes. The fat fool claims it by reason of a trace of royal blood. Conan makes a bad mistake in letting men live who still boast descent from the old dynasty, from which he tore the crown of Aquilonia.

"Volmana wishes to be reinstated in royal favor as he was under the old regime, so that he may lift his poverty-ridden estates to their former grandeur. Gromel hates Pallantides, commander of the Black Dragons, and desires the command of the whole army, with all the stubbornness of the Bossonian. Alone of us all, Rinaldo has no personal ambition. He sees in Conan a red-handed, rough-footed barbarian who came out of the north to plunder a civilized land. He idealizes the king whom Conan killed to get the crown, remembering only that he occasionally patronized the arts, and forgetting the evils of his reign, and he is making the people forget. Already they openly sing *The Lament for the King* in which Rinaldo lauds the sainted villain and denounces Conan as 'that black-hearted savage from the abyss.' Conan laughs, but the people snarl."

"Why does he hate Conan?"

"Poets always hate those in power. To them perfection is always just behind the last corner, or beyond the next. They escape the present in dreams of the past and future. Rinaldo is a flaming torch of idealism, rising, as he thinks, to overthrow a tyrant and liberate the people. As for me—well, a few months ago I had lost all ambi-

174

tion but to raid the caravans for the rest of my life; now old dreams stir. Conan will die; Dion will mount the throne. Then he, too, will die. One by one, all who oppose me will die—by fire, or steel, or those deadly wines you know so well how to brew. Ascalante, king of Aquilonia! How like you the sound of it?"

The Stygian shrugged his broad shoulders.

"There was a time," he said with unconcealed bitterness, "when I, too, had my ambitions, beside which yours seem tawdry and childish. To what a state I have fallen! My old-time peers and rivals would stare indeed could they see Thoth-Amon of the Ring serving as the slave of an outlander, and an outlaw at that; and aiding in the petty ambitions of barons and kings!"

"You laid your trust in magic and mummery," answered Ascalante carelessly. "I trust my wits and my sword."

"Wits and swords are as straws against the wisdom of the Darkness," growled the Stygian, his dark eyes flickering with menacing lights and shadows. "Had I not lost the Ring, our positions might be reversed."

"Nevertheless," answered the outlaw impatiently, "you wear the stripes of my whip on your back, and are likely to continue to wear them."

"Be not so sure!" the fiendish hatred of the Stygian glittered for an instant redly in his eyes. "Some day, somehow, I will find the Ring again, and when I do, by the serpent-fangs of Set, you shall pay—"

The hot-tempered Aquilonian started up and struck him heavily across the mouth. Thoth reeled back, blood starting from his lips.

"You grow over-bold, dog," growled the outlaw. "Have a care; I am still your master who knows your dark secret. Go upon the housetops and shout that Ascalante is in the city plotting against the king—if you dare."

"I dare not," muttered the Stygian, wiping the blood from his lips.

"No, you do not dare," Ascalante grinned bleakly. "For, if I die by your stealth or treachery, a hermit priest in the southern desert will know of it and will break the seal of a manuscript I left in his hands. And having read, a word will be whispered in Stygia, and a wind will creep up from the south by midnight. And where will you hide your head, Thoth-Amon?"

The slave shuddered and his dusky face went ashen.

"Enough!" Ascalante changed his tone peremptorily. "I have work for you. I do not trust Dion. I bade him ride to his country estate and remain there until the work tonight is done. The fat fool could never conceal his nervousness before the king today. Ride after him and, if you do not overtake him on the road, proceed to his estate and remain with him until we send for him. Don't let him out of your sight. He is mazed with fear and might bolt—might even rush to Conan in a panic, and reveal the whole plot, hoping thus to save his own hide. Go!"

The slave bowed, hiding the hate in his eyes, and did as he was bidden. Ascalante turned again to his wine. Over the jeweled spires was rising a dawn crimson as blood.

2.

When I was a fighting-man, the kettle-drums
    they beat,
The people scattered gold-dust before my horse's
    feet;
But now I am a great king, the people hound
    my track
With poison in my wine-cup, and daggers at my
    back.
                    —*The Road of Kings*

The room was large and ornate, with rich tapestries
on the polished-panelled walls, deep rugs on the ivory
floor, and with the lofty ceiling adorned with intricate
carvings and silver scrollwork. Behind an ivory, gold-in-
laid writing-table sat a man whose broad shoulders and
sun-browned skin seemed out of place among those
luxuriant surroundings. He seemed more a part of the
sun and winds and high places of the outlands. His
slightest movement spoke of steel-spring muscles knit
to a keen brain with the coordination of a born fighting
man. There was nothing deliberate or measured about
his actions. Either he was perfectly at rest—still as a
bronze statue—or else he was in motion, not with the
jerky quickness of over-tense nerves, but with a catlike
speed that blurred the sight which tried to follow him.

His garments were of rich fabric, but simply made. He

wore no ring or ornaments, and his square-cut black mane was confined merely by a cloth-of-silver band about his head.

Now he laid down the golden stylus with which he had been laboriously scrawling on waxed tablets, rested his chin on his fist, and fixed his smoldering blue eyes enviously on the man who stood before him. This person was occupied in his own affairs at the moment, for he was taking up the laces of his gold-chased armor, and abstractedly whistling—a rather unconventional performance, considering that he was in the presence of a king.

"Prospero," said the man at the table, "these matters of state-craft weary me as all the fighting I have done never did."

"All part of the game, Conan," answered the dark-eyed Poitainian. "You are king—you must play the part."

"I wish I might ride with you to Nemedia," said Conan enviously. "It seems ages since I had a horse between my knees—but Publius says that affairs in the city require my presence. Curse him!

"When I overthrew the old dynasty," he continued, speaking with the easy familiarity which existed only between the Poitainian and himself, "it was easy enough, though it seemed bitter hard at the time. Looking back now over the wild path I followed, all those days of toil, intrigue, slaughter, and tribulation seem like a dream.

"I did not dream far enough, Prospero. When King Numedides lay dead at my feet and I tore the crown from his gory head and set it on my own, I had reached the ultimate border of my dreams. I had prepared myself to take the crown, not to hold it. In the old free days all I wanted was a sharp sword and a straight path to my enemies. Now no paths are straight and my sword is useless.

"When I overthrew Numedides, *then* I was the Liberator—now they spit at my shadow. They have put a statue

178

of that swine in the temple of Mitra, and people go and wail before it, hailing it as the holy effigy of a saintly monarch who was done to death by a red-handed barbarian. When I led her armies to victory as a mercenary, Aquilonia overlooked the fact that I was a foreigner, but now she cannot forgive me.

"Now in Mitra's temple there come to burn incense to Numedides' memory, men whom his hangmen maimed and blinded, men whose sons died in his dungeons, whose wives and daughters were dragged into his seraglio. The fickle fools!"

"Rinaldo is largely responsible," answered Prospero, drawing up his sword-belt another notch. "He sings songs that make men mad. Hang him in his jester's garb to the highest tower in the city. Let him make rimes for the vultures."

Conan shook his lion head. "No, Prospero, he's beyond my reach. A great poet is greater than any king. His songs are mightier than my scepter; for he has near ripped the heart from my breast when he chose to sing for me. I shall die and be forgotten, but Rinaldo's songs will live for ever.

"No, Prospero," the king continued, a somber look of doubt shadowing his eyes, "there is something hidden, some undercurrent of which we are not aware. I sense it as in my youth I sensed the tiger hidden in the tall grass. There is a nameless unrest throughout the kingdom. I am like a hunter who crouches by his small fire amid the forest, and hears stealthy feet padding in the darkness, and almost sees the glimmer of burning eyes. If I could but come to grips with something tangible, that I could cleave with my sword! I tell you, it's not by chance that the Picts have of late so fiercely assailed the frontiers, so that the Bossonians have called for aid to beat them back. I should have ridden with the troops."

"Publius feared a plot to trap and slay you beyond

the frontier," replied Prospero, smoothing his silken surcoat over his shining mail, and admiring his tall lithe figure in a silver mirror. "That's why he urged you to remain in the city. These doubts are born of your barbarian instincts. Let the people snarl! The mercenaries are ours, and the Black Dragons, and every rogue in Poitain swears by you. Your only danger is assassination, and that's impossible, with men of the imperial troops guarding you day and night. What are you working at there?"

"A map," Conan answered with pride. "The maps of the court show well the countries of south, east, and west, but in the north they are vague and faulty. I am adding the northern lands myself. Here is Cimmeria, where I was born. And—"

"Asgard and Vanaheim," Prospero scanned the map. "By Mitra, I had almost believed those countries to have been fabulous."

Conan grinned savagely, involuntarily touching the scars on his dark face. "You had known otherwise, had you spent your youth on the northern frontiers of Cimmeria! Asgard lies to the north, and Vanaheim to the northwest of Cimmerdia, and there is continual war along the borders."

"What manner of men are these northern folk?" asked Prospero.

"Tall and fair and blue-eyed. Their god is Ymir, the frost giant, and each tribe has its own king. They are wayward and fierce. They fight all day and drink ale and roar their wild songs all night."

"Then I think you are like them," laughed Prospero. "You laugh greatly, drink deep, and bellow good songs; though I never saw another Cimmerian who drank aught but water, or who ever laughed, or ever sang save to chant dismal dirges."

"Perhaps it's the land they live in," answered the king. "A gloomier land never was—all of hills, darkly wooded, under skies nearly always gray, with winds moaning drearily down the valleys."

"Little wonder men grow moody there," quoth Prospero with a shrug of his shoulders, thinking of the smiling, sun-washed plains and blue, lazy rivers of Poitain, Aquilonia's southernmost province.

"They have no hope here or hereafter," answered Conan. "Their gods are Crom and his dark race, who rule over a sunless place of everlasting mist, which is the world of the dead. Mitra! The ways of the Æsir were more to my liking."

"Well," grinned Prospero, "the dark hills of Cimmeria are far behind you. And now I go. I'll quaff a goblet of white Nemedian wine for you at Numa's court."

"Good," grunted the king, "but kiss Numa's dancing-girls for yourself only, lest you involve the states!"

His gusty laughter followed Prospero out of the chamber.

3.

Under the caverned pyramids great Set coils
    asleep;
Among the shadows of the tombs his dusky people
    creep.
I speak the Word from the hidden gulfs that
    never knew the sun—
Send me a servant for my hate, O scaled and
    shining One!

The sun was setting, etching the green and hazy blue
of the forest in brief gold. The waning beams glinted
on the thick golden chain which Dion of Attalus twisted
continually in his pudgy hand as he sat in the flaming
riot of blossoms and flower-trees which was his garden.
He shifted his fat body on his marble seat and glanced
furtively about, as if in quest of a lurking enemy. He sat
within a circular grove of slender trees, whose interlap-
ping branches cast a thick shade over him. Near at hand,
a fountain tinkled silverly, and other unseen fountains
in various parts of the great garden whispered an everlasting symphony.

Dion was alone except for the great dusky figure which
lounged on a marble bench close at hand, watching the
baron with deep somber eyes. Dion gave little thought to
Thoth-Amon. He vaguely knew that he was a slave in
whom Ascalante reposed much trust, but like so many

rich men, Dion paid scant heed to men below his own station in life.

"You need not be so nervous," said Thoth. "The plot cannot fail."

"Ascalante can make mistakes as well as another," snapped Dion, sweating at the mere thought of failure.

"Not he," grinned the Stygian savagely, "else I had not been his slave, but his master."

"What talk is this?" peevishly returned Dion, with only half a mind on the conversation.

Thoth-Amon's eyes narrowed. For all his iron self-control, he was near bursting with long pent-up shame, hate, and rage, ready to take any sort of a desperate chance. What he did not reckon on was the fact that Dion saw him, not as a human being with a brain and a wit, but simply a slave and, as such, a creature beneath notice.

"Listen to me," said Thoth. "You will be king. But you little know the mind of Ascalante. You cannot trust him, once Conan is slain. I can help you. If you will protect me when you come to power, I will aid you.

"Listen, my lord. I was a great sorcerer in the south. Men spoke of Thoth-Amon as they spoke of Rammon. King Ctesphon of Stygia gave me great honor, casting down the magicians from the high places to exalt me above them. They hated me, but they feared me, for I controlled beings from *outside* which came at my call and did my bidding. By Set, mine enemy knew not the hour when he might awake at midnight to feel the taloned fingers of a nameless horror at his throat! I did dark and terrible magic with the Serpent Ring of Set, which I found in a nighted tomb a league beneath the earth, forgotten before the first man crawled out of the slimy sea.

"But a thief stole the Ring and my power was broken. The magicians rose up to slay me, and I fled. Disguised

183

as a camel-driver, I was travelling in a caravan in the land of Koth, when Ascalante's reavers fell upon us. All in the caravan were slain except myself; I saved my life by revealing my identity to Ascalante and swearing to serve him. Bitter has been that bondage!

"To hold me fast, he wrote of me in a manuscript, and sealed it and gave it into the hands of a hermit who dwells on the southern borders of Koth. I dare not strike a dagger into him while he sleeps, or betray him to his enemies, for then the hermit would open the manuscript and read—thus Ascalante instructed him. And he would speak a word in Stygia—"

Again Thoth shuddered, and an ashen hue tinged his dusky skin.

"Men knew me not in Aquilonia," he said. "But should my enemies in Stygia learn my whereabouts, not the width of half a world between us would suffice to save me from such a doom as would blast the soul of a bronze statue. Only a king with castles and hosts of swordsmen. could protect me. So I have told you my secret, and urge that you make a pact with me. I can aid you with my wisdom, and you can protect me. And some day I shall find the Ring—"

"Ring? Ring?" Thoth had underestimated the man's utter egoism. Dion had not even been listening to the slave's words, so completely engrossed was he in his own thoughts, but the final word stirred a ripple in his self-centeredness.

"Ring?" he repeated. "That makes me remember—my ring of good fortune. I had it from a Shemitish thief, who swore he stole it from a wizard far to the south, and that it would bring me luck. I paid him enough, Mitra knows. By the gods, I need all the luck I can have, what with Volmana and Ascalante dragging me into their bloody plots—I'll see to the ring."

Thoth sprang up, blood mounting darkly to his face, while his eyes flamed with the stunned fury of a man who suddenly realizes the full depths of a fool's swinish stupidity. Dion never heeded him. Lifting a secret lid in the marble seat, he fumbled for a moment among a heap of gewgaws of various kinds—barbaric charms, bits of bones, pieces of tawdry jewelry—luck-pieces and conjures which the man's superstitious nature had prompted him to collect.

"Ah, here it is!" He triumphantly lifted a ring of curious make. It was of a metal like copper and was made in the form of a scaled serpent, coiled in three loops, with its tail in its mouth. Its eyes were yellow gems which glittered balefully. Thoth-Amon cried out as if he had been struck, and Dion wheeled and gaped, his face suddenly bloodless. The slave's eyes were blazing, his mouth wide, his huge dusky hands outstretched like talons.

"The Ring! By Set! The Ring!" he shrieked. "My Ring—stolen from me—"

Steel glittered in the Stygian's hand, and with a heave of his great dusky shoulders he drove the dagger into the baron's fat body. Dion's high thin squeal broke in a strangled gurgle and his whole flabby frame collapsed like melted butter. A fool to the end, he died in mad terror, not knowing why. Flinging aside the crumpled corpse, already forgetful of it, Thoth grasped the ring in both hands, his dark eyes blazing with a fearful avidness.

"My Ring!" he whispered in terrible exultation. "My power!"

How long he crouched over the baleful thing, motionless as a statue, drinking the evil aura of it into his dark soul, not even the Stygian knew. When he shook himself from his revery and drew back his mind from the nighted abysses where it had been questing, the moon was rising,

185

casting long shadows across the smooth marble back of the garden-seat, at the foot of which sprawled the darker shadow which had been the lord of Attálus.

"No more, Ascalante, no more!" whispered the Stygian, and his eyes burned red as a vampire's in the gloom. Stooping, he cupped a handful of congealing blood from the sluggish pool in which his victim sprawled, and rubbed it in the copper serpent's eyes until the yellow sparks were covered by a crimson mask.

"Blind your eyes, mystic serpent," he chanted in a blood-freezing whisper. "Blind your eyes to the moonlight and open them on darker gulfs! What do you see, O serpent of Set? Whom do you call from the gulfs of the Night? Whose shadow falls on the waning Light? Call him to me, O serpent of Set!"

Stroking the scales with a peculiar circular motion of his fingers, a motion which always carried the fingers back to their starting place, his voice sank still lower as he whispered dark names and grisly incantations forgotten the world over save in the grim hinterlands of dark Stygia, where monstrous shapes move in the dusk of the tombs.

There was a movement in the air about him, such a swirl as is made in water when some creature rises to the surface. A nameless, freezing wind blew on him briefly, as if from an opened Door. Thoth felt a presence at his back, but he did not look about. He kept his eyes fixed on the moonlit space of marble, on which a tenuous shadow hovered. As he continued his whispered incantations, this shadow grew in size and clarity, until it stood out distinct and horrific. Its outline was not unlike that of a gigantic baboon, but no such baboon ever walked the earth, not even in Stygia. Still Thoth did not look, but drawing from his girdle a sandal of his master—always carried in the dim hope that he might be able to put it to such use—he cast it behind him.

"Know it well, slave of the Ring!" he exclaimed. "Find him who wore it and destroy him! Look into his eyes and blast his soul, before you tear out his throat! Kill him! Aye," in a blind burst of passion, "and all with him!"

Etched on the moonlit wall, Thoth saw the horror lower its misshapen head and take the scent like some hideous hound. Then the grisly head was thrown back, and the thing wheeled and was gone like a wind through the trees. The Stygian flung up his arms in maddened exultation, and his teeth and eyes gleamed in the moonlight.

A soldier on guard without the walls yelled in startled horror as a great loping black shadow with flaming eyes cleared the wall and swept by him with a swirling rush of wind. But it was gone so swiftly that the bewildered warrior was left wondering whether it had been a dream or an hallucination.

4.

When the world was young and men were weak,
    and the fiends of the night walked free,
I strove with Set by fire and steel and the juice of
    the upas-tree;
Now that I sleep in the mount's black heart, and
    the ages take their toll,
Forget ye him who fought with the Snake to save
    the human soul?

Alone in the great sleeping chamber with its high golden dome, King Conan slumbered and dreamed. Through swirling gray mists he heard a curious call, faint and far, and though he did not understand it, it seemed not within his power to ignore it. Sword in hand, he went through the gray mist, as a man might walk through clouds, and the voice grew more distinct as he proceeded until he understood the word it spoke—it was his own name that was being called across the gulfs of Space or Time.

Now the mists grew lighter, and he saw that he was in a great, dark corridor that seemed to be cut in solid black stone. It was unlighted, but by some magic he could see plainly. The floor, ceiling, and walls were highly polished and gleamed dully, and they were carved with the figures of ancient heroes and half-forgotten gods. He shuddered to see the vast shadowy outlines of the Nameless Old

Ones, and he knew somehow that mortal feet had no traversed the corridor for centuries.

He came upon a wide stair carved in the solid rock, and the sides of the shaft were adorned with esoteric symbols so ancient and horrific that King Conan's skin crawled. The steps were carven each with the abhorrent figure of the Old Serpent, Set, so that at each step he planted his heel on the head of the Snake, as it was intended from old times. But he was none the less at ease for all that.

But the voice called him on, and at last, in darkness that would have been impenetrable to his material eyes, he came into a strange crypt, and saw a vague, white-bearded figure sitting on a tomb. Conan's hair rose up and he grasped his sword, but the figure spoke in sepulchral tones.

"O man, do you know me?"

"Not I, by Crom!" swore the king.

"Man," said the ancient, "I am Epemitreus."

"But Epemitreus the Sage has been dead for fifteen hundred years!" stammered Conan.

"Harken!" spoke the other commandingly. "As a pebble cast into a dark lake sends ripples to the further shores, happenings in the Unseen World have broken like waves on my slumber. I have marked you well, Conan of Cimmeria, and the stamp of mighty happenings and great deeds is upon you. But dooms are loose in the land, against which your sword cannot aid you."

"You speak in riddles," said Conan uneasily. "Let me see my foe and I'll cleave his skull to the teeth."

"Loose your barbarian fury against your foes of flesh and blood," answered the ancient. "It is not against men I must shield you. There are dark worlds barely guessed by man, wherein formless monsters stalk—fiends which may be drawn from the Outer Voids to take material shape and rend and devour at the bidding of evil ma-

189

gicians. There is a serpent in your house, O king—an adder in your kingdom, come up from Stygia, with the dark wisdom of the shadows in his murky soul. As a sleeping man dreams of the serpent which crawls near him, I have felt the foul presence of Set's neophyte. He is drunk with terrible power, and the blows he strikes at his enemy may well bring down the kingdom. I have called you to me, to give you a weapon against him and his hell-hound pack."

"But why?" bewilderedly asked Conan. "Men say you sleep in the black heart of Golamira, whence you send forth your ghost on unseen wings to aid Aquilonia in times of need, but I—I am an outlander and a barbarian."

"Peace!" the ghostly tones reverberated through the great shadowy cavern. "Your destiny is one with Aquilonia. Gigantic happenings are forming in the web and the womb of Fate, and a blood-mad sorcerer shall not stand in the path of imperial destiny. Ages ago Set coiled about the world like a python about its prey. All my life, which was as the lives of three common men, I fought him. I drove him into the shadows of the mysterious south, but in dark Stygia men still worship him who to us is the arch-demon. As I fought Set, I fight his worshippers and his votaries and his acolytes. Hold out your sword."

Wondering, Conan did so, and on the great blade, close to the heavy silver guard, the ancient traced with a bony finger a strange symbol that glowed like white fire in the shadows. And on the instant crypt, tomb, and ancient vanished, and Conan, bewildered, sprang from his couch in the great golden-domed chamber. And as he stood, bewildered at the strangeness of his dream, he realized that he was gripping his sword in his hand. And his hair prickled at the nape of his neck, for on the broad blade was carven a symbol—the outline of a phoenix. And he remembered that on the tomb in the crypt he had seen what he had thought to be a similar figure, carven of stone. Now he wondered if it had been but a stone figure, and his skin crawled at the strangeness of it all.

Then as he stood, a stealthy sound in the corridor outside brought him to life, and without stopping to investigate, he began to don his armor; again he was the barbarian, suspicious and alert as a gray wolf at bay.

5.

What do I know of cultured ways, the gilt, the
    craft and the lie?
I, who was born in a naked land and bred in the
    open sky.
The subtle tongue, the sophist guile, they fail
    when the broadswords sing;
Rush in and die, dogs—I was a man before I
    was a king.
                      —*The Road of Kings*

Through the silence which shrouded the corridor of the royal palace stole twenty furtive figures. Their stealthy feet, bare or cased in soft leather, made no sound either on thick carpet or bare marble tile. The torches which stood in niches along the halls gleamed red on dagger, sword, and keen-edged ax.

"Easy all!" hissed Ascalante. "Stop that cursed loud breathing, whoever it is! The officer of the night guard has removed most of the sentries from these halls and made the rest drunk, but we must be careful, just the same. Back! Here come the guard!"

They crowded back behind a cluster of carven pillars, and almost immediately ten giants in black armor swung by at a measured pace. Their faces showed doubt as they glanced at the officer who was leading them away from their post of duty. This officer was rather pale; as the guard passed the hiding-places of the conspirators, he was seen to wipe the sweat from his brow with a shaky hand. He was young, and this betrayal of a king did not come easy to him. He mentally cursed the vainglorious extravagance which had put him in debt to the moneylenders and made him a pawn of scheming politicians.

The guardsmen clanked by and disappeared up the corridor.

"Good!" grinned Ascalante. "Conan sleeps unguarded. Haste! If they catch us killing him, we're undone—but few men will espouse the cause of a dead king."

"Aye, haste!" cried Rinaldo, his blue eyes matching the gleam of the sword he swung above his head. "My blade is thirsty! I hear the gathering of the vultures! On!"

They hurried down the corridor with reckless speed and stopped before a gilded door, which bore the royal dragon symbol of Aquilonia.

"Gromel!" snapped Ascalante. "Break me this door open!"

The giant drew a deep breath and launched his mighty frame against the panels, which groaned and bent at the impact. Again he crouched and plunged. With a snapping of bolts and a rending crash of wood, the door splintered and burst inward.

"In!" roared Ascalante, on fire with the spirit of the deed.

"In!" yelled Rinaldo. "Death to the tyrant!"

They stopped short. Conan faced them, not a naked man roused mazed and unarmed out of deep sleep to be butchered like a sheep, but a barbarian wide-awake and at bay, partly armored, and with his long sword in his hand.

For an instant the tableau held—the four rebel noblemen in the broken door, and the horde of wild hairy faces crowding behind them—all held momentarily frozen by the sight of the blazing-eyed giant standing sword in hand in the middle of the candle-lighted chamber. In that instant Ascalante beheld, on a small table near the royal couch, the silver scepter and the slender gold circlet which was the crown of Aquilonia, and the sight maddened him with desire.

"In, rogues!" yelled the outlaw. "He is one to twenty and he has no helmet!"

True; there had been lack of time to don the heavy plumed casque, or to lace in place the side-plates of the cuirass, nor was there now time to snatch the great shield from the wall. Still, Conan was better protected than any of his foes except Volmana and Gromel, who were in full armor.

The king glared, puzzled as to their identity. Ascalante he did not know; he could not see through the closed vizors of the armored conspirators, and Rinaldo had pulled his slouch cap down above his eyes. But there was no time for surmise. With a yell that rang to the roof, the killers flooded into the room, Gromel first. He came like a charging bull, head down, sword low for the disembowelling thrust. Conan sprang to meet him, and all his tigerish strength went into the arm that swung the sword. In a whistling arc the great blade flashed through the air and crashed on the Bossonian's helmet. Blade and casque shivered together, and Gromel rolled lifeless on the floor. Conan bounded back, still gripping the broken hilt.

"Gromel!" he spat, his eyes blazing in amazement, as the shattered helmet disclosed the shattered head; then the rest of the pack were upon him. A dagger point raked along his ribs between breastplate and backplate, a sword-edge flashed before his eyes. He flung aside the dagger-wielder with his left arm, and smashed his broken hilt like a cestus into the swordsman's temple. The man's brains spattered in his face.

"Watch the door, five of you!" screamed Ascalante, dancing about the edge of the singing steel whirlpool, for he feared that Conan might smash through their midst and escape. The rogues drew back momentarily, as their leader seized several and thrust them toward the single door, and in that brief respite Conan leaped to the wall and tore therefrom an ancient battle-ax which, untouched by time, had hung there for half a century.

With his back to the wall he faced the closing ring for a flashing instant, then leaped into the thick of them. He was no defensive fighter; even in the teeth of overwhelming odds he always carried the war to the enemy. Any other man would have already died there, and Conan himself did not hope to survive, but he did ferociously wish to inflict as much damage as he could before he fell. His barbaric soul was ablaze, and the chants of old heroes were singing in his ears.

As he sprang from the wall, his ax dropped an outlaw with a severed shoulder, and the terrible back-hand return crushed the skull of another. Swords whined venomously about him, but death passed him by breathless margins. The Cimmerian moved in a blur of blinding speed. He was like a tiger among baboons as he leaped, side-stepped, and spun, offering an ever-moving target, while his ax wove a shining wheel of death about him.

For a brief space, the assassins crowded him fiercely, raining blows blindly and hampered by their own numbers; then they gave back suddenly—two corpses on the floor gave mute evidence of the king's fury, though Conan himself was bleeding from wounds on arm, neck and legs.

"Knaves!" screamed Rinaldo, dashing off his feathered cap, his wild eyes glaring. "Do ye shrink from the combat? Shall the despot live? Out on it!"

He rushed in, hacking madly, but Conan, recognizing him, shattered his sword with a short terrific chop and with a powerful push of his open hand sent him reeling to the floor. The king took Ascalante's point in his left arm, and the outlaw barely saved his life by ducking and springing backward from the swinging ax. Again the wolves whirled in and Conan's ax sang and crushed. A hairy rascal stooped beneath its stroke and dived at the king's legs, but after wrestling for a brief instant at what seemed a solid iron tower, glanced up in time to see the ax falling, but not in time to avoid it. In the interim, one of his comrades lifted a broadsword with both hands and hewed through the king's left shoulder-plate, wounding the shoulder beneath. In an instant Conan's cuirass was full of blood.

Volmana, flinging the attackers right and left in his savage impatience, came plowing through and hacked murderously at Conan's unprotected head. The king ducked deeply and the sword shaved off a lock of his black hair as it whistled above him. Conan pivoted on his heel and struck in from the side. The ax crunched through the steel cuirass, and Volmana crumpled with his whole left side saved in.

"Volmana!" gasped Conan breathlessly. "I'll know that dwarf in Hell—"

He straightened to meet the maddened rush of Rinaldo, who charged in wild and wide open, armed only with a dagger. Conan leaped back, lifting his ax.

"Rinaldo!" his voice was strident with desperate urgency. "Back! I would not slay you—"

195

"Die, tyrant!" screamed the mad minstrel, hurling himself headlong on the king. Conan delayed the blow he was loath to deliver, until it was too late. Only when he felt the bite of the steel in his unprotected side did he strike, in a frenzy of blind desperation.

Rinaldo dropped with his skull shattered, and Conan reeled back against the wall, blood spurting from between the fingers which gripped his wound.

"In, now, and slay him!" yelled Ascalante.

Conan put his back against the wall and lifted his ax. He stood like an image of the unconquerable primordial —legs braced far apart, head thrust forward, one hand clutching the wall for support, the other gripping the ax on high, with the great corded muscles standing out in iron ridges, and his features frozen in a death snarl of fury—his eyes blazing terribly through the mist of blood which veiled them. The men faltered—wild, criminal, and dissolute though they were, yet they came of a breed men called civilized, with a civilized background; here was the barbarian—the natural killer. They shrank back —the dying tiger could still deal death.

Conan sensed their uncertainty and grinned mirthlessly and ferociously.

"Who dies first?" he mumbled through smashed and bloody lips.

Ascalante leaped like a wolf, halted almost in midair with incredible quickness and fell prostrate to avoid the death which was hissing toward him. He frantically whirled his feet out of the way and rolled clear as Conan recovered from his missed blow and struck again. This time the ax sank inches deep into the polished floor close to Ascalante's revolving legs.

Another misguided desperado chose this instant to charge, followed half-heartedly by his fellows. He intended killing Conan before the Cimmerian could wrench his ax from the floor, but his judgment was faulty. The red ax lurched up and crashed down and a crimson caricature of a man catapulted back against the legs of the attackers.

At that instant a fearful scream burst from the rogues at the door as a black misshapen shadow fell across the wall. All but Ascalante wheeled at that cry; and then, howling like dogs, they burst blindly through the door in a raving, blaspheming mob and scattered through the corridors in screaming flight.

Ascalante did not look toward the door; he had eyes only for the wounded king. He supposed that the noise of the fray had at last roused the palace, and that the loyal guards were upon him, though even in that moment it seemed strange that his hardened rogues should scream so terribly in their flight. Conan did not look toward the door because he was watching the outlaw with the burning eyes of a dying wolf. In this extremity Ascalante's cynical philosophy did not desert him.

"All seems to be lost, particularly honor," he murmured. "However, the king is dying on his feet—and—" Whatever other cogitation might have passed through his mind is not to be known; for, leaving the sentence uncompleted, he ran lightly at Conan just as the Cimmerian was perforce employing his ax-arm to wipe the blood from his blinded eyes.

But even as he began his charge, there was a strange rushing in the air and a heavy weight struck terrifically between his shoulders. He was dashed headlong, and great talons sank agonizingly in his flesh. Writhing desperately beneath his attacker, he twisted his head about and stared into the face of Nightmare and lunacy. Upon him crouched a great black thing which, he knew, was born in no sane or human world. Its slavering black fangs were near his throat and the glare of its yellow eyes shrivelled his limbs as a killing wind shrivels young corn.

The hideousness of its face transcended mere bestiality. It might have been the face of an ancient, evil mummy,

197

quickened with demoniac life. In those abhorrent features the outlaw's dilated eyes seemed to see, like a shadow in the madness that enveloped him, a faint and terrible resemblance to the slave Thoth-Amon. Then Ascalante's cynical and all-sufficient philosophy deserted him, and with a ghastly cry he gave up the ghost before those slavering fangs touched him.

Conan, shaking the blood-drops from his eyes, stared frozen. At first he thought it was a great black hound which stood above Ascalante's distorted body; then as his sight cleared he saw that it was neither a hound nor a baboon.

With a cry that was like an echo of Ascalante's death-shriek, he reeled away from the wall and met the leaping horror with a cast of his ax that had behind it all the desperate power of his electrified nerves. The flying weapon glanced singing from the slanting skull it should have crushed, and the king was hurled half-way across the chamber by the impact of the giant body.

The slavering jaws closed on the arm Conan flung up to guard his throat, but the monster made no effort to secure a death-grip. Over his mangled arm it glared fiendishly into the king's eyes, in which there began to be mirrored a likeness of the horror which stared from the dead eyes of Ascalante. Conan felt his soul shrivel and begin to be drawn out of his body, to drown in the yellow wells of cosmic horror which glimmered spectrally in the formless chaos that was growing about him and engulfing all life and sanity. Those eyes grew and became gigantic, and in them the Cimmerian glimpsed the reality of all the abysmal and blasphemous horrors that lurk in the outer darkness of formless voids and nighted gulfs. He opened his bloody lips to shriek his hate and loathing, but only a dry rattle burst from his throat.

But the horror that paralyzed and destroyed Ascalante roused in the Cimmerian a frenzied fury akin to madness. With a volcanic wrench of his whole body he plunged backward, heedless of the agony of his torn arm, dragging the monster bodily with him. And his outflung hand struck something his dazed fighting-brain recognized as the hilt of his broken sword. Instinctively he gripped it and struck with all the power of nerve and thew, as a man stabs with a dagger. The broken blade sank deep, and Conan's arm was released as the abhorrent mouth gaped as in agony. The king was hurled violently aside, and lifting himself on one hand he saw, as one mazed, the terrible convulsions of the monster, from which thick blood was gushing through the great wound his broken blade had torn. And as he watched, its struggles ceased and it lay jerking spasmodically, staring upward with its grisly dead eyes. Conan blinked and shook the blood from his own eyes; it seemed to him that the thing was melting and disintegrating into a slimy, unstable mass.

Then a medley of voices reached his ears, and the room was thronged with the finally roused people of the court —knights, peers, ladies, men-at-arms, councillors—all babbling and shouting and getting in one another's way. The Black Dragons were on hand, wild with rage, swearing and ruffling, with their hands on their hilts and foreign oaths in their teeth. Of the young officer of the door guard nothing was seen, nor was he found then or later, though earnestly sought after.

"Gromel! Volmana! Rinaldo!" exclaimed Publius, the high councillor, wringing his fat hands among the corpses. "Black treachery! Some one shall dance for this! Call the guard."

"The guard is here, you old fool!" cavalierly snapped Callantides, commander of the Black Dragons, forgetting Publius' rank in the stress of the moment. "Best stop your caterwauling and aid us to bind the king's wounds. He's like to bleed to death."

"Yes, yes!" cried Publius, who was a man of plans rather than action. "We must bind his wounds. Send for every leech of the court! Oh, my lord, what a black shame on the city! Are you entirely slain?"

"Wine!" gasped the king from the couch where they had laid him. They put a goblet to his bloody lips and he drank like a man half dead of thirst.

"Good!" he grunted, falling back. "Slaying is cursed dry work."

They had stanched the flow of blood, and the innate vitality of the barbarian was asserting itself.

"See first to the dagger-wound in my side," he bade the court physicians. "Rinaldo wrote me a deathly song there, and keen was the stylus."

"We should have hanged him long ago," gibbered Publius. "No good can come of poets—who is this?"

He nervously touched Ascalante's body with his sandalled toe.

"By Mitra!" ejaculated the commander. "It is Ascalante, once count of Thune! What devil's work brought *him* up from his desert haunts?"

"But why does he stare so?" whispered Publius, drawing away, his own eyes wide and a peculiar prickling among the short hairs at the back of his fat neck. The others fell silent as they gazed at the dead outlaw.

"Had you seen what he and I saw," growled the king, sitting up despite the protests of the leeches, "you had not wondered. Blast your own gaze by looking at—" He stopped short, his mouth gaping, his finger pointing fruitlessly. Where the monster had died, only the bare floor met his eyes.

"Crom!" he swore. "The thing's melted back into the foulness which bore it!"

"The king is delirious," whispered a noble. Conan heard and swore with barbaric oaths.

"By Badb, Morrigan, Macha, and Nemain!" he concluded wrathfully. "I am sane! It was like a cross between a Stygian mummy and a baboon. It came through the door, and Ascalante's rogues fled before it. It slew Ascalante, who was about to run me through. Then it came upon me and I slew it—how I know not, for my ax glanced from it as from a rock. But I think that the Sage Epemitreus had a hand in it—"

"Hark how he names Epemitreus, dead for fifteen hundred years!" they whispered to each other.

"By Ymir!" thundered the king. "This night I talked with Epemitreus! He called to me in my dreams, and I walked down a black stone corridor carved with old gods, to a stone stair on the steps of which were the outlines of Set, until I came to a crypt, and a tomb with a phoenix carved on it—"

"In Mitra's name, lord king, be silent!" It was the high priest of Mitra who cried out, and his countenance was ashen.

Conan threw up his head like a lion tossing back its mane, and his voice was thick with the growl of the angry lion.

"Am I a slave, to shut my mouth at your command?"

"Nay, nay, my lord!" The high-priest was trembling, but not through fear of the royal wrath. "I meant no offense." He bent his head close to the king and spoke in a whisper that carried only to Conan's ears.

"My lord, this is a matter beyond human understanding. Only the inner circle of the priestcraft know of the black stone corridor carved in the black heart of Mount Golamira, by unknown hands, or of the phoenix-guarded tomb where Epemitreus was laid to rest fifteen hundred years ago. And since that time no living man has entered it, for his chosen priests, after placing the Sage in the crypt, blocked up the outer entrance of the corridor so that no man could find it, and today not even the high priests know where it is. Only by word of mouth, handed down by the high priests to the chosen few, and jealously guarded, does the inner circle of Mitra's acolytes know of the resting-place of Epemitreus in the black heart of Golamira. It is one of the Mysteries, on which Mitra's cult stands."

"I cannot say by what magic Epemitreus brought me to him," answered Conan. "But I talked with him, and he made a mark on my sword. Why that mark made it deadly to demons, or what magic lay behind the mark, I know not; but though the blade broke on Gromel's helmet, yet the fragment was long enough to kill the horror."

"Let me see your sword," whispered the high priest from a throat gone suddenly dry.

Conan held out the broken weapon, and the high priest cried out and fell to his knees.

"Mitra guard us against the powers of darkness!" he gasped. "The king has indeed talked with Epemitreus this night! There on the sword—it is the secret sign none might make but him—the emblem of the immortal phoenix which broods for ever over his tomb! A candle, quick! Look again at the spot where the king said the goblin died!"

It lay in the shade of a broken screen. They threw the screen aside and bathed the floor in a flood of candlelight. And a shuddering silence fell over the people as they looked. Then some fell on their knees calling on Mitra, and some fled screaming from the chamber.

There on the floor where the monster had died, there lay, like a tangible shadow, a broad dark stain that could not be washed out; the thing had left its outline clearly etched in its blood, and that outline was of no being of a sane and normal world. Grim and horrific it brooded there, like the shadow cast by one of the apish gods that squat on the shadowy altars of dim temples in the dark land of Stygia.

The Scarlet Citadel

No sooner have the mutterings of civil war died down, than Conan receives an urgent plea for help from Aquilonia's ally, King Amalrus of Ophir. King Strabonus of Koth is demonstrating against Ophir's borders, and Conan rides to the rescue with five thousand of Aquilonia's bravest knights, but finds both kings treacherously allied against him on the plain of Shamu.

1.

They trapped the Lion on Shamu's plain
They weighted his limbs with an iron chain,
They cried aloud in the trumpet-blast,
They cried, "The Lion is caged at last!"
Wo to the cities of river and plain
If ever the Lion stalks again!

— *Old Ballad*

THE ROAR of battle had died away; the shout of victory
mingled with the cries of the dying. Like gay-hued leaves
after an autumn storm, the fallen littered the plain; the
sinking sun shimmered on burnished helmets, gilt-worked
mail, silver breastplates, broken swords, and the heavy
regal folds of silken standards, overthrown in pools of
curdling crimson. In silent heaps lay war horses and their
steel-clad riders, flowing manes and blowing plumes
stained alike in the red tide. About them and among
them, like the drift of a storm, were strewn slashed and
trampled bodies in steel caps and leather jerkins—archers
and pikemen.

The oliphants sounded a fanfare of triumph over all
the plain, and the hoofs of the victors crunched in the
breasts of the vanquished as all the straggling, shining
lines converged inward like the spokes of a glittering
wheel, to the spot where the last survivor still waged
unequal strife.

That day Conan, king of Aquilonia, had seen the pick

of his chivalry cut to pieces, smashed and hammered to bits, and swept into eternity. With five thousand knights he had crossed the southeastern border of Aquilonia and ridden into the grassy meadowlands of Ophir, to find his former ally, King Amalrus of Ophir, drawn up against him with the hosts of Strabonus, king of Koth. Too late he had seen the trap. All that a man might do he had done with his five thousand cavalrymen against the thirty thousand knights, archers, and spearmen of the conspirators.

Without bowmen or infantry, he had hurled his armored horsemen against the oncoming host, had seen the knights of his foes in their shining mail go down before his lances, had torn the opposing center to bits, driving the riven ranks headlong before him, only to find himself caught in a vise as the untouched wings closed in. Strabonus' Shemitish bowmen had wrought havoc among his knights, feathering them with shafts that found every crevice in their armor, shooting down the horses, the Kothian pikemen rushing in to spear the fallen riders. The mailed lancers of the routed center had re-formed, reinforced by the riders from the wings, and had charged again and again, sweeping the field by sheer weight of numbers.

The Aquilonians had not fled; they had died on the field, and of the five thousand knights who had followed Conan southward, not one left the plain of Shamu alive. And now the king himself stood at bay among the slashed bodies of his house-troops, his back against a heap of dead horses and men. Ophirean knights in gilded mail leaped their horses over mounds of corpses to slash at the solitary figure; squat Shemites with blue-black beards, and dark-faced Kothian knights ringed him on foot. The clangor of steel rose deafeningly; the black-mailed figure of the western king loomed among his swarming foes, dealing blows like a butcher wielding a great cleaver.

Riderless horses raced down the field; about his iron-clad feet grew a ring of mangled corpses. His attackers drew back from his desperate savagery, panting and livid.

Now through the yelling, cursing lines rode the lords of the conquerors—Strabonus, with his broad dark face and crafty eyes; Amalrus, slender, fastidious, treacherous, dangerous as a cobra; and the lean vulture Tsotha-lanti, clad only in silken robes, his great black eyes glittering from a face that was like that of a bird of prey. Of this Kothian wizard dark tales were told; tousle-headed women in northern and western villages frightened children with his name, and rebellious slaves were brought to abased submission quicker than by the lash, with the threat of being sold to him. Men said that he had a whole library of dark works bound in skin flayed from living human victims, and that in nameless pits below the hill whereon his palace sat, he trafficked with the powers of darkness, trading screaming girl slaves for unholy secrets. He was the real ruler of Koth.

Now he grinned bleakly as the kings reined back a safe distance from the grim, iron-clad figure looming among the dead. Before the savage blue eyes blazing murderously from beneath the crested, dented helmet, the boldest shrank. Conan's dark, scarred face was darker yet with passion; his black armor was hacked to tatters and splashed with blood; his great sword red to the cross-piece. In this stress all the veneer of civilization had faded; it was a barbarian who faced his conquerors. Conan was a Cimmerian by birth, one of those fierce, moody hillmen who dwelt in their gloomy, cloudy land in the north. His saga, which had led him to the throne of Aquilonia, was the basis of a whole cycle of hero-tales.

So now the kings kept their distance, and Strabonus called on his Shemitish archers to loose their arrows at his foe from a distance; his captains had fallen like ripe grain before the Cimmerian's broadsword, and Strabonus, penurious of his knights as of his coins, was frothing with fury. But Tsotha shook his head.

"Take him alive."

"Easy to say!" snarled Strabonus, uneasy lest in some way the black-mailed giant might hew a path to them through the spears. "Who can take a man-eating tiger alive? By Ishtar, his heel is on the necks of my finest swordsmen! It took seven years and stacks of gold to train each, and there they lie, so much kite's meat. Arrows, I say!"

"Again, nay!" snapped Tsotha, swinging down from his horse. He laughed coldly. "Have you not learned by this time that my brain is mightier than any sword?"

He passed through the lines of the pikemen, and the giants in their steel caps and mail brigandines shrank back fearfully, lest they so much as touch the skirts of his robe. Nor were the plumed knights slower in making room for him. He stepped over the corpses and came face to face with the grim king. The hosts watched in tense silence, holding their breath. The black-armored figure loomed in terrible menace over the lean, silk-robed shape, the notched, dripping sword hovering on high.

"I offer you life, Conan," said Tsotha, a cruel mirth bubbling at the back of his voice.

"I give you death, wizard," snarled the king, and backed by iron muscles and ferocious hate the great sword swung in a stroke meant to shear Tsotha's lean torso in half. But even as the hosts cried out, the wizard stepped in, too quick for the eye to follow, and apparently merely laid an open hand on Conan's left forearm, from the rigid muscles of which the mail had been hacked away. The whistling blade veered from its arc, and the mailed giant crashed heavily to earth, to lie motionless. Tsotha laughed silently.

"Take him up and fear not; the lion's fangs are drawn."

The kings reined in and gazed in awe at the fallen lion. Conan lay stiffly, like a dead man, but his eyes glared up at them, wide open and blazing with helpless fury.

"What have you done to him?" asked Amalrus uneasily.

Tsotha displayed a broad ring of curious design on his finger. He pressed his fingers together and on the inner side of the ring a tiny steel fang darted out like a snake's tongue.

"It is steeped in the juice of the purple lotus, which grows in the ghost-haunted swamps of southern Stygia," said the magician. "Its touch produces temporary paralysis. Put him in chains and lay him in a chariot. The sun sets, and it is time we were on the road for Khorshemish."

Strabonus turned to his general Arbanus.

"We return to Khorshemish with the wounded. Only a troop of the royal cavalry will accompany us. Your orders are to march at dawn to the Aquilonian border and invest the city of Shamar. The Ophireans will supply you with food along the march. We will rejoin you as soon as possible, with reinforcements."

So the host, with its steel-sheathed knights, its pikemen and archers and camp-servants, went into camp in the meadowlands near the battlefield. And through the starry night, the two kings and the sorcerer who was greater than any king rode to the capital of Strabonus, in the midst of the glittering palace troop, and accompanied by a long line of chariots, loaded with the wounded. In one of these chariots lay Conan, king of Aquilonia, weighted with chains, the tang of defeat in his mouth, the blind fury of a trapped tiger in his soul.

The poison which had frozen his mighty limbs to helplessness had not paralyzed his brain. As the chariot in which he lay rumbled over the meadowlands, his mind revolved maddeningly about his defeat. Amalrus had sent an emissary imploring aid against Strabonus, who, he said, was ravaging his western domain, which lay like a tapering wedge between the border of Aquilonia and the vast southern kingdom of Koth. He asked only a thousand horsemen and the presence of Conan, to hearten his demoralized subjects. Conan now blasphemed mentally. In his generosity he had come with five times the number the treacherous monarch had asked. In good faith he had ridden into Ophir, and had been confronted by the supposed rivals allied against him. It spoke significantly of his prowess that they had brought up a whole host to trap him and his five thousand.

A red cloud veiled his vision; his veins swelled with fury, and in his temples a pulse throbbed maddeningly. In all his life he had never known greater and more helpless wrath. In swift-moving scenes, the pageant of his life passed fleetingly before his mental eye—a panorama wherein moved shadowy figures which were himself, in many guises and conditions—a skin-clad barbarian; a mercenary swordsman in horned helmet and scale-mail corselet; a corsair in a dragon-prowed galley that trailed a crimson wake of blood and pillage along southern coasts; a captain of hosts in burnished steel, on a rearing black charger; a king on a golden throne with the lion banner flowing above, and throngs of gay-hued courtiers and ladies on their knees. But always the jouncing and rumbling of the chariot brought his thoughts back to revolve with maddering monotony about the treachery of Amalrus and the sorcery of Tsotha. The veins nearly burst in his temples and the cries of the wounded in the chariots filled him with ferocious satisfaction.

Before midnight they crossed the Ophirean border, and at dawn the spires of Khorshemish stood up gleaming and rose-tinted on the southeastern horizon, the slim towers overawed by the grim scarlet citadel that at a distance was like a splash of bright blood in the sky. That was the castle of Tsotha. Only one narrow street, paved with marble and guarded by heavy iron gates, led up to it, where it crowned the hill dominating the city. The sides of that hill were too sheer to be climbed elsewhere. From the walls of the citadel one could look down on the broad white streets of the city, on minaretted mosques, shops, temples, mansions, and markets. One could look down, too, on the palaces of the king, set in broad gardens, high-walled, luxurious riots of fruit trees and blossoms, through which artificial streams murmured, and silvery fountains rippled incessantly. Over all brooded the citadel, like a condor stooping above its prey, intent on its own dark meditations.

The mighty gates between the huge towers of the outer wall clanged open, and the king rode into his capital between lines of glittering spearmen, while fifty trumpets pealed salute. But no throngs swarmed the white-paved streets to fling roses before the conqueror's hoofs. Strabonus had raced ahead of news of the battle, and the people, just rousing to the occupations of the day, gaped to see their king returning with a small retinue and were in doubt as to whether it portended victory or defeat.

Conan, life sluggishly moving in his veins again, craned his neck from the chariot floor to view the wonders of this city, which men called the Queen of the South. He had thought to ride some day through these golden-chased gates at the head of his steel-clad squadrons, with the great lion banner flowing over his helmeted head. Instead he entered in chains, stripped of his armor, and thrown like a captive slave on the bronze floor of his conqueror's chariot. A wayward devilish mirth of mockery

210

rose above his fury, but to the nervous soldiers who drove
the chariot his laughter sounded like the muttering of
a rousing lion.

2.

Gleaming shell of an outworn lie; fable of Right
    divine—
You gained your crowns by heritage, but Blood
    was the price of mine.
The throne that I won by blood and sweat, by
    Crom, I will not sell
For promise of valleys filled with gold, or threat
    of the Halls of Hell!
                —*The Road of Kings*

In the citadel, in a chamber with a domed ceiling of
carven jet, and the fretted arches of doorways glimmering
with strange dark jewels, a strange conclave came to
pass. Conan of Aquilonia, blood from unbandaged
wounds caking his huge limbs, faced his captors. On
either side of him stood a dozen black giants, grasping
their long-shafted axes. In front of him stood Tsotha,
and on divans lounged Strabonus and Amalrus in their
silks and gold, gleaming with jewels, naked slave-boys
beside them pouring wine into cups carved of a single sap-
phire. In strong contrast stood Conan, grim, blood-
stained, naked but for a loin-cloth, shackles on his mighty
limbs, his blue eyes blazing beneath the tangled black

mane that fell over his low, broad forehead. He dominated the scene, turning to tinsel the pomp of the conquerors by the sheer vitality of his elemental personality, and the kings in their pride and splendor were aware of it each in his secret heart and were not at ease. Only Tsotha was not disturbed.

"Our desires are quickly spoken, king of Aquilonia," said Tsotha. "It is our wish to extend our empire."

"And so you swine want my kingdom," rasped Conan.

"What are you but an adventurer, seizing a crown to which you had no more claim than any other wandering barbarian?" parried Amalrus. "We are prepared to offer you suitable compensation—"

"Compensation?" It was a gust of deep laughter from Conan's mighty chest. "The price of infamy and treachery! I am a barbarian, so I shall sell my kingdom and its people for life and your filthy gold? Ha! How did you come to your crown, you and that black-faced pig beside you? Your fathers did the fighting and the suffering, and handed their crowns to you on golden platters. What you inherited without lifting a finger—except to poison a few brothers—I fought for.

"You sit on satin and guzzle wine the people sweat for, and talk of divine rights of sovereignty—bah! I climbed out of the abyss of naked barbarism to the throne, and in that climb I split my blood as freely as I split that of others. If either of us has the right to rule men, by Crom, it is I! How have you proved yourself my superior?

"I found Aquilonia in the grip of a pig like you—one who traced his genealogy for a thousand years. The land was torn with the wars of the barons, and the people cried out under suppression and taxation. Today no Aquilonian noble dares maltreat the humblest of my subjects, and the taxes of the people are lighter than anywhere else in the world.

"What of you? Your brother, Amalrus, holds the eastern half of your kingdom and defies you. And you, Strabonus, your soldiers are even now besieging castles of a dozen or more rebellious barons. The people of both your kingdoms are crushed into the earth by tyrannous taxes and levies. And you would loot mine—ha! Free my hands and I'll varnish this floor with your brains!"

Tsotha grinned bleakly to see the rage of his kingly companions.

"All this, truthful though it be, is beside the point. Our plans are no concern of yours. Your responsibility is at an end when you sign this parchment, which is an abdication in favor of Prince Arpello of Pellia. We will give you arms and horse, and five thousand golden lunas, and escort you to the eastern frontier."

"Setting me adrift where I was when I rode into Aquilonia to take service in her armies, except with the added burden of a traitor's name!" Conan's laugh was like the deep, short bark of a timber wolf. "Arpello, eh? I've had suspicions of that butcher of Pellia. Can you not even steal and pillage frankly and honestly, but you must have an excuse, however thin? Arpello claims a trace of royal blood; so you use him as an excuse for theft, and a satrap to rule through! I'll see you in Hell first."

"You're a fool!" exclaimed Amalrus. "You are in our hands, and we can take both crown and life at our pleasure!"

Conan's answer was neither kingly nor dignified, but characteristically instinctive in the man, whose barbaric nature had never been submerged in his adopted culture. He spat full in Amalrus' eyes. The king of Ophir leaped up with a scream of outraged fury, groping for his slender sword. Drawing it, he rushed at the Cimmerian, but Tsotha intervened.

"Wait, Your Majesty; this man is *my* prisoner."

"Aside, wizard!" shrieked Amalrus, maddened by the glare in the Cimmerian's blue eyes.

"Back, I say!" roared Tsotha, roused to awesome wrath. His lean hand came from his sleeve and cast a shower of dust into the Ophirean's contorted face. Amalrus cried out and staggered back, clutching at his eyes, the sword falling from his hand. He dropped limply on the divan, while the Kothian guards looked on stolidly and King Strabonus hurriedly gulped another goblet of wine, holding it with hands that trembled. Amalrus lowered his hands and shook his head violently, intelligence slowly sifting back into his gray eyes.

"I went blind," he growled. "What did you do to me, wizard?"

"Merely a gesture to convince you who was the real master," snapped Tsotha, the mask of his formal pretense dropped, revealing the naked, evil personality of the man. "Strabonus has learned his lesson—let you learn yours. It was but a dust I found in a Stygian tomb which I flung into your eyes—if I brush out their sight again, I will leave you to grope in darkness for the rest of your life."

Amalrus shrugged his shoulders, smiled whimsically, and reached for a goblet, dissembling his fear and fury. A polished diplomat, he was quick to regain his poise. Tsotha turned to Conan, who had stood imperturbably during the episode. At the wizard's gesture, the blacks laid hold of their prisoner and marched him behind Tsotha, who led the way out of the chamber through an arched doorway into a winding corridor, whose floor was of many-hued mosaics, whose walls were inlaid with gold tissue and silver chasing, and from whose fretted, arched ceiling swung golden censers, filling the corridor with dreamy, perfumed clouds. They turned down a smaller corridor, done in jade and black jet, gloomy and awful, which ended at a brass door, over whose arch a human skull grinned horrifically. At this door stood a fat, repellent figure, dangling a bunch of

214

keys—Tsotha's chief eunuch, Shukeli, of whom grisly tales were whispered—a man with whom a bestial lust for torture took the place of normal human passions.

The brass door let onto a narrow stair that seemed to wind down into the very bowels of the hill on which the citadel stood. Down these stairs went the band, to halt at last at an iron door, the strength of which seemed unnecessary. Evidently it did not open on outer air, yet it was built as if to withstand the battering of mangonels and rams. Shukeli opened it, and as he swung back the ponderous portal, Conan noted the evident uneasiness among the black giants who guarded him; nor did Shukeli seem altogether devoid of nervousness as he peered into the darkness beyond. Inside the great door there was a second barrier, composed of great steel bars. It was fastened by an ingenious bolt which had no lock and could be worked only from the outside; this bolt shot back, the grille slid into the wall. They passed through, into a broad corridor, the floor, walls, and arched ceiling of which seemed to be cut out of solid stone. Conan knew he was far underground, even below the hill itself. The darkness pressed in on the guardsmen's torches like a sentient, animate thing.

They made the king fast to a ring in the stone wall. Above his head in a niche in the wall they placed a torch, so that he stood in a dim semicircle of light. The blacks were anxious to be gone; they muttered among themselves and cast fearful glances at the darkness. Tsotha motioned them out, and they filed through the door in stumbling haste, as if fearing the darkness might take tangible form and spring upon their backs. Tsotha turned toward Conan, and the king noticed uneasily that the wizard's eyes shone in the semi-darkness, and that his teeth much resembled the fangs of a wolf, gleaming whitely in the shadows.

215

"And so, farewell, barbarian," mocked the sorcerer. "I must ride to Shamar, and the siege. In ten days I shall be in your palace in Tarantia, with my warriors. What word from you shall I say to your women, before I flay their dainty skins for scrolls whereon to chronicle the triumphs of Tsotha-lanti?"

Conan answered with a searing Cimmerian curse that would have burst the very eardrums of an ordinary man, and Tsotha laughed thinly and withdrew. Conan had a glimpse of his vulturelike figure through the thick-set bars, as he slid home the grate; then the heavy outer door clanged, and silence fell like a pall.

3.

The Lion strode through the halls of Hell;
Across his path grim shadows fell
Of many a mowing, nameless shape—
Monsters with dripping jaws agape.
The darkness shuddered with scream and yell
When the Lion stalked through the halls of Hell.
—*Old Ballad*

King Conan tested the ring in the wall and the chain that bound him. His limbs were free, but he knew that his shackles were beyond even his iron strength. The links of the chain were as thick as his thumb and were fastened to a band of steel about his waist, a band broad as his hand and half an inch thick. The sheer weight of his shackles would have slain a lesser man with exhaustion. The locks that held band and chain were massive affairs that a sledge hammer could hardly have dented. As for the ring, evidently it went clear through the wall and was clinched on the other side.

Conan cursed, and panic surged through him as he glared into the darkness that pressed against the half-circle of light. All the superstitious dread of the barbarian slept in his soul, untouched by civilized logic. His primitive imagination peopled the subterranean darkness with grisly shapes. Besides, his reason told him that he had not been placed there merely for confinement. His captors had no reason to spare him. He had been placed in these pits for a definite doom. He cursed himself for his refusal of their offer, even while his stubborn manhood revolted at the thought, and he knew that were he taken forth and given another chance, his reply would be the same. He would not sell his subjects to the butcher. And yet it had been with no thought of anyone's gain but his own that he had seized the kingdom originally. Thus subtly does the instinct of sovereign responsibility enter even a red-handed plunderer sometimes.

Conan thought of Tsotha's last abominable threat, and groaned in sick fury, knowing it was no idle boast. Men and women were to the wizard no more than the writhing insect is to the scientist. Soft white hands that had caressed him, red lips that had been pressed to his, dainty white bosoms that had quivered to his hot fierce kisses, to be stripped of their delicate skin, white as ivory and pink as young petals—from Conan's lips burst a yell so frightful and inhuman in its mad fury that a listener would have stared in horror to know that it came from a human throat.

The shuddering echoes made him start and brought back his own situation vividly to the king. He glared fearsomely at the outer gloom and thought of all the grisly tales he had heard of Tsotha's necromantic cruelty, and it was with an icy sensation down his spine that he realized that these must be the very Halls of Horror named in shuddering legendry, the tunnels and dungeons wherein Tsotha performed horrible experiments with beings human, bestial, and, it was whispered, demoniac, tampering blasphemously with the naked basic elements of life itself. Rumor said that the mad poet Rinaldo had visited these pits and been shown horrors by the wizard, and that the nameless monstrosities of which he hinted in his awful poem, *The Song of the Pit*, were no mere fantasies of a disordered brain. That brain had crashed to dust beneath Conan's battle-ax on the night the king had fought for his life with the assassins the mad rimer had led into the betrayed palace, but the shuddersome words of that grisly song still rang in the king's ears as he stood there in his chains.

Even with the thought, the Cimmerian was frozen by a soft rustling sound, blood-freezing in its implication. He tensed in an attitude of listening, painful in its intensity. An icy hand stroked his spine. It was the unmistakable sound of pliant scales slithering softly over stone. Cold sweat beaded his skin, as beyond the ring of dim light he saw a vague and colossal form, awful even in its indistinctness. It reared upright, swaying slightly, and yellow eyes burned icily on him from the shadows. Slowly a huge, hideous, wedge-shaped head took form before his dilated eyes, and from the darkness oozed, in flowing scaly coils, the ultimate horror of reptilian development.

It was a snake that dwarfed all Conan's previous ideas of snakes. Eighty feet it stretched from its pointed tail to its triangular head, which was bigger than that of a horse. In the dim light its scales glistened coldly, white as hoar-frost. Surely this reptile was one born and grown in darkness, yet its eyes were full of evil and sure sight. It looped its titan coils in front of the captive, and the great head on the arching neck swayed a matter of inches from his face. Its forked tongue almost brushed his lips as it darted in and out, and its fetid odor made his senses reel with nausea. The great yellow eyes burned into his, and Conan gave back the glare of a trapped wolf. He fought frenziedly against the mad impulse to grasp the great arching neck in his tearing hands. Strong beyond the comprehension of civilized man, he had broken the neck of a python in a fiendish battle on the Stygian coast, in his corsair days. But this reptile was venomous; he saw the great fangs, a foot long, curved like scimitars. From them dripped a colorless liquid that he instinctively knew was death. He might conceivably crush that wedge-shaped skull with a desperate clenched fist, but he knew that at his first hint of movement, the monster would strike like lightning.

It was not because of any logical reasoning process that Conan remained motionless, since reason might have told him—since he was doomed anyway—to goad the snake into striking and get it over with; it was the blind, black instinct of self-preservation that held him rigid as a statue blasted out of iron. Now the great barrel reared up and the head was poised high above his own, as the monster investigated the torch. A drop of venom fell on his naked thigh, and the feel of it was like a white-hot dagger driven into his flesh. Red jets of agony shot through Conan's brain, yet he held himself immovable; not by the twitching of a muscle or the flicker of an eyelash did he betray the pain of the hurt that left a scar he bore to the day of his death.

The serpent swayed above him, as if seeking to ascertain whether there were in truth life in this figure which stood so deathlike still. Then suddenly, unexpectedly, the outer door, all but invisible in the shadows, clanged stridently. The serpent, suspicious as all its kind, whipped about with a quickness incredible for its bulk and vanished with a long-drawn slithering down the corridor.

The door swung open and remained open. The grille was withdrawn, and a huge, dark figure was framed in the glow of torches outside. The figure glided in, pulling the grille partly to behind it, leaving the bolt poised. As it moved into the light of the torch over Conan's head, the king saw that it was a gigantic black man, stark naked, bearing in one hand a huge sword and in the other a bunch of keys. The black spoke in a sea-coast dialect, and Conan replied; he had learned the jargon while a corsair on the coasts of Kush.

"Long have I wished to meet you, Amra," the black gave Conan the name by which the Cimmerian had been known to the Kushites in his piratical days—Amra, the Lion. The slave's woolly skull split in an animal-like grin, showing white tusks, but his eyes glinted redly in the torchlight. "I have dared much for this meeting. Look! The keys to your chains! I stole them from Shukeli. What will you give me for them?"

He dangled the keys in front of Conan's eyes.

"Ten thousand golden lunas," answered the king quickly, new hope surging fiercely in his breast.

"Not enough!" cried the black, a ferocious exultation shining on his ebon countenance. "Not enough for the risks I take. Tsotha's pets might come out of the dark and eat me, and if Shukeli finds out I stole his keys, he'll hang me up by my—well, what will you give me?"

"Fifteen thousand lunas and a palace in Poitain," offered the king.

The black yelled and stamped in a frenzy of barbaric gratification.

"More!" he cried. "Offer me more! What will you give me?"

"You black dog!" a red mist of fury swept across Conan's eyes. "Were I free I'd give you a broken back! Did Shukeli send you here to mock me?"

"Shukeli knows nothing of my coming, white man," answered the black, craning his thick neck to peer into Conan's savage eyes. "I know you from of old, since the days when I was a chief among a free people, before the Stygians took me and sold me into the north. Do you not remember the sack of Abombi, when your seawolves swarmed in? Before the palace of King Ajaga you slew a chief and a chief fled from you. It was my brother who died; it was I who fled. I demand of you a blood-price, Amra!"

"Free me and I'll pay you your weight in gold pieces," growled Conan.

The red eyes glittered, the white teeth flashed wolf-ishly in the torchlight.

"Aye, you white dog, you are like all your race; but to a black man gold can never pay for blood. The price I ask is—your head!"

The word was a maniacal shriek that sent the echoes shivering. Conan tensed, unconsciously straining against his shackles in his abhorrence of dying like a sheep; then he was frozen by a greater horror. Over the black's shoulder he saw a vague horrific form swaying in the darkness.

"Tsotha will never know!" laughed the black fiend-ishly, too engrossed in his gloating triumph to take heed of anything else, too drunk with hate to know that Death swayed behind his shoulder. "He will not come into the vaults until the demons have torn your bones from their chains. I will have your head, Amra!"

He braced his knotted legs like ebon columns and

swung up the massive sword in both hands, his great
black muscles rolling and cracking in the torchlight.
And at that instant the titanic shadow behind him
darted down and out, and the wedge-shaped head smote
with an impact that re-echoed down the tunnels. Not
a sound came from the thick blubbery lips that flew wide
in fleeting agony. With the thud of the stroke, Conan
saw the life go out of the wide black eyes with the sud-
denness of a candle blown out. The blow knocked the
great black body clear across the corridor, and horribly
the gigantic sinuous shape whipped around it in glistening coils that hid it from view, and the snap and splintering of bones came plainly to Conan's ears. Then
something made his heart leap madly. The sword and
the keys had flown from the black's hands to crush and
jangle on the stone—and the keys lay almost at the
king's feet.

He tried to bend to them, but the chain was too short;
almost suffocated by the mad pounding of his heart, he
slipped one foot from its sandal, and gripped them with
his toes; drawing his foot up, he grasped them fiercely,
barely stifling the yell of ferocious exultation that rose
instinctively to his lips.

An instant's fumbling with the huge locks and he was
free. He caught up the fallen sword and glared about.
Only empty darkness met his eyes, into which the serpent had dragged a mangled, tattered object that only
faintly resembled a human body. Conan turned to the
open door. A few quick strides brought him to the
threshold—a squeal of high-pitched laughter shrilled
through the vaults, and the grille shot home under his
very fingers, the bolt crashed down. Through the
bars peered a face like a fiendishly mocking carven gar-
goyle—Shukeli the eunuch, who had followed his stolen
keys. Surely he did not, in his gloating, see the sword in
the prisoner's hand. With a terrible curse, Conan struck

as a cobra strikes; the great blade hissed between the bars, and Shukeli's laughter broke in a death-scream. The fat eunuch bent at the middle, as if bowing to his killer, and crumpled like tallow, his pudgy hands clutching vainly at his spilling entrails.

Conan snarled in savage satisfaction; but he was still a prisoner. His keys were futile against the bolt which could be worked only from the outside. His experienced touch told him the bars were hard as the sword; an attempt to hew his way to freedom would only splinter his one weapon. Yet he found dents on those adamantine bars, like the marks of incredible fangs, and wondered with an involuntary shudder what nameless monsters had assailed the barriers so terribly. Regardless, there was but one thing for him to do, and that was to seek some other outlet. Taking the torch from the niche, he set off down the corridor, sword in hand. He saw no sign of the serpent or its victim, only a great smear of blood on the stone floor.

Darkness stalked on noiseless feet about him, scarcely driven back by his flickering torch. On either hand he saw dark openings, but he kept to the main corridor, watching the floor ahead of him carefully, lest he fall into some pit. And suddenly he heard the sound of a woman, weeping piteously. Another of Tsotha's victims, he thought, cursing the wizard anew, and turning aside, followed the sound down a smaller tunnel, dank and damp.

The weeping grew nearer as he advanced and, lifting his torch, he made out a vague shape in the shadows. Stepping closer, he halted in sudden horror at the anthropomorphic bulk which sprawled before him. Its unstable outlines somewhat suggested an octopus, but its malformed tentacles were too short for its size, and its substance was a quaking, jelly-like stuff which made him physically sick to look at. From among this loathsome, gelid mass reared up a frog-like head, and he was frozen with nauseated horror to realize that the sound of weeping was coming from those obscene blubbery lips. The noise changed to an abominable high-pitched tittering as the great unstable eyes of the monstrosity rested on him, and it hitched its quaking bulk toward him.

He backed away and fled up the tunnel, not trusting his sword. The creature might be composed of terrestrial matter, but it shook his very soul to look upon it, and he doubted the power of man-made weapons to harm it. For a short distance, he heard it flopping and floundering after him, screaming with horrible laughter. The unmistakably human note in its mirth almost staggered his reason. It was exactly such laughter as he had heard bubble obscenely from the fat lips of the salacious women of Shadizar, City of Wickedness, when captive girls were stripped naked on the public auction block. By what hellish arts had Tsotha brought this unnatural being into life? Conan felt vaguely that he had looked on blasphemy against the eternal laws of nature.

He ran toward the main corridor, but before he reached it he crossed a sort of small square chamber, where two tunnels crossed. As he reached this chamber, he was flashingly aware of some small squat bulk on the floor ahead of him; then before he could check his flight or swerve aside, his foot struck something yielding that squalled shrilly, and he was precipitated headlong, the torch flying from his hand and being extinguished as it struck the stone floor. Half stunned by his fall, Conan rose and groped in the darkness. His sense of direction was confused, and he was unable to decide in which direction lay the main corridor. He did not look for the torch, as he had no means of rekindling it. His groping hands found the openings of the tunnels, and he chose one at random. How long he traversed it in utter darkness, he never knew, but suddenly his barbarian's instinct of near peril halted him short.

He had the same feeling he had had when standing on the brink of great precipices in the darkness. Dropping to all fours, he edged forward, and presently his outflung hand encountered the edge of a well, into which the tunnel floor apparently dropped abruptly. As far down as he could reach, the sides fell away sheerly, dank and slimy to his touch. He stretched out an arm in the darkness and could barely touch the opposite edge with the point of his sword. He could leap across it then, but there was no point in that. He had taken the wrong tunnel, and the main corridor lay somewhere behind him.

Even as he thought this, he felt a faint movement of air; a shadowy wind, rising from the well, stirred his black mane. Conan's skin crawled. He tried to tell himself that this well connected somehow with the outer world, but his instincts told him it was a thing unnatural. He was not merely inside the hill; he was below it, far below the level of the city streets. How then could an outer wind find its way into the pits and blow up from *below*? A faint throbbing pulsed on that ghostly wind, like drums beating far, far below. A strong shudder shook the king of Aquilonia.

He rose to his feet and backed away, and as he did *something* floated up out of the well. What it was, Conan did not know. He could see nothing in the darkness, but he distinctly felt a presence—an invisible, intangible intelligence which hovered malignly near him. Turning, he fled the way he had come. Far ahead he saw a tiny red spark. He headed for it, and long before he thought to have reached it, he caromed headlong into a solid wall and saw the spark at his feet. It was his torch, the flame extinguished, but the end a glowing coal. Carefully he took it up and blew upon it, fanning it into flame again. He gave a sigh as the tiny blaze leaped up.

225

He was back in the chamber where the tunnels crossed, and his sense of direction came back.

He located the tunnel by which he had left the main corridor, and even as he started toward it, his torch-flame flickered wildly as if blown upon by unseen lips. Again he felt a presence, and he lifted his torch, glaring about.

He saw nothing; yet he sensed, somehow, an invisible, bodiless thing that hovered in the air, dripping slimily and mouthing obscenities that he could not hear but was in some instinctive way aware of. He swung viciously with his sword and it felt as if he were cleaving cobwebs. A cold horror shook him then, and he fled down the tunnel, feeling a foul burning breath on his naked back as he ran.

But when he came out into the broad corridor, he was no longer aware of any presence, visible or invisible. Down it he went, momentarily expecting fanged and taloned fiends to leap at him from the darkness. The tunnels were not silent. From the bowels of the earth in all directions came sounds that did not belong in a sane world. There were titterings, squeals of demoniac mirth, long shuddering howls, and once the unmistakable squalling laughter of a hyena ended awfully in human words of shrieking blasphemy. He heard the pad of stealthy feet, and in the mouths of the tunnels caught glimpses of shadowy forms, monstrous and abnormal in outline.

It was as if he had wandered into Hell—a hell of Tsotha-lanti's making. But the shadowy things did not come into the great corridor, though he distinctly heard the greedy sucking-in of slavering lips and felt the burning glare of hungry eyes. And presently he knew why. A slithering sound behind him electrified him, and he leaped to the darkness of a near-by tunnel, shaking out his torch. Down the corridor he heard the great serpent

226

crawling, sluggish from its recent grisly meal. From his very side something whimpered in fear and shrank away in the darkness. Evidently the main corridor was the great snake's hunting-ground, and the other monsters gave it room.

To Conan the serpent was the least horror of them; he almost felt a kinship with it when he remembered the weeping, tittering obscenity, and the dripping, mouthing thing that came out of the well. At least it was of earthly matter; it was a crawling death, but it threatened only physical extinction, whereas these other horrors menaced mind and soul as well.

After it had passed on down the corridor, he followed, at what he hoped was a safe distance, blowing his torch into flame again. He had not gone far when he heard a low moan that seemed to emanate from the black entrance of a tunnel near by. Caution warned him on, but curiosity drove him to the tunnel, holding high the torch that was now little more than a stump. He was braced for the sight of anything, yet what he saw was what he had least expected.

He was looking into a broad cell, and a space of this was caged off with closely set bars extending from floor to ceiling, set firmly in the stone. Within these bars lay a figure, which, as he approached, he saw was either a man, or the exact likeness of a man, twined and bound about with the tendrils of a thick vine which seemed to grow through the solid stone of the floor. It was covered with strangely pointed leaves and crimson blossoms —not a satiny red of natural petals, but a livid, unnatural crimson, like a perversity of flower-life. Its clinging, pliant branches wound about the man's naked body and limbs, seeming to caress his shrinking flesh with lustful avid kisses. One great blossom hovered exactly over his mouth. A low bestial moaning drooled from the loose lips; the head rolled as if in unbearable agony, and the eyes looked full at Conan. But there was no light of intelligence in them; they were blank, glassy, the eyes of an idiot.

Now the great crimson blossom dipped and pressed its petals over the writhing lips. The limbs of the wretch twisted in anguish; the tendrils of the plant quivered as if in ecstasy, vibrating their full snaky lengths. Waves of changing hues surged over them; their color grew deeper, more venomous.

Conan did not understand what he saw, but he knew that he looked on Horror of some kind. Man or demon, the suffering of the captive touched Conan's wayward and impulsive heart. He sought for entrance and found a grille-like door in the bars, fastened with a heavy lock, for which he found a key among the keys he carried, and entered. Instantly the petals of the livid blossoms spread like the hood of a cobra, the tendrils reared menacingly and the whole plant shook and swayed toward him. Here was no blind growth of natural vegetation. Conan sensed a strange, malignant intelligence; the plant could see him, and he felt its hate emanate from it in almost tangible waves. Stepping warily nearer, he marked the root-stem, a repulsively supple stalk thicker than his thigh, and even as the long tendrils arched toward him with a rattle of leaves and hiss, he swung his sword and cut through the stem with a single stroke.

Instantly the wretch in its clutches was thrown violently aside as the great vine lashed and knotted like a beheaded serpent, rolling into a huge irregular ball. The tendrils thrashed and writhed, the leaves shook and rattled like castanets, and petals opened and closed convulsively; then the whole length straightened out limply, the vivid colors paled and dimmed, and a reeking white liquid oozed from the severed stump.

Conan stared, spellbound; then a sound brought him round, sword lifted. The freed man was on his feet, surveying him. Conan gaped in wonder. No longer were the eyes in the worn face expressionless. Dark and meditative, they were alive with intelligence, and the expression of imbecility had dropped from the face like a mask. The head was narrow and well-formed, with a high splendid forehead. The whole build of the man was aristocratic, evident no less in his tall slender frame than in his small trim feet and hands. His first words were strange and startling.

"What year is this?" he asked, speaking in Kothian.

"Today is the tenth day of the month Yuluk, of the year of the Gazelle," answered Conan.

"Yagkoolan Ishtar!" murmured the stranger. "Ten years!" He drew a hand across his brow, shaking his head as if to clear his brain from cobwebs. "All is dim yet. After a ten-year emptiness, the mind cannot be expected to begin functioning clearly at once. Who are you?"

"Conan, once of Cimmeria. Now king of Aquilonia."

The other's eyes showed surprise.

"Indeed? And Numedides?"

"I strangled him on his throne, the night I took the royal city," answered Conan.

A certain naïveté in the king's reply twitched the stranger's lips.

"Pardon, Your Majesty. I should have thanked you for the service you have done me. I am like a man woken suddenly from sleep deeper than death and shot with nightmares of agony more fierce than Hell, but I understand that you delivered me. Tell me—why did you cut the stem of the plant Yothga instead of tearing it up by the roots?"

"Because I learned long ago to avoid touching with my flesh that which I do not understand," answered the Cimmerian.

"Well for you," said the stranger. "Had you been able to tear it up, you might have found things clinging to

229

the roots against which not even your sword would prevail. Yothga's roots are set in Hell."

"But who are you?" demanded Conan.

"Men called me Pelias."

"What!" cried the king. "Pelias the sorcerer, Tsotha-lanti's rival, who vanished from the earth ten years ago?"

"Not entirely from the earth," answered Pelias with a wry smile. "Tsotha preferred to keep me alive, in shackles more grim than rusted iron. He pent me in here with this devil-flower, whose seeds drifted down through the black cosmos from Yag the Accursed, and found fertile field only in the maggot-writing corruption that seethes on the floors of Hell.

"I could not remember my sorcery and the words and symbols of my power, with that cursed thing gripping me and drinking my soul with its loathsome caresses. It sucked the contents of my mind day and night, leaving my brain as empty as a broken wine-jug. Ten years! Ishtar preserve us!"

Conan found no reply, but stood holding the stump of the torch and trailing his great sword. Surely the man was mad—yet there was no madness in the strange dark eyes that rested so calmly on him.

"Tell me, is the black wizard in Khorshemish? But no —you need not reply. My powers begin to wake, and I sense in your mind a great battle and a king trapped by treachery. And I see Tsotha-lanti riding hard for the Tybor with Strabonus and the king of Ophir. So much the better. My art is too frail from the long slumber to face Tsotha yet. I need time to recruit my strength, to assemble my powers. Let us go forth from these pits."

Conan jangled his keys discouragedly.

"The grille to the outer door is made fast by a bolt which can only be worked from outside. Is there no other exit from these tunnels?"

"Only one which neither of us would care to use, seeing that it goes down and not up," laughed Pelias. "But no matter. Let us see to the grille."

He moved toward the corridor with uncertain steps, as of long-unused limbs, which gradually became more sure. As he followed, Conan said uneasily, "There is a cursed big snake creeping about this tunnel. Let us be wary lest we step into his mouth."

"I remember him of old," answered Pelias grimly, "the more as I was forced to watch while ten of my acolytes were fed to him. He is Satha, the Old One, chiefest of Tsotha's pets."

"Did Tsotha dig these pits for no other reason than to house his cursed monstrosities?" asked Conan.

"He did not dig them. When the city was founded three thousand years ago, there were ruins of an earlier city on and about this hill. King Khossus V, the founder, built his palace on the hill, and digging cellars beneath it, came upon a walled-up doorway, which he broke into and discovered the pits, which were about as we see them now. But his grand vizier came to such a grisly end in them that Khossus in a fright walled up the entrance again. He said the vizier fell into a well—but he had the cellars filled in, and later abandoned the palace itself, and built himself another in the suburbs, from which he fled in a panic on discovering some black mold scattered on the marble floor of his chamber one morning.

"He then departed with his whole court to the eastern corner of the kingdom and built a new city. The palace on the hill was not used and fell into ruins. When Akkutho I revived the lost glories of Khorshemish, he built a fortress there. It remained for Tsotha-lanti to rear the scarlet citadel and open the way to the pits again. Whatever fate overtook the grand vizier of Khossus, Tsotha avoided it. He fell into no well, though he did descend into a well he found, and came out with a strange expression which has not since left his eyes.

"I have seen that well, but I do not care to seek in it for wisdom. I am a sorcerer, and older than men reckon, but I am human. As for Tsotha—men say that a dancing-girl of Shadizar slept too near the pre-human ruins on Dagoth Hill and woke in the grip of a black demon; from that unholy union was spawned an accursed hybrid men call Tsotha-lanti——"

Conan cried out sharply and recoiled, thrusting his companion back. Before them rose the great shimmering white form of Satha, an ageless hate in its eyes. Conan tensed himself for one mad berserker onslaught—to thrust the glowing faggot into that fiendish countenance and throw his life into the ripping sword-stroke. But the snake was not looking at him. It was glaring over his shoulder at the man called Pelias, who stood with his arms folded, smiling. And in the great, cold, yellow eyes slowly the hate died out in a glitter of pure fear—the only time Conan ever saw such an expression in a reptile's eyes. With a swirling rush like the sweep of a strong wind, the great snake was gone.

"What did he see to frighten him?" asked Conan, eyeing his companion uneasily.

"The scaled people see what escapes the mortal eye," answered Pelias cryptically. "You see my fleshly guise; he saw my naked soul."

An icy trickle disturbed Conan's spine, and he wondered if, after all, Pelias were a man, or merely another demon of the pits in a mask of humanity. He contemplated the advisability of driving his sword through his companion's back without further hesitation. But while he pondered, they came to the steel grille, etched blackly in the torches beyond, and the body of Shukeli, still slumped against the bars in a curdled welter of crimson.

Pelias laughed, and his laugh was not pleasant to hear.

"By the ivory hips of Ishtar, who is our doorman? Lo, it is no less than the noble Shukeli himself, who hanged

232

my young men by their feet and skinned them with squeals of laughter! Do you sleep, Shukeli? Why do you lie so stiffly, with your fat belly sunk in like a dressed pig's?"

"He is dead," muttered Conan, ill at ease to hear these wild words.

"Dead or alive," laughed Pelias, "he shall open the door for us."

He clapped his hands sharply and cried, "Rise, Shukeli! Rise from Hell and rise from the bloody floor and open the door for your masters! Rise, I say!"

An awful groan reverberated through the vaults. Conan's hair stood on end, and he felt clammy sweat bead his hide. For the body of Shukeli stirred and moved, with infantile gropings of the fat hands. The laug*.ter of Pelias was merciless as a flint hatchet, as the form of the eunuch reeled upright, clutching at the bars of the grille. Conan, glaring at him, felt his blood turn to ice, and the marrow of his bones to water; for Shukeli's wide-open eyes were glassy and empty, and from the great gash in his belly his entrails hung limply to the floor. The eunuch's feet stumbled among his entrails as he worked the bolt, moving like a brainless automaton. When he had first stirred, Conan had thought that by some incredible chance the eunuch was alive; but the man was dead —had been dead for hours.

Pelias sauntered through the opened grille, and Conan crowded through behind him, sweat pouring from his body, shrinking away from the awful shape that slumped on sagging legs against the grate it held open. Pelias passed on without a backward glance, and Conan followed him, in the grip of nightmare and nausea. He had not taken half a dozen strides when a sodden thud brought him round. Shukeli's corpse lay limply at the foot of the grille.

"His task is done, and Hell gapes for him again," re-

233

marked Pelias pleasantly, politely, affecting not to notice the strong shudder which shook Conan's mighty frame.

He led the way up the long stairs and through the brass skull-crowned door at the top. Conan gripped his sword, expecting a rush of slaves, but silence gripped the citadel. They passed through the black corridor and came into that in which the censers swung, billowing forth their everlasting incense. Still they saw no one.

"The slaves and soldiers are quartered in another part of the citadel," remarked Pelias. "Tonight, their master being away, they doubtless lie drunk on wine or lotus-juice."

Conan glanced through an arched, golden-silled window that let out upon a broad balcony, and swore in surprise to see the dark-blue, star-flecked sky. It had been shortly after sunrise when he was thrown into the pits. Now it was past midnight. He could scarcely realize he had been so long underground. He was suddenly aware of thirst and a ravenous appetite. Pelias led the way into a golden-domed chamber, floored with silver, its lapis-lazuli walls pierced by the fretted arches of many doors.

With a sigh, Pelias sank onto a silken divan.

"Silks and gold again," he sighed. "Tsotha affects to be above the pleasures of the flesh, but he is half devil. I am human, despite my black arts. I love ease and good cheer—that's how Tsotha trapped me. He caught me helpless with drink. Wine is a curse—by the ivory bosom of Ishtar, even as I speak of it, the traitor is here! Friend, please pour me a goblet—hold! I forgot you are a king. I will pour."

"The devil with that," growled Conan, filling a crystal goblet and proffering it to Pelias. Then, lifting the jug, he drank deeply from the mouth, echoing Pelias' sigh of satisfaction.

"The dog knows good wine," said Conan, wiping his mouth with the back of his hand. "But by Crom, Pelias, are we to sit here until his soldiers awake and cut our throats?"

"No fear," answered Pelias. "Would you like to see how fortune holds with Strabonus?"

Blue fire burned in Conan's eyes and he gripped his sword until his knuckles showed blue. "Oh, to be at sword-points with him!" he rumbled.

Pelias lifted a great shimmering globe from an ebony table.

"Tsotha's crystal. A childish toy, but useful when there is lack of time for higher science. Look in, Your Majesty."

He laid it on the table before Conan's eyes. The king looked into cloudy depths which deepened and expanded. Slowly images crystallized out of mist and shadows. He was looking on a familiar landscape. Broad plains ran to a wide winding river, beyond which the level lands ran up quickly into a maze of low hills. On the northern bank of the river stood a walled town, guarded by a moat connected at each end with the river.

"By Crom!" ejaculated Conan. "It's Shamar! The dogs besiege it!"

The invaders had crossed the river; their pavilions stood in the narrow plain between the city and the hills. Their warriors swarmed about the walls, their mail gleaming palely under the moon. Arrows and stones rained on them from the towers and they staggered back, but came on again.

Even as Conan cursed, the scene changed. Tall spires and gleaming domes stood up in the mist, and he looked on his own capital of Tarantia, where all was confusion. He saw the steel-clad knights of Poitain, his staunchest supporters, whom he had left in charge of the city, riding out of the gate, hooted and hissed by the multitude which swarmed the streets. He saw looting and rioting, and men-at-arms, whose shields bore the insignia of

235

Pellia, manning the towers and swaggering through the markets. Over all, like a fantasmal picture, he saw the dark, triumphant face of Prince Arpello of Pellia. The images faded.

"So!" cursed Conan. "My people turn on me the moment my back is turned——"

"Not entirely," broke in Pelias. They have heard that you are dead. There is no one to protect them from outer enemies and civil war, they think. Naturally, they turn to the strongest noble, to avoid the horrors of anarchy. They do not trust the Poitainians, remembering former wars. But Arpello is on hand, and the strongest prince of the central realm."

"When I come to Aquilonia again he will be but a headless corpse rotting on Traitor's Common." Conan ground his teeth.

"Yet before you can reach your capital," reminded Pelias, "Strabonus may be before you. At least his riders will be ravaging your kingdom."

"True!" Conan paced the chamber like a caged lion. "With the fastest horse I could not reach Shamar before midday. Even there, I could do no good except to die with the people, when the town falls—as fall it will in a few days at most. From Shamar to Tarantia is five days' ride, even if you kill your horses on the road. Before I could reach my capital and raise an army, Strabonus would be hammering at the gates; because raising an army is going to be hell—all my damnable nobles will have scattered to their own cursed fiefs at the word of my death. And since the people have driven out Trocero of Poitain, there's none to keep Arpello's greedy hands off the crown—and the crown-treasure. He'll hand the country over to Strabonus, in return for a mock-throne —and as soon as Strabonus' back is turned, he'll stir up revolt. But the nobles won't support him, and it will only give Strabonus excuse for annexing the kingdom openly. Oh, Crom, Ymir, and Set! If I but had wings to fly like lightning to Tarantia!"

Pelias, who sat tapping the jade table-top with his fingernails, halted suddenly, and rose as with a definite purpose, beckoning Conan to follow. The king complied, sunk in moody thoughts, and Pelias led the way out of the chamber and up a flight of marble, gold-worked stairs that let out on the pinnacle of the citadel, the roof of the tallest tower. It was night, and a strong wind was blowing through the star-filled skies, stirring Conan's black mane. Far below them twinkled the lights of Khorshemish, seemingly farther away than the stars above them. Pelias seemed withdrawn and aloof here, one in cold, unhuman greatness with the company of the stars.

"There are creatures," said Pelias, "not alone of earth and sea, but of air and the far reaches of the skies as well, dwelling apart, unguessed of men. Yet to him who holds the Master-words and Signs and the Knowledge underlying all, they are not malignant nor inaccessible. Watch, and fear not."

He lifted his hands to the skies and sounded a long weird call that seemed to shudder endlessly out into space, dwindling and fading, yet never dying out, only receding farther and farther into some unreckoned cosmos. In the silence that followed, Conan heard a sudden beat of wings in the stars, and recoiled as a huge batlike creature alighted beside him. He saw its great, calm eyes regarding him in the starlight; he saw the forty-foot spread of its giant wings. And he saw it was neither bat nor bird.

"Mount and ride," said Pelias. "By dawn it will bring you to Tarantia."

"By Crom!" muttered Conan. "Is this all a nightmare

from which I shall presently awaken in my palace at Tarantia? What of you? I would not leave you alone among your enemies."

"Be at ease regarding me," answered Pelias. "At dawn the people of Khorshemish will know they have a new master. Doubt not what the gods have sent you. I will meet you in the plain by Shamar."

Doubtfully Conan clambered upon the ridged back, gripping the arched neck, still convinced that he was in the grasp of a fantastic nightmare. With a great rush and thunder of titan wings, the creature took the air, and the king grew dizzy as he saw the lights of the city dwindle far below him.

4.

"The sword that slays the king
cuts the cords of the empire."
—*Aquilonian proverb*

The streets of Tarantia swarmed with howling mobs, shaking fists and rusty pikes. It was the hour before dawn of the second day after the battle of Shamar, and events had occurred so swiftly as to daze the mind. By means known only to Tsotha-lanti, word had reached Tarantia of the king's death, within half a dozen hours after the battle. Chaos had resulted. The barons had deserted the royal capital, galloping away to secure their castles

238

against marauding neighbors. The well-knit kingdom Conan had built up seemed tottering on the edge of dissolution, and commoners and merchants trembled at the imminence of a return of the feudalistic regime. The people howled for a king to protect them against their own aristocracy no less than foreign foes. Count Trocero, left by Conan in charge of the city, tried to reassure them, but in their unreasoning terror they remembered old civil wars, and how this same count had besieged Tarantia fifteen years before. It was shouted in the streets that Trocero had betrayed the king; that he planned to plunder the city. The mercenaries began looting the quarters, dragging forth screaming merchants and terrified women.

Trocero swept down on the looters, littered the streets with their corpses, drove them back into their quarter in confusion, and arrested their leaders. Still the people rushed wildly about, with brainless squawks, screaming that the count had incited the riot for his own purposes.

Prince Arpello came before the distracted council and announced himself ready to take over the government of the city until a new king could be decided upon, Conan having no son. While they debated, his agents stole subtly among the people, who snatched at a shred of royalty. The council heard the storm outside the palace windows, where the multitude roared for Arpello the Rescuer. The council surrendered.

Trocero at first refused the order to give up his baton of authority, but the people swarmed about him, hissing and howling, hurling stones and offal at his knights. Seeing the futility of a pitched battle in the streets with Arpello's retainers, under such conditions, Trocero hurled the baton in his rival's face, hanged the leaders of the mercenaries in the market-square as his last official act, and rode out of the southern gate at the head of his fifteen hundred steel-clad knights. The gates slammed behind him, and Arpello's suave mask fell away to reveal the grim visage of the hungry wolf.

With the mercenaries cut to pieces or hiding in their barracks, his were the only soldiers in Tarantia. Sitting his war horse in the great square, Arpello proclaimed himself king of Aquilonia, amid the clamor of the deluded multitude.

Publius the Chancellor, who opposed this move, was thrown into prison. The merchants, who had greeted the proclamation of a king with relief, now found with consternation that the new monarch's first act was to levy a staggering tax on them. Six rich merchants, sent as a delegation of protest, were seized and their heads slashed off without ceremony. A shocked and stunned silence followed this execution. The merchants, as is the habit of merchants when confronted by a power they cannot control with money, fell on their fat bellies and licked their oppressor's boots.

The common people were not perturbed at the fate of the merchants, but they began to murmur when they found that the swaggering Pellian soldiery, pretending to maintain order, were as bad as Turanian bandits. Complaints of extortion, murder, and rape poured in to Arpello, who had taken up his quarters in Publius' palace, because the desperate councillors, doomed by his order, were holding the royal palace against his soldiers. He had taken possession of the pleasure-palace, however, and Conan's girls were dragged to his quarters. The people muttered at the sight of the royal beauties writhing in the brutal hands of the iron-clad retainers—dark-eyed damsels of Poitain, slim black-haired wenches from Zamora, Zingara, and Hyrkania, Brythunian girls with tousled yellow heads, all weeping with fright and shame, unused to brutality.

Night fell on a city of bewilderment and turmoil, and

before midnight word spread mysteriously in the street that the Kothians had followed up their victory and were hammering at the walls of Shamar. Somebody in Tsotha's mysterious secret service had babbled. Fear shook the people like an earthquake, and they did not even pause to wonder at the witchcraft by which the news had been so swiftly transmitted. They stormed at Arpello's doors, demanding that he march southward and drive the enemy back over the Tybor. He might have subtly pointed out that his force was not sufficient, and that he could not raise an army until the barons recognized his claim to the crown. But he was drunk with power, and laughed in their faces.

A young student, Athemides, mounted a column in the market, and with burning words accused Arpello of being a catspaw for Strabonus, painting a vivid picture of existence under Kothian rule, with Arpello as satrap. Before he finished, the multitude was screaming with fear and howling with rage. Arpello sent his soldiers to arrest the youth, but the people caught him up and fled with him, deluging the pursuing retainers with stones and dead cats. A volley of crossbow quarrels routed the mob, and a charge of horsemen littered the market with bodies, but Athemides was smuggled out of the city to plead with Trocero to retake Tarantia and march to aid Shamar.

Athemides found Trocero breaking his camp outside the walls, ready to march to Poitain, in the far southwestern corner of the kingdom. To the youth's urgent pleas he answered that he had neither the force necessary to storm Tarantia, even with the aid of the mob inside, nor to face Strabonus. Besides, avaricious nobles would plunder Poitain behind his back, while he was fighting the Kothians. With the king dead, each man must protect his own. He was riding to Poitain, there to defend it as best he might against Arpello and his foreign allies.

While Athemides pleaded with Trocero, the mob still raved in the city with helpless fury. Under the great tower beside the royal palace the people swirled and milled, screaming their hate at Arpello, who stood on the turrets and laughed down at them while his archers ranged the parapets, bolts drawn and fingers on the triggers of their arbalests.

The prince of Pellia was a broad-built man of medium height, with a dark stern face. He was an intriguer, but he was also a fighter. Under his silken jupon with its gilt-braided skirts and jagged sleeves, glimmered burnished steel. His long black hair was curled and scented, and bound back with a cloth-of-silver band, but at his hip hung a broadsword the jeweled hilt of which was worn with battles and campaigns.

"Fools! Howl as you will! Conan is dead and Arpello is king!"

What if all Aquilonia were leagued against him? He had men enough to hold the mighty walls until Strabonus came up. But Aquilonia was divided against itself. Already the barons were girding themselves each to seize his neighbor's treasure. Arpello had only the helpless mob to deal with. Strabonus would carve through the loose lines of the warring barons as a galley-ram through foam, and until his coming, Arpello had only to hold the royal capital.

"Fools! Arpello is king!"

The sun was rising over the eastern towers. Out of the crimson dawn came a flying speck that grew to a bat, then to an eagle. Then all who saw screamed in amazement, for over the walls of Tarantia swooped a shape such as men knew only in half-forgotten legends, and from between its titan-wings sprang a human form as it roared over the great tower. Then with a deafening thunder of wings it was gone, and the folk blinked, wondering if they dreamed. But on the turret stood a wild barbaric figure, half naked, blood-stained, brandishing a great sword. And from the multitude rose a roar that rocked the very towers, "The king! It is the king!"

Arpello stood transfixed; then with a cry he drew and leaped at Conan. With a lion-like roar the Cimmerian parried the whistling blade, then dropping his own sword, gripped the prince and heaved him high above his head by crotch and neck.

"Take your plots to hell with you!" he roared, and like a sack of salt, he hurled the prince of Pellia far out, to fall through empty space for a hundred and fifty feet. The people gave back as the body came hurtling down, to smash on the marble pave, spattering blood and brains, and lie crushed in its splintered armor, like a mangled beetle.

The archers on the tower shrank back, their nerve broken. They fled, and the beleaguered councilmen sallied from the palace and hewed into them with joyous abandon. Pellian knights and men-at-arms sought safety in the streets, and the crowd tore them to pieces. In the streets the fighting milled and eddied, plumed helmets and steel caps tossed among the tousled heads and then vanished; swords hacked madly in a heaving forest of pikes, and over all rose the roar of the mob, shouts of acclaim mingling with screams of blood-lust and howls of agony. And high above all, the naked figure of the king rocked and swayed on the dizzy battlements, mighty arms brandished, roaring with gargantuan laughter that mocked all mobs and princes, even himself.

5.

A long bow and a strong bow, and let the sky
    grow dark!
The cord to the nock, the shaft to the ear, and
    the king of Koth for a mark!
          —*Song of the Bossonian archers*

The midafternoon sun glinted on the placid waters of
the Tybor, washing the southern bastions of Shamar.
The haggard defenders knew that few of them would
see that sunrise again. The pavilions of the besiegers
dotted the plain. The people of Shamar had not been
able successfully to dispute the crossing of the river, outnumbered as they were. Barges, chained together, made
a bridge over which the invader poured his hordes. Strabonus had not dared march on into Aquilonia with
Shamar, unsubdued, at his back. He had sent his light
riders, his spahis, inland to ravage the country and had
reared up his siege engines in the plain. He had anchored
a flotilla of boats, furnished him by Amalrus, in the middle of the stream, over against the river-wall. Some of
these boats had been sunk by stones from the city's
ballistae, which crashed through their decks and ripped
out their planking, but the rest held their places, and
from their bows and mast-heads, protected by mantlets, archers raked the riverward turrets. These were

244

Shemites, born with bows in their hands, not to be matched by Aquilonian bowmen.

On the landward side, mangonels rained boulders and tree-trunks among the defenders, shattering through roofs and crushing human beings like beetles; rams pounded incessantly at the stones; sappers burrowed like moles in the earth, sinking their mines beneath the towers. The moat had been dammed at the upper end and, emptied of its water, had been filled up with boulders, earth, and dead horses and men. Under the walls the mailed figures swarmed, battering at the gates, rearing up scaling-ladders, pushing storming-towers, thronged with spearmen, against the turrets.

Hope had been abandoned in the city, where a bare fifteen hundred men resisted forty thousand warriors. No word had come from the kingdom whose outpost the city was. Conan was dead, so the invaders shouted exultantly. Only the strong walls and the desperate courage of the defenders had kept them so long at bay, and that could not suffice for ever. The western wall was a mass of rubbish on which the defenders stumbled in hand-to-hand conflict with the invaders. The other walls were buckling from the mines beneath them, the towers leaning drunkenly.

Now the attackers were massing for a storm. The oliphants sounded, the steel-clad ranks drew up on the plain. The storming-towers, covered with raw bull-hides, rumbled forward. The people of Shamar saw the banners of Koth and Ophir, flying side by side, in the center, and made out, among their gleaming knights, the slim, lethal figure of the golden-mailed Amalrus and the squat, black-armored form of Strabonus. And between them was a shape that made the bravest blench with horror—a lean vulture figure in a filmy robe. The pikemen moved forward, flowing over the ground like the glinting waves of a river of molten steel; the knights cantered forward, lances lifted, guidons streaming. The warriors on the walls drew a long breath, consigned their souls to Mitra, and gripped their notched and red-stained weapons.

Then, without warning, a bugle-call cut the din. A drum of hoofs rose above the rumble of the approaching host. North of the plain across which the army moved, rose ranges of low hills, mounting northward and westward like giant stair-steps. Now down out of these hills, like spume blown before a storm, shot the spahis who had been laying waste the countryside, riding low and spurring hard, and behind them the sun shimmering on moving ranks of steel. They moved into full view, out of the defiles—mailed horsemen, the great lion banner of Aquilonia floating over them.

From the electrified watchers on the towers, a great shout rent the skies. In ecstasy, warriors clashed their notched swords on their riven shields, and the people of the town, ragged beggars and rich merchants, harlots in red kirtles and dames in silks and satins, fell to their knees and cried out for joy to Mitra, tears of gratitude streaming down their faces.

Strabonus, frantically shouting orders, with Arbanus, that would wheel around the ponderous lines to meet this unexpected menace, grunted, "We still outnumber them, unless they have reserves hidden in the hills. The men on the battle-towers can mask any sorties from the city. These are Poitainians—we might have guessed Trocero would try some such mad gallantry."

Amalrus cried out in unbelief.

"I see Trocero and his captain Prospero—but who rides between them?"

"Ishtar preserve us!" shrieked Strabonus, paling. "It is King Conan!"

"You are mad!" squalled Tsotha, starting convulsively. "Conan has been in Satha's belly for days!" He stopped short, glaring wildly at the host which was drop-

246

ping down, file by file, into the plain. He could not mistake the giant figure in black, gilt-worked armor on the great black stallion, riding beneath the billowing silken folds of the great banner. A scream of feline fury burst from Tsotha's lips, flecking his beard with foam. For the first time in his life, Strabonus saw the wizard completely upset, and shrank from the sight.

"Here is sorcery!" screamed Tsotha, clawing madly at his beard. "How could he have escaped and reached his kingdom in time to return with an army so quickly? This is the work of Pelias, curse him! I feel his hand in this! May I be cursed for not killing him when I had the power!"

The kings gaped at the mention of a man they believed ten years dead, and panic, emanating from the leaders, shook the host. All recognized the rider on the black stallion. Tsotha felt the superstitious dread of his men, and fury made a hellish mask of his face.

"Strike home!" he screamed, brandishing his lean arms madly. "We are still the stronger! Charge and crush these dogs! We shall yet feast in the ruins of Shamar tonight! O Set!" he lifted his hands and invoked the serpent-god to even Strabonus' horror, "grant us victory and I swear I will offer up to thee five hundred virgins of Shamar, writhing in their blood!"

Meanwhile the opposing host had debouched onto the plain. With the knights came what seemed a second, irregular army on tough, swift ponies. These dismounted and formed their ranks on foot—stolid Bossonian archers, and keen pikemen from Gunderland, their tawny locks blowing from under their steel caps.

It was a motley army Conan had assembled, in the wild hours following his return to his capital. He had beaten the frothing mob away from the Pellian soldiers who held the outer walls of Tarantia, and impressed them into his service. He had sent a swift rider after

Trocero to bring him back. With these as a nucleus of an army, he had raced southward, sweeping the countryside for recruits and for mounts. Nobles of Tarantia and the surrounding countryside had augmented his forces, and he had levied recruits from every village and castle along his road. Yet it was but a paltry force he had gathered to dash against the invading hosts, though of the quality of tempered steel.

Nineteen hundred armored horsemen followed him, the main bulk of which consisted of the Poitainian knights. The remnants of the mercenaries and professional soldiers in the trains of loyal noblemen made up his infantry—five thousand archers and four thousand pikemen. This host now came on in good order—first the archers, then the pikemen, behind them the knights, moving at a walk.

Over against them Arbanus ordered his lines, and the allied army moved forward like a shimmering ocean of steel. The watchers on the city walls shook to see that vast host, which overshadowed the powers of the rescuers. First marched the Shemitish archers, then the Kothian spearmen, then the mailed knights of Strabonus and Amalrus. Arbanus' intent was obvious—to employ his footmen to sweep away the infantry of Conan, and open the way for an overpowering charge of his heavy cavalry.

The Shemites opened fire at five hundred yards, and arrows flew like hail between the hosts, darkening the sun. The western archers, trained by a thousand years of merciless warfare with the Pictish savages, came stolidly on, closing their ranks as their comrades fell. They were far outnumbered, and the Shemitish bow had the longer range; but in accuracy the Bossonians were equal to their foes, and they balanced sheer skill in archery by superiority in morale, and in excellence of armor. Within good range they loosed, and the Shemites went down by whole ranks. The blue-bearded warriors in their light mail shirts could not endure punishment as could the heavier-armored Bossonians. They broke, throwing away their bows, and their flight disordered the ranks of the Kothian spearmen behind them.

Without the support of the archers, these men-at-arms fell by the hundreds before the shafts of the Bossonians and, charging in madly to close quarters, they were met by the spears of the pikemen. No infantry was a match for the wild Gundermen, whose homeland, the northernmost province of Aquilonia, was but a day's ride across the Bossonian marches from the borders of Cimmeria, and who, born and bred to battle, were the purest blood of all the Hyborian peoples. The Kothian spearmen, dazed by their losses from arrows, were cut to pieces and fell back in disorder.

Strabonus roared in fury as he saw his infantry repulsed, and shouted for a general charge. Arbanus demurred, pointing out the Bossonians re-forming in good order before the Aquilonian knights, who had sat their steeds motionless during the mêlée. The general advised a temporary retirement, to draw the western knights out of the cover of the bows, but Strabonus was mad with rage. He looked at the long shimmering ranks of his knights, he glared at the handful of mailed figures over against him, and he commanded Arbanus to give the order to charge.

The general commended his soul to Ishtar and sounded the golden oliphant. With a thunderous roar the forest of lances dipped, and the great host rolled across the plain, gaining momentum as it came. The whole plain shook to the rumbling avalanche of hoofs, and the shimmer of gold and steel dazzled the watchers on the towers of Shamar.

The squadrons clave the loose ranks of the spearmen, riding down friend and foe alike, and rushed into the teeth of a blast of arrows from the Bossonians. Across the plain they thundered, grimly riding the storm that scattered their way with gleaming knights like autumn leaves. Another hundred paces and they would ride among the Bossonians and cut them down like corn; but flesh and blood could not endure the rain of death that now ripped and howled among them. Shoulder to shoulder, feet braced wide, stood the archers, drawing shaft to ear and loosing as one man, with deep short shouts.

The whole front rank of the knights melted away, and over the pin-cushioned corpses of horses and riders, their comrades stumbled and fell headlong. Arbanus was down, an arrow through his throat, his skull smashed by the hoofs of his dying war horse, and confusion ran through the disordered host. Strabonus was screaming an order, Amalrus another, and through all ran the superstitious dread the sight of Conan had awakened.

And while the gleaming ranks milled in confusion, the trumpets of Conan sounded, and through the opening ranks of the archers crashed home the terrible charge of the Aquilonian knights.

The hosts met with a shock like that of an earthquake, that shook the tottering towers of Shamar. The disordered squadrons of the invaders could not withstand the solid steel wedge, bristling with spears, that rushed like a thunderbolt against them. The long lances of the attackers ripped their ranks to pieces, and into the heart of their host rode the knights of Poitain, swinging their terrible two-handed swords.

The clash and clangor of steel was as that of a million sledges on as many anvils. The watchers on the walls were stunned and deafened by the thunder as they gripped the battlements and watched the steel maelstrom swirl and eddy, where plumes tossed high among the flashing swords, and standards dipped and reeled.

Amalrus went down, dying beneath the trampling hoofs, his shoulder-bone hewn in twain by Prospero's two-handed sword. The invaders' numbers had engulfed the nineteen hundred knights of Conan, but about this compact wedge, which hewed deeper and deeper into the looser formation of their foes, the knights of Koth and Ophir swirled and smote in vain. They could not break the wedge.

Archers and pikemen, having disposed of the Kothian infantry which was strewn in disorderly flight across the plain, came to the edges of the fight, loosing their arrows point-blank, running in to slash at girths and horses' bellies with their knives, thrusting upward to spit the riders on their long pikes.

At the tip of the steel wedge Conan roared his heathen battle-cry and swung his great sword in glittering arcs of death that made naught of steel burganet or mail haburgeon. Straight through a thundering waste of steel-sheathed foes he rode, and the knights of Koth closed in behind him, cutting him off from his warriors. As a thunderbolt strikes, Conan struck, hurtling through the ranks by sheer power and velocity, until he came to Strabonus, livid, among his palace troops. Now here the battle hung in balance, for with his superior numbers, Strabonus still had opportunity to pluck victory from the knees of the gods.

But he screamed when he saw his arch-foe within arm's length at last, and lashed out wildly with his ax. It clanged on Conan's helmet, striking fire, and the Cimmerian reeled and struck back. The five-foot blade crushed Strabonus' casque and skull, and the king's charger reeled screaming, hurling a limp and sprawling corpse from the saddle. A great cry went up from the host, which faltered and gave back. Trocero and his house troops, hewing desperately, cut their way to

Conan's side, and the great banner of Koth went down. Then behind the dazed and stricken invaders went up a mighty clamor and the blaze of a huge conflagration. The defenders of Shamar had made a desperate sortie, cut down the men masking the gates, and were raging among the tents of the besiegers, cutting down the camp followers, burning the pavilions, and destroying the siege engines. It was the last straw. The gleaming army melted away in flight, and the furious conquerors cut them down as they ran.

The fugitives raced for the river, but the men on the flotilla, harried sorely by the stones and shafts of the revived citizens, cast loose and pulled for the southern shore, leaving their comrades to their fate. Of these many gained the shore, racing across the barges that served as a bridge, until the men of Shamar cut these adrift and severed them from the shore. Then the fight became a slaughter. Driven into the river to drown in their armor, or hacked down along the bank, the invaders perished by thousands. No quarter they had promised; no quarter they got.

From the foot of the low hills to the shores of the Tybor, the plain was littered with corpses, and the river, whose tide ran red, floated thick with the dead. Of the nineteen hundred knights who had ridden south with Conan, scarcely five hundred lived to boast of their scars, and the slaughter among the archers and pikemen was ghastly. But the great and shining host of Strabonus and Amalrus was hacked out of existence, and those that fled were less than those that died.

While the slaughter yet went on along the river, the final act of a grim drama was being played out in the meadowland beyond. Among those who had crossed the barge-bridge before it was destroyed was Tsotha, riding like the wind on a gaunt, weird-looking steed whose stride no natural horse could match. Ruthlessly riding down friend and foe, he gained the southern bank, and then a glance backward showed him a grim figure on a great black stallion in mad pursuit. The lashings had already been cut, and the barges were drifting apart, but Conan came recklessly on, leaping his steed from boat to boat as a man might leap from one cake of floating ice to another. Tsotha screamed a curse, but the great stallion took the last leap with a straining groan and gained the southern bank. Then the wizard fled away into the empty meadowland, and on his trail came the king, riding madly and silently, swinging the great sword that spattered his trail with crimson drops.

On they fled, the hunted and the hunter, and not a foot could the black stallion gain, though he strained each nerve and thew. Through a sunset land of dim light and illusive shadows they fled, till sight and sound of the slaughter died out behind them. Then in the sky appeared a dot, that grew into a huge eagle as it approached. Swooping down from the sky, it drove at the head of Tsotha's steed, which screamed and reared, throwing his rider.

Old Tsotha rose and faced his pursuer, his eyes those of a maddened serpent, his face an inhuman mask of awful fury. In each hand he held something that shimmered, and Conan knew he held death there.

The king dismounted and strode toward his foe, his armor clanking, his great sword gripped high.

"Again we meet, wizard!" he grinned savagely.

"Keep off!" screamed Tsotha like a blood-mad jackal. "I'll blast the flesh from your bones! You cannot conquer me—if you hack me in pieces, the bits of flesh and bone will reunite and haunt you to your doom! I see the hand of Pelias in this, but I defy ye both! I am Tsotha, son of—"

Conan rushed, sword gleaming, eyes slits of wariness.

Tsotha's right hand came back and forward, and the king ducked quickly. Something passed by his helmeted head and exploded behind him, searing the very sands with a flash of hellish fire. Before Tsotha could toss the globe in his left hand, Conan's sword sheared through his lean neck. The wizard's head shot from his shoulders on an arching fount of blood, and the robed figure staggered and crumpled drunkenly. Yet the mad black eyes glared up at Conan with no dimming of their feral light, the lips writhed awfully, and the hands groped hideously, as if searching for the severed head. Then with a swift rush of wings, something swooped from the sky—the eagle which had attacked Tsotha's horse. In its mighty talons it snatched up the dripping head and soared skyward, and Conan stood struck dumb, for from the eagle's throat boomed human laughter, in the voice of Pelias the sorcerer.

Then a hideous thing came to pass, for the headless body reared up from the sand, and staggered away in awful flight on stiffening legs, hands outstretched blindly toward the dot speeding and dwindling in the dusky sky. Conan stood like one turned to stone, watching until the swift reeling figure faded in the dusk that purpled the meadows.

"Crom!" his mighty shoulders twitched. "A murrain on these wizardly feuds! Pelias has dealt well with me, but I care not if I see him no more. Give me a clean sword and a clean foe to flesh it in. Damnation! What would I not give for a flagon of wine!"

CONAN

☐ 11577-2	**CONAN, #1**	$2.50
☐ 11595-0	**CONAN OF CIMMERIA, #2**	$2.50
☐ 11614-0	**CONAN THE FREEBOOTER, #3**	$2.50
☐ 11596-9	**CONAN THE WANDERER, #4**	$2.50
☐ 11598-5	**CONAN THE ADVENTURER, #5**	$2.50
☐ 11599-3	**CONAN THE BUCCANEER, #6**	$2.50
☐ 11616-7	**CONAN THE WARRIOR, #7**	$2.50
☐ 11602-7	**CONAN THE USURPER, #8**	$2.50
☐ 11603-5	**CONAN THE CONQUEROR, #9**	$2.50
☐ 11608-6	**CONAN THE AVENGER, #10**	$2.50
☐ 11612-4	**CONAN OF AQUILONIA, #11**	$2.50
☐ 11613-2	**CONAN OF THE ISLES, #12**	$2.50

A-04